Betty Rowlands trained as a secretary, gained a diploma in French and a certificate in further education, and worked for some years in business administration. When her husband's office moved to Gloucestershire, Betty began teaching business French and English at a nearby language school and also wrote course material which was later published as a series of textbooks for foreign students of English.

Her fiction includes a number of short stories, one of which was judged Crime Short Story of the Year, and seven mystery novels featuring Melissa Craig, crime writer and amateur sleuth. She is an active member of the Crime Writers' Association and a local writers' circle, regularly appears on panels at writers' conferences and runs workshops on creative writing.

DEATH AT DEARLEY MANOR

Paul Reynolds' second marriage has turned into a nightmare; nowadays, his wealthy wife, Myrna, treats him more like an employee than a husband. When she is found brutally murdered, Paul is the obvious suspect. But Myrna's obsession with money and power has endeared her to so few that there is no shortage of others with possible motives . . . For scene of crime officer Sukey Reynolds, who discovers the body after what appears to be a routine break-in, the case brings terrible dilemmas as she is forced to confront accusations and suspicions about the man to whom she was once married . . .

BETTY ROWLANDS

DEATH AT DEARLEY MANOR

Complete and Unabridged

ULVERSCROFT
Leicester

First published in Great Britain in 1998 by
Severn House Publishers Limited
Surrey

First Large Print Edition
published 1999
by arrangement with
Severn House Publishers Limited
Surrey

The right of Betty Rowlands to be identified
as author of this work has been asserted
by her in accordance with the
Copyright, Designs and Patents Act 1988

British Library CIP Data

Rowlands, Betty
    Death at Dearley Manor.—Large print ed.—
Ulverscroft large print series: mystery
1. Detective and mystery stories
2. Large type books
I. Title
823.9′14 [F]

ISBN 0–7089–4112–5

Published by
F. A. Thorpe (Publishing) Ltd.
Anstey, Leicestershire

Set by Words & Graphics Ltd.
Anstey, Leicestershire
Printed and bound in Great Britain by
T. J. International Ltd., Padstow, Cornwall

This book is printed on acid-free paper

1

Paul Reynolds approached the front door of Dearley Manor with his latchkey at the ready, although he knew he would have no need of it. Sure enough, he had barely reached the top step when the door swung open and the housekeeper stood there with a smile of welcome on her face.

'Good-evening, Sir,' she said in her warm, Gloucestershire voice. She stood aside while he entered, then closed the door behind him with her inevitable question, 'Have you had a good day?'

He forced himself to return her smile and her greeting. 'Not too bad, thank you, Mrs Little,' he replied, also as usual. At least she enquired, even if she wasn't really interested — something his wife no longer troubled to do. And he had nothing against the woman personally; on the contrary. She was no oil painting, but he found her unfailingly pleasant and obliging. He had more than once mentioned that it was unnecessary for her to be so punctilious about listening out for the car so that she could spare him the necessity of opening the door for himself, but

1

she had merely replied, 'Madam's instructions, Sir', with the slightly deferential smile that always accompanied any reference to the mistress of the house. *And what Madam says, goes*, had been his resentful, unspoken retort.

Mrs Little took his coat, which she would later brush and hang up in his wardrobe, saying, 'Madam is in her boudoir.' This time he had to turn his head away to conceal his exasperation. Why did Myrna have to insist on such a bloody arty-farty name for what was to all intents and purposes an office?

'Thank you,' he called over his shoulder as he made his way upstairs. He went to the bathroom, *en suite* with the room where he had slept alone ever since Myrna made it clear that she no longer required him to share her bed. It had taken him some time to realise that there were just two reasons why she had married him: sex, plus an exceptional financial acumen which had been instrumental in expanding and developing Maxford Domestic Fittings Limited, the business she had inherited from her father, to the point where it had recently attracted a substantial takeover bid. Five years on, she was no longer interested in sex — not with him, at any rate — but his accountant's brain would continue to be useful to her until she found someone else who fulfilled both functions.

After that — what? A demand for a divorce, consigning him to the scrapheap along with his two predecessors? His thoughts were bitter as he washed and changed into jeans and a sweatshirt before making his way along the landing to the private sanctum where his wife kept as tight a rein over the affairs of the company as she did over the running of her household.

Dearley Manor, dating from the early part of the eighteenth century, lay in a wooded valley in the Cotswolds. In the early days of his marriage to Myrna, the days when he believed without question her passionate declarations of love for him, this room had been one of Paul's favourite places. It was centrally placed at the back of the house, overlooking the garden, and the view from the tall casement windows had a special appeal to his love of symmetry and order. The classical, lichen-covered stone balustrade along the paved terrace was surmounted by a series of regularly-spaced Grecian urns and centrally pierced by a flight of stone steps leading down to the lawn, where a flagged path led to a lily pond with a fountain in the middle. A perfectly balanced arrangement of flower beds made a brilliant show during the summer and a careful planting of trees and shrubs gave colour and interest during the winter.

Myrna had very soon made it clear to Paul that his rôle in the running of the company would be strictly advisory and she steadfastly refused to make him a shareholder. Nevertheless, to enter her domain, to be consulted and made party to the most confidential aspects of its affairs, still gave him a certain satisfaction. At least he continued to wield influence, if not power. He derived pleasure from the understated opulence of the decor and the expensive electronic gadgetry which gave its owner instant access to every part of her small but immensely lucrative empire. Most of the furniture was custom-made and strictly functional, but the term 'boudoir' upon which Myrna insisted, was justified by an arrangement of armchairs, a couch, a cocktail cabinet and a music centre at the far end. In the early days of their tempestuous marriage the two of them often sat there with a drink, discussing some aspect of company business. Later, when he had dealt with all the points she raised and answered all her questions, she would dim the lights and switch on some soft, sensuous music while they made love on the couch. But that was a long time ago . . . .

When he entered, Myrna was sitting at her reproduction regency desk with an open file in front of her. Without looking up she said, 'There you are. The draft annual accounts came today. I'd like you to go over them as soon as possible.' She reached for the half-smoked cigarette burning on a heavy onyx ashtray and continued to study the file for several moments before tapping the top sheet with a poppy-red fingernail and saying, 'According to this, our pretax profits are only marginally above last year's level. It isn't good enough; if we want to extend the factory, we'll have to raise more capital.'

Paul frowned. 'Surely, that's no longer a problem. Once the Headwaters takeover goes through — '

'Oh, that!' Myrna's tone was dismissive, as though the offer for her company by the country's leading specialist in domestic plumbing supplies was of little consequence. 'I've decided to vote against acceptance.'

'You what?' Paul could hardly believe his ears. 'I thought it was as good as settled.'

'So did my fellow directors.' Her eyes sparkled with a glee that was almost malevolent. 'Brad and Sam have already planned how they're going to spend their hand-outs — or rather, their wives have. I can't wait to see their faces when I tell them the deal's off.'

'But why?'

She assumed a self-righteous expression. 'I don't think Father would have approved of my handing over control to outsiders.'

Some of Paul's pent-up frustration exploded at this display of hypocrisy and double standards. 'Why don't you admit it's got nothing to do with what your father would have wanted?' he demanded. 'The truth is, *you* don't want to give up playing God, do you? You enjoy running the show — it gives you the chance to manipulate people's lives, gives you power over them — '

He broke off, almost choking on the raw emotion that threatened to swamp him. As if she had not heard, Myrna drew on her cigarette, her attention once more on the file. He fought the urge to snatch it up and trample it underfoot. After a few moments of uneasy silence he said, 'Well, if you've made up your mind — '

'I have.'

' — and you want to extend the factory, of course there are other ways of raising the money. The company came through the recession on a pretty sound footing and the potential for growth is obviously there or Headwaters wouldn't be interested. We can approach a finance company, or maybe the bank — '

'I'm not thinking of a loan, not with

interest rates the way they are.'

'So what do you have in mind?'

She stubbed out her cigarette and for the first time turned to face him. 'I'm going to sell Dearley's Acres,' she said. 'Land prices are beginning to rise and I've had a good offer from some developers that should more than cover the extension, even allowing for an increase in costs between now and the millennium.'

Paul stared at her in disbelief. 'You can't sell that land . . . your father insisted it had to remain part of the estate . . . you gave an undertaking — '

'There was never anything in writing.'

'Only because he died before he had time to make it a condition in his will. There's such a thing as a moral obligation — '

'Moral obligation my foot! Father had absolutely no concept of the problems of running a business — or an estate — in the nineties. His ideas were positively feudal.'

'He made enough money to build up a flourishing company — ' Paul began, but his wife made a dismissive gesture.

'It was Grandfather who founded the company and built it up,' she interrupted, 'and it was Grandfather who insisted on appointing me to the Board and giving me control before he died because he could see

7

that his talent for business had skipped a generation. That's one thing poor Father did *not* inherit.'

'He inherited your grandfather's humanity and sense of fair play, and he cared about his employees.'

'Exactly.' Myrna assumed a sanctimonious expression. 'The takeover would almost certainly mean redundancies.'

'Oh, I see, what you're really concerned about is the welfare of the workforce.' Recalling some ruthless decisions she had taken in the past, Paul was unable to keep the sarcasm out of his voice. 'But you're prepared to sell your estate workers' cottages over their heads. Where are they going to find other jobs? And what about poor old Pussy Willow, for example? She's lived in Holly Cottage ever since she married Albert. It'll break her heart to move out.'

'That dotty old thing . . . she can go into a home or something. That's the least of the problems.'

'For God's sake, she's not dotty, just a bit eccentric. And she's barely sixty and still active — why should she go into a home?'

'Well, she can't stay in the cottage if it's going to be demolished, that's for sure. She'll find somewhere . . . anyway, she should be thankful I didn't give her notice when her husband died.'

'You would have done if it hadn't needed so much spending on it before anyone else would agree to live in it.'

'I don't remember hearing any complaints.'

'Probably because she was scared of losing her pension.'

Myrna's carefully lipsticked mouth turned down at the corners. 'She needn't have worried about that . . . I looked into it, but Father made sure it was secure.'

'You mean, you'd have stopped it if you could — a few measly quid a week out of what you're worth?'

'The state pension would have been quite enough for her needs.'

'You really are a hard-nosed bitch.'

'And you're a soft, sentimental fool.'

Paul swallowed, fighting a second outburst. He tried another line of attack. 'Have you given any thought to how local people will feel about the sale? There's a bridle path across one of the fields and ramblers use it all the time. It's green belt land we're talking about — there's bound to be opposition.'

'So what? Footpaths can be diverted or accommodated somehow — they'll have to get used to it.'

'What about planning consent?'

'Don't you read the papers? The County

Council has got to find space to build thousands of new houses and this land is ideally situated. It's near the motorway and there's already development less than two miles away. I've been assured there'll be no difficulty.'

'Assured by whom?'

Myrna gave an impatient shake of her reddish-gold head. 'Never you mind. Just stick to what you're best at and leave the big decisions to me. And by the way, you are not to mention a word of this to anyone until I've made a formal announcement.' Her jaw was set in a hard line and the eyes he had once found so enchanting were like sea-green marbles. 'Do you hear me?'

'I hear you.' He turned away and stared out of the window, but the view had lost its appeal. The rage and resentment that had been fermenting within him over the past few months burned in his stomach and brought the sour taste of bile to his mouth. There were times when she provoked him almost beyond endurance. In the early days of their marriage the rows had always ended in passionate reconciliation, when he could thrust to the back of his mind the creeping suspicion that he had made a ghastly mistake. Now, suspicion had become a reality; it stared him in the face, mocked him whenever he tried to stand up to her and saw the sardonic curve of her mouth as she taunted him with his dependence on her. '*Well darling*', she would say, '*if you don't like living here with me you can always go back to your ex and that gangling oaf of a son you think so highly of*'.

And of course, he couldn't — and she knew it. Even if Susan would have him back, which seemed highly unlikely now that she was involved with that policeman, his pride wouldn't let him. And it wasn't only pride; he was reluctant even to consider exchanging his present luxurious lifestyle for the humdrum domesticity and the problems of balancing the household budget that had been a constant feature of his first marriage. It had been all right at first, when they were both working, but after Fergus was born and Susan had insisted on giving up her job to be a full-time mother . . .

Myrna brought him back to the present by standing up and thrusting the file into his reluctant hands. 'By the way,' she added over her shoulder as she went back to the desk and began stowing papers in a filing cabinet disguised as a regency tallboy, 'Leonie will be here for dinner this evening. I know she's not exactly your cup of tea — '

'She's hardly any man's cup of tea, is she?'

'There's no need to be offensive.'

'I don't mean to be. I've nothing against the girl personally, but men don't go for dykes any more than dykes go for men. I wouldn't have thought she was *your* type, either,' he added, this time with studied irony.

Myrna looked down her nose at him. 'We have business matters to discuss,' she said coldly.

'What's wrong with the office?'

'*Confidential* business matters.' Her implication was obvious, even before she added, 'I'd appreciate it if you'd leave us on our own after dinner.'

This time, he made no attempt to conceal his anger. 'If you want to talk secrets with Leonie or anyone else, you can either do it during office hours or when I *choose* not to be around. I'm your husband, not a bloody lodger!'

'You're quite right darling — we mustn't tell the world about our differences, must we? Of *course* you're still my husband.' Her voice had become silky, almost conciliatory, as if she realised that she had pushed him too far. All the same, her tone and the look in her eyes said, '*Just remember who pays the bills, won't you?*' so unmistakably that the words might have been spoken aloud.

Paul looked down at the file in his hands. Without realising, he had gripped it so hard that the manila folder was buckled at the edges. 'Don't worry, I won't be here to cramp your style over the weekend,' he muttered. 'I'm taking Fergus to watch a cricket match on Saturday and Sunday.'

'How nice,' Myrna purred. She glanced at her watch. 'Drinks at seven-thirty; that leaves you almost an hour to start going through those figures.'

2

When Fergus arrived home on Sunday night, Susan Reynolds — known to her family, friends and colleagues as Sukey — was sitting on the couch in the front room with her feet up, watching the late television news. She'd had an ear cocked for him since ten o'clock and was beginning to feel faintly uneasy. It was ridiculous, really; he had been spending the weekend with his father, so he could hardly have come to any harm. It was always like this when he was out at night; he was sixteen, sensible and mature for his age, yet her mother-hen instinct kept her on the alert until her one chick was safely back in the nest. And Paul was usually so meticulous about sticking to the agreed time.

Unless it was raining, he was in the habit of dropping Fergus off on the corner rather than driving right up to the front door. When the weather was fine, as on this warm August evening, the first indication of his arrival would normally be the clang of the front gate, followed by the sound of his key in the lock, a series of thuds as he dumped his possessions on the hall floor and the resounding slam as the front door closed behind him. Like any normal teenage youth he seemed incapable of entering or leaving the house quietly.

Tonight, however, the first indication that he was home came when he entered the room and said, 'Hi, Mum.'

'Gus! You made me jump!' One thing she had learned some time ago was to avoid any suggestion that she had been watching the clock. She swung her feet to the floor to make room for him to sit beside her. That was something else she had trained herself to accept: you didn't chase your adolescent son off to bed the minute he arrived home, no matter how late. 'You practising to become a cat-burglar or something?'

He gave a faint smile but made no answering wisecrack, which was also unusual. 'How was your weekend?' he asked. 'Did you see Jim?'

'We went to the theatre yesterday evening and then out to supper. He's been on duty today so I've spent most of it in the garden.' She did not mention that Jim had stayed the night, but she knew Fergus would take it for granted that he had. In the magnanimous fashion of a young adult in the euphoria of his own first love affair, he had signalled his acceptance of hers, even before it had started.

He gestured at the TV, where a round-up

of the day's sporting events was being shown. Normally, he would have settled down to follow it with interest; tonight he picked up the remote control and said, 'Are you watching this?'

'Not especially, if you want to talk.'

He pressed the 'Off' button and sat for several moments in silence, staring at the blank screen. Sukey waited, guessing that something was troubling him and that he was trying to find the right words to tell her what was on his mind. Several minutes passed; sensing that he needed help, she said, 'How was the cricket?'

'Oh, the cricket was brilliant!' His mood lightened as he launched into an enthusiastic account of the day's play. 'I just wish I could be there tomorrow, it's turning into a really exciting match.'

'Did Dad enjoy it too?'

It was the lead-in he needed. His face clouded again as he answered glumly, 'As much as he seems to enjoy anything these days.'

'As bad as that?' From remarks Fergus had let drop after previous weekends spent with his father and step-mother, Sukey had divined that the turbulent interludes in her ex-husband's second marriage were becoming more frequent, but she was under the

16

impression that they were short-lived and amicably resolved. She gave her son a searching glance; he had his hands clasped together and seemed to be mesmerised by the sight of his interlocked fingers moving restlessly up and down in a series of V-shapes. She put her own hand over them and they became still again. 'Tell me,' she said gently.

'Oh, Mum!' He turned and faced her, his young face troubled. 'He's so unhappy. She's destroying him . . . she treats him like dirt . . . orders him about as if he was a servant. And he takes it, that's what gets up my nose. Why doesn't he stand up to her like he used to? Who does she think she is?'

'She's Queen Bee — and she holds the purse-strings.'

'He doesn't need her money. He's got a good job, now he's got a partnership — '

'His income is a flea-bite compared to what Myrna's worth. You don't imagine Dad could afford what it takes to run her place, do you?'

'I know . . . she's filthy rich, but she won't hear of a joint bank account. She even makes him contribute to the housekeeping. I once overheard them arguing about it.'

'Yes, I remember him telling me, after the divorce. He used to trot out that same old excuse whenever I tried to get him to part with a little extra cash.' Sukey gave a wry smile, remembering Paul's self-righteous manner as he proclaimed, '*You don't imagine I'm living entirely on my wife's money, do you? I have my pride.*' It still rankled to think of her struggle to make ends meet before Fergus had been old enough for her to go back to work, but looking back and picturing the scene she found it almost laughable to think how naïve he had been while under Myrna's spell — a willing fly walking into her gilded, silken web. It had been part of her strategy in those early days to feed his self-esteem while making sure of his subservience to her every whim.

'So what's the trouble this time?' she asked.

Fergus shrugged. 'I don't know all the details. Something to do with a takeover by some big company — '

'Headwaters?'

'That's it. How did you know?'

'There was something about it in the local paper. The workers are anxious about job losses. Not that that's likely to worry Myrna, as long as she gets her pretty little hands on the dosh.'

'It isn't going to happen.'

'What? I thought it was all settled.'

'Myrna's backed out and the deal can't go ahead without her agreement.'

'That doesn't sound like her — passing up

the chance to fill her coffers. What's the catch?'

'She's going to raise money by selling some land to developers. That's what they've been rowing about. Dad says it's going to mean some of the estate workers and an elderly widow having to move out of their houses.'

'Dad told you all this? Does he often talk to you about the business?'

'Not usually, but this has really got under his skin. It's not official yet and he's supposed to keep it to himself until the old bat gives the word, but he was so choked he just exploded as soon as we were on our own. You won't tell anyone, will you Mum, not even Jim? She'd give him hell if she knew he'd told me.'

'Of course I won't . . . and I wouldn't worry about it, Gus. There's nothing you can do.'

'It's Dad I'm worried about. There's something strange going on. There was a woman staying at the house — her name's Leonie but she likes to be called Leo.'

'What about her?'

'She's a les.'

'Gus! What are you suggesting?'

'I don't know.' Fergus stood up and began prowling restlessly round the little sitting-room with his hands thrust into the front pockets of his jeans. 'They weren't being lovey-dovey or anything like that . . . Dad explained that this Leo woman's some sort of secretary and she and Myrna were supposed to have business to talk about that was too confidential for the office. He kept saying it was no big deal, but I could tell he was really pissed off about it.' Fergus swung round to face his mother and his voice, so recently broken that it was still liable to crack and squeak under stress, was unsteady. 'Mum, I'm afraid for Dad.'

'You mean, you think Myrna and Leo are having an affair?'

'They could be, I suppose, but that's not what's worrying me.'

'Then what is it?'

'I'm afraid Dad might . . . do something stupid.'

It wasn't the first time Fergus had come home with tales of ructions between Paul and Myrna. There had been a time when Sukey experienced a certain spiteful satisfaction on learning of the cracks in the idyllic relation-ship which her ex-husband, with no apparent regard for her own feelings, had so confidently and enthusiastically described as he announced that he was leaving her. '*Myrna and I were destined for each other* ', he had told her. '*I'm sorry, Susan*', — he had always avoided using her nickname, saying it

20

sounded childish — *'I'll make provision for you and Fergus, of course, but there's no future for you and me any more'.* And he had packed his bags and walked out of the house leaving her too dazed with shock even to weep, although she had shed plenty of tears since.

Time had helped the wounds to heal — time and her renewed relationship with Jim Castle, which had ended long ago when they both married other people. Their work — his as a Detective Inspector in the County Police Force, hers as a Scene of Crime Officer — had brought them into contact again. Recently their friendship had blossomed into an affair, and the happiness they shared made her more tolerant towards Paul. At times, she even found herself sympathising with him in his disillusionment, however well-deserved. To give him his due, he had spent more time with Fergus since the lad was old enough for them to have shared interests. It worried her sometimes that their son was being torn in two directions: anxious to build a loving relationship with his father while not saying or doing anything to hurt his mother. On the whole, she felt, he was coping pretty well, despite having to witness the occasional marital spat. Normally, he shrugged them off; this one, she sensed, was more serious.

'Whatever do you mean — something stupid?' she asked. 'What actually happened?'

'Not a lot, really, not while I was there, but there was a horrible atmosphere at dinner on Friday evening. That was the only time the four of us were together, which was just as well or I think Dad would have exploded.'

'Was there an argument then?'

'Not exactly. Myrna made her usual snide wisecracks about cricket and what a stupid game it is, and she and Leo sort of giggled together. She's got a way of kind of mocking Dad with her eyes . . . and now and again she and this Leo woman exchanged glances as if they shared some sort of secret. And Dad just sat there stony-faced, saying hardly anything, but I could tell he was seething inside. That's what's worrying me. He always used to defend his corner . . . there'd be an almighty run-in and then they'd make it up, but just lately he's been different. Mum,' Fergus sat down again and took one of his mother's hands in both his own. 'I really believe he hates her and I think . . . I'm afraid he might — '

Sukey felt a contraction in her throat as she looked at her son. He was still so young, with his unlined face, the wisp of down on the upper lip and a sprinkle of teenage spots round the mouth, yet anxiety and apprehension made him look suddenly ten years older.

'Might do what?' she asked gently, as he seemed afraid to go on.

'Sometimes he looks at her as if he'd like to kill her,' he muttered.

'I dare say he would at times — I know I used to feel like it, and I never even met the woman,' said Sukey cheerfully, but he gave no answering smile.

'If you'd seen the look on his face — ' he began.

'Listen!' Sukey put both hands on his shoulders. 'Gus, I know your father. We lived together for over eleven years, remember, and we had our rows like everyone else, but he never said or did anything to suggest he might be capable of violence. He probably kept his feelings buttoned up the other evening because of Leo being there. You mustn't worry, truly. They're probably making it up at this very moment.'

'I doubt it. They don't share a room any more.'

The revelation took Sukey by surprise. 'Since when?'

'I don't know. Since last time I spent a weekend there, but that was quite a long time ago.'

'I'm sorry to hear that,' Sukey sighed. 'It

looks as though the marriage is cracking, but I don't suppose for a moment that Dad would so much as contemplate violence. I expect what made him angry was the game Myrna was playing with Leo — hinting at a lesbian relationship, I mean — in front of you. He probably thinks you're still an innocent little cherub and from what you've told me about Myrna, it's just the sort of trick she would play. I'd try and forget about it if I were you.' She yawned and stretched. 'I don't know about you, my son, but I'm going to bed. Tomorrow's a working day for us both.'

'Right.' He stood up and she was relieved to see that some of the tension had faded. 'Is it okay if Anita has supper with us tomorrow? Her Mum's got some committee meeting at the house in the evening and she says it's an awful bore — '

'Of course.'

'Thanks. Good-night, Mum.' He dropped a kiss on her cheek and made for the door. 'Is the water hot enough for a shower?'

'Sure.'

He clattered up the stairs, his fears apparently allayed after her confident reassurance. But as she went round the house switching off lights, checking windows and locking the front door, Sukey found herself wondering whether, after all, those fears might be justified. It was true that Paul had never shown any tendency to violence. But neither had he, until the day he broke the news that he was leaving her, given any sign of having been unfaithful, although the affair with Myrna had been going on for months. Then she told herself that it was hardly a valid comparison and went upstairs to get ready for bed.

3

The following week Sukey was on the early shift, finishing at four o'clock in the afternoon, which meant that she and Fergus — who, after finishing his GCSE exams had found a holiday job in a local supermarket — left the house at the same time each morning and arrived home within a few minutes of each other in the afternoon. For once the week passed uneventfully, with no serious crimes reported. On the Friday news reached the Scene of Crime Office at Police Headquarters that Sukey's work on a bungled raid a few weeks previously, during which a badly cut suspect had left bloodstained fingerprints all over some of his abandoned haul, had led to the recovery of several thousand pounds' worth of stolen property and gained the Scientific Support Department a pat on the back from their Superintendent. By way of celebration, on Friday evening Jim and Sukey went out to dinner; on Saturday, after a day spent alternately working and relaxing in the garden, they went to a concert in Cheltenham and on Sunday afternoon they watched a cricket match in which Fergus was playing for a local club against a neighbouring village.

The weather was fine throughout, Fergus made thirty runs, took two wickets and was lovingly congratulated by his girlfriend, Anita. All was sweetness and light; there were no further references to his melodramatic forebodings of the previous weekend and the whole episode had sunk to the back of Sukey's mind.

When she reported for duty shortly before eight o'clock on Monday morning there was nothing to suggest that it was going to be anything but a normal day. The officer in charge, Sergeant George Barnes, was riffling through the computer print-outs containing details of incidents that had been reported since the previous evening. When Sukey entered, he greeted her with something less than his normal joviality.

'What's up, Sarge?' she asked, as she dumped her handbag on her desk and sat down. 'You're not looking your radiant self this morning.'

'Didn't get much sleep, did I?' he growled. 'The baby was crying half the night.'

'Colic?'

'That's what they tell Jane at the clinic.' After the early death of his first wife and several years as a childless widower, George was now married to a woman fifteen years his junior and the somewhat surprised father of a three-month-old baby boy. 'They say he'll grow out of it, but it's taking a hell of a time,' he went on morosely.

'That's tough,' Sukey sympathised, remembering a few sleepless nights when Fergus was that age. 'Can I get you a cup of tea?'

'Don't bother specially, but if you're making one for yourself — ' He wasn't speaking out of politeness; the words were sincerely meant. That was one of the nice things about George; as far as the job was concerned he insisted that his officers do everything by the book, but there was nothing sexist about him.

'That's okay, I could do with one to wake me up,' she said. 'I had a slightly disturbed night as well.'

'Oh? What's your problem? Trouble with the boyfriend?'

'Nothing so interesting, I'm afraid — just some amorous cats having a party in my back garden.' Sukey, on her way to the door, glanced round in time to catch what struck her as a slightly prurient smirk replacing his downcast expression. It could have been simply a throwaway remark with no deliberate attempt to pry, but she often wondered how much, if anything, he — or any of the others in the department, come to that — had guessed about the nature of her relationship with DI Castle.

From the outset, they had been careful to maintain a strictly professional attitude to one another during working hours, but more than once, after Jim had been into the office to discuss a case with her, she had caught George looking at her with a slightly quizzical expression. It was something she had noticed only after his own whirlwind courtship and marriage, as if the rebirth of romance in his own life had made him more aware of its potential effect on others.

By the time she returned to the office with two mugs of tea, the rest of the morning's shift had arrived: PC Ted Field, who had recently joined the department, and Mandy Parfitt, its longest-serving member apart from George and a civilian like herself. In between gulps of tea, George began allocating the morning's jobs.

'RTA on Cleeve Hill, two vehicles involved, ambulance on the scene, sounds nasty,' he said, scanning a sheet of paper before handing it to the constable. 'You'd better take that, Ted. Mandy, another couple of break-ins in Hopley village . . . same MO as before by the looks of it.'

'House broken into, keys taken and car

29

nicked?' Mandy guessed.

'You've got it. A BMW and a Range Rover this time. CID are pretty sure the Jackson boys are behind it — they reckon they're running a car-ringing racket and they'll be very grateful if you can find them some nice fat clues.' George, his normal good humour apparently restored by the sweet, strong tea, gave a sardonic chuckle. 'Those buggers have been giving our lot the runaround for months.'

'Didn't we nick them a while back for handling stolen radios?'

'We did; they got three months apiece and were out in six weeks, greatly refreshed and eager to start work again. CID are convinced they're behind the theft of the cars, but they've managed to keep several jumps ahead of us up to now. See what you can turn up this time, Mandy.'

'I'll do my best, Sarge.' Mandy put the reports in her handbag and made for the door. 'Catch you guys later,' she said to the room at large, and she and Ted departed on their respective assignments.

'So what have you got for me?' Sukey asked.

'Barn fire at Dearley Farm, off the Cirencester road. Fire service alerted a little after ten-thirty last night.'

'Dearley Farm?' Sukey's interest was aroused. 'That rings a bell.'

'You know it?'

'I know of it. Presumably it's part of the Dearley Manor estate.' Sukey saw no reason to reveal her somewhat tenuous connection with the estate's owner. She ran her eye over the report and commented, 'I imagine arson is suspected, but I don't recall any other incidents recently so it doesn't look as if we're looking for a serious fire-bug.'

'On the face of it, no,' George agreed. 'Could just be kids being careless with their joints, of course, but you never know. Might be the start of a run of similar incidents, possibly someone with a grudge. Either way, we have to take it seriously.'

'Sure. Anything else for me?'

George nodded and handed over another sheet. 'The dreaded wheeler-dealers have struck again, although this time they weren't so lucky. The owner woke up and challenged them and they scarpered before they could get the wheels off the car. They left their jack behind so you might get some prints.'

'Same village as before,' Sukey commented as she scanned the details. 'Didn't their Neighbourhood Watch report some lads in a car seen acting suspiciously a few days earlier?'

'They did . . . and they got the number. And guess what?'

'The car had been nicked?'

'Right. The locals have been asked to report any further sightings, but it'll probably be found torched somewhere and the villains will have taken another for their next job. I wonder sometimes why we bother.' The cloud of depression settled once again on George's brow. 'Okay, Sukey, that's your lot for the moment. On your way.'

On this fine August morning after an enjoyable weekend, Sukey was in an optimistic frame of mind as she stepped out into the sunshine and crossed the yard to collect her van. The spaces on either side were empty; evidently, Ted and Mandy had already left. The rush-hour was not yet over and traffic was heavy, so it was almost a quarter of an hour before she reached the roundabout at the top of Crickley Hill and joined the procession of cars and lorries streaming up the Cirencester road.

It was an undulating route, carving across the Cotswolds between wide areas of upland pasture and fields of ripening crops, interspersed with wooded hollows. The traffic on the main road was still too heavy and fast-moving to allow Sukey an opportunity to appreciate the countryside, but about five miles from Cirencester she turned left into a narrow lane that meandered along a valley, with gently sloping fields on one side and mixed woodland on the other. She rolled down the window to admit the light breeze, still early-morning fresh and carrying the sound of birdsong and a distant clatter of farm machinery.

After half a mile or so she passed a wide metal gate on her left bearing the words 'Private Property — Dearley Estates', beyond which piles of felled timber lay at the side of a track running through the trees. As she drove slowly past, a tractor appeared dragging a trailer with a further load.

Round the next bend, a wisp of smoke drifting upwards from behind a stone wall told her that she had almost reached her destination. Another track, this time to the right, led across a field dotted with grazing sheep which scattered, bleating in agitation, as the van bumped along the uneven, stony surface. The land dipped and revealed the source of the smoke: a barn standing at the edge of a field of stubble dotted with neatly bound bales and separated from the first by a stone wall. The sound of a nearby tractor and a ribbon of freshly turned earth running the width of the field told Sukey that no time was being lost in ploughing a firebreak. She parked the van and began a preliminary survey of the scene.

It was a sight she had encountered a number of times before and it never failed to depress her. Blackened bales lay scattered over the ground, some only partially burned, a few still smouldering, all unusable. Being country bred, she understood better than most of her colleagues the value — not just in terms of money but also in long hours of toil — of the produce of the land and the frustration caused by its wanton destruction. Lambs with their throats torn out by dogs allowed by heedless owners to run free; the disappearance overnight of livestock faithfully tended for months in fair weather and foul; broken fences that had taken days to erect. Today's target was a valuable building, its structure badly damaged and its contents — fortunately, because of the season, not a full year's supply of straw, but more than any farmer would want to lose — reduced to a stinking ruin as the result of some careless or malicious action.

The barn was an old one, partly constructed of wood, with a more recent, steel-framed structure alongside. Judging by the state of the blackened beams, the fire appeared to have started in one corner and spread, probably fanned by a breeze blowing through the open sides, towards the wall of the adjacent building, which was scorched but apparently undamaged. Evidently, fire-fighters had reached the scene in time. Sukey spent several minutes examining and photo-graphing the seat of the fire, and was so absorbed in her task that the appearance of a black and white dog sniffing round her feet took her by surprise. She looked up and saw a Land Rover parked a short distance away, its approach evidently drowned by the noise of the tractor. A man was picking his way over the debris towards her.

He was, she judged, in his fifties; a typical countryman, sturdily built with a ruddy complexion and a ring of greying hair encircling a shining, copper-coloured pate. He was dressed like the average farm worker in a checked shirt, cotton trousers and heavy boots, but he had an upright, almost an authoritative bearing and the hand grasping the carved handle of a stout walking stick was clean and well-cared for.

'You from the police?' he asked.

'That's right. Sukey Reynolds, Scene of Crime examiner. And you are — ?'

'Ezra Hampton, Estate Manager. I was over at the timber yard and saw your van turn into the field.' He glanced round at the remains of the fire. 'Started deliberately, of course,' he observed. His tone, as he made the brief pronouncement, had a flat finality, as if he was in no doubt of its truth.

'Have you any idea who might have done it?' Sukey asked.

'I can think of several.' She waited for him to enlarge on this cryptic statement, but instead he turned and gestured with his stick at the locked building. 'Just as well the fire didn't get to that. Lot of valuable machinery in there.'

'Who raised the alarm?'

'One of the estate workers spotted it on his way home from the pub. He alerted me and I contacted several of the others. We got some tractors and trailers out . . . luckily we hadn't brought in the new crop of straw so there wasn't that much in the barn anyway. We managed to salvage quite a bit of what was left before the fire-fighters got here.' While he was speaking, his eyes moved restlessly over the depressing scene. 'Framework's badly charred, don't know if it can be repaired,' he muttered.

'It sounds as if it was started only a little while before — what time was the alarm raised?'

'I got the call about ten-thirty.'

'I see.' Sukey began examining the ground. 'Not much chance of finding shoeprints, the ground's too dry. I wonder which way they came.' She gestured towards a gate in the hedge on the far side of the field. 'Where does that lead?'

'Into a private lane leading to the Manor. There's a public bridleway off it that cuts through woodland and comes out in Dearley village.'

'My guess is that whoever started the fire probably approached from that direction,' Sukey speculated. 'They'd be less likely to be seen from the road. I wonder if they used an accelerant?' she added, half to herself.

Ezra shrugged. 'Can't say I smelt anything like that.'

'You were probably too busy tackling the fire to think of it,' she pointed out. 'If they did, they must have brought it in a container — I don't suppose you noticed one lying around?'

'Never thought to look.'

'Well, let's see if we can find anything.' The pair of them hunted among the wreckage for a while without success. 'They might have dumped it on their way back,' Sukey said. 'We'd better look a bit further afield.' She set off towards the gate, peering behind the bales as she went but with little hope of finding anything, while Ezra followed at her heels and the dog bounded ahead. On reaching the gate, she was about to open it and continue her search on the far side when something in the undergrowth beneath the hedge caught her eye. Ezra spotted it at the same time — a green plastic container. Before she could stop him he snatched it up and sniffed the empty interior.

'Petrol!' he pronounced, holding it up in triumph.

'Please, put it down without handling it any further,' she said, trying not to sound impatient. 'We might be able to get some prints off it.'

He looked slightly affronted, as if he expected congratulation instead of an implied reproof, but he did as she asked and laid it on the ground. 'Sorry, didn't think,' he muttered.

Sukey broke a twig off an elder tree growing by the wall and used it to pick up the container by its handle. 'I don't suppose you've seen it before, by any chance? It seems to have contained some garden chemical and it's quite a distinctive colour.'

Ezra shrugged. 'Might have done . . . all sorts of containers knocking about on a farm . . . couldn't be sure though.'

'Perhaps you'd try and find out if there's one missing from any of your stores?' she suggested and Ezra gave a slightly sullen nod, as if he resented being given instructions by a woman considerably younger than himself. 'I'll have a hunt round for the cap,' she went on as they made their way back to the barn. 'With any luck we'll find it under one of the bales.'

It was several minutes before the missing cap came to light, almost entirely concealed by trampled straw. Sukey put on rubber gloves, lifted it carefully with one finger and carried it to the van, where she bagged and labelled both their finds. She closed the rear doors and went round to the front.

'That it then?' said Ezra as she settled into the driver's seat.

'I've done all I can for the time being,' she told him. 'You'll be hearing from us again very soon. And if you should happen to think of anything else, perhaps you'll let us know? Here's the office number.'

He took the card she gave him and stood watching her, his expression inscrutable, while she reversed and drove past the Land Rover on her way back to the road. On reaching it, she took the opportunity, while waiting for a line of traffic caught behind a slow-moving tractor to pass, to contact the control room. 'Just finished with the barn fire at Dearley,' she told the officer who answered her call. 'On my way to the wheel-snatching job.'

'Forget that for the moment, there's another one just up the road from where you are. Break-in at Dearley Manor. Uniformed already attending. Informant the house-keeper, Mrs Little.'

'Right, I'm on my way.' It wasn't Myrna's lucky day, she thought as she turned right instead of left. Two attacks on her property within a few hours was probably a coincidence, but she recalled Ezra's cryptic reply when asked if he had any idea who might have started the fire: '*I can think of several* '.

4

For the whole of the six years that she and Paul had been divorced, Sukey had made a point of avoiding Dearley village, its manor and estates. Although her work had occasionally taken her to within a short distance of it, this was going to be the first time she had so much as set eyes on the house, let alone passed through the imposing gateway. When, after over a year of severely limited contact with his son, Paul had suddenly begun inviting him to his new home for occasional weekends, she stubbornly refused either to drive the boy there or to collect and bring him back, using the excuse that her car was old and none too reliable, that she depended on it for getting to work and that she couldn't afford to buy a better one. This, of course, was intended to prick Paul's conscience and to point up the difference in their circumstances now that he had found a rich wife, but although he had once grudgingly settled an unusually heavy garage repair bill he continued to insist that there was no question of giving her the money for a replacement. He paid her allowance regularly and on time, she had a job; she ought to be able to manage.

After his first visit to Dearley Manor, which had taken place over a weekend when his stepmother was away on a business trip, Fergus had come home quite overwhelmed with his father's new abode, describing in the graphic language of an eleven-year-old the luxury of its furniture and appointments and the beauty of its setting. 'I had a smashing bedroom and a bathroom all to myself!' he told his mother, his young face aglow. 'And you'd love the kitchen — it's brill, like the pictures in magazines . . . and there's a nice lady called Mrs Little, only she isn't little, she's big and fat and she comes to work on a bicycle . . . and she gives me homemade biscuits and lemonade and cooks really yummy nosh . . . and there's acres and acres of gardens and a tennis court and a swimming pool . . . and there was a cricket match in the village, Dad took me to watch — ' And on and on, while Sukey listened, smiling and doing her best to sound interested, hiding her bitter resentment, determined to say or do nothing to mar her child's delight in the renewed contact with his father, although every word of boyish prattle was like a sharp instrument driven into an open wound.

As Fergus grew older and more perceptive, and began bringing home accounts of disagreements between Paul and Myrna, Sukey could not help feeling a certain grim satisfaction in the knowledge that flaws were beginning to show in the once idyllic marriage. *'Serves the bastard right!'* she would mutter to herself — although never in front of Fergus. Then she would reproach herself for being unchristian. It wasn't Paul's fault that he was weak and impressionable and had been dazzled by Myrna's wealth and beauty. Her own hurt had lessened with time and she guessed that now, after over five sometimes very difficult years, she was more content and could look forward to the future with greater confidence than he.

With these thoughts running through her head, Sukey found herself for the first time driving along the gravelled approach to the Manor, a broad avenue lined with trees and bordered on either side by smooth lawns dotted with beds bright with flowers. She had half expected a large, imposing pile; instead she saw a comparatively modest but well proportioned house of Cotswold stone with a gabled roof and mullioned windows. Roses covered the walls and wisteria framed the porch, above which was a stone slab carved with a coat of arms. Her feelings as she

43

parked her van alongside the police car already there were mixed: a certain excitement on seeing at first hand the house where her ex-husband now lived and about which she had heard so much; a twinge of apprehension that she might have to come face to face with the woman who had taken him from her. Although it was unlikely that Myrna would recognise the person who came to investigate a break-in at her home as the former wife of her husband, one could never be sure. It might be better if another SOCO attended the scene. For a moment, she considered calling Sergeant Barnes and asking him to assign the job to one of her colleagues, but curiosity, coupled with a reluctance to reveal this aspect of her private life, got the better of her. She went to the door and rang the bell.

It seemed a long time before there was any movement within the house. She was about to ring again when she heard approaching footsteps; the lock clicked and the studded oak door swung open to reveal a stocky, middle-aged police constable in shirtsleeves. His glance went from her face to the bag of kit in her hand. 'You the SOCO?' he asked.

'That's right. Sukey Reynolds.' She showed her ID and he stood aside to let her in. 'I take it you're the local bobby?'

'That's right. PC Kevin Riley, at your service.'

'So what happened here?'

'We had a call about nine o'clock from the housekeeper to say the house had been broken into. She says she arrived later than usual, five or ten minutes to nine she thinks, found the back door smashed open, got back on her bicycle, belted hell for leather back home and called us.'

'Why didn't she call from here?'

'Said she was scared the intruders might still be in the house.'

'Understandable. Did she see a strange car or anyone hanging about?'

'No, but I don't think she waited to look. She just saw the broken door and panicked. There was certainly no car here when I arrived — that was the first thing I looked for — and I'm pretty sure there's no one in the house. I've been trying to get a statement from her, but there doesn't seem to be much more she can tell me. She seems pretty upset — keeps on about it was her fault for being late and she'll probably lose her job.'

'What about the owners — are they up and about?'

'Haven't set eyes on them. He's gone to work, she's still in bed having given instructions not to be disturbed. Probably sleeping it off — seems there was a party over the weekend.'

'Looks like it.' Sukey glanced round, pulling a face. While speaking, the constable was leading the way across a wide entrance hall with a carved staircase on one side leading to a galleried landing. A chandelier hung from an elaborate plaster ceiling and on the walls were several landscapes and portraits in heavy gilded frames, but the effect was marred by a scattering of crumpled rugs, broken glass and spilt wine on the polished wooden floor and a smell of stale tobacco smoke and vomit in the air. 'Is the rest of the place in this sort of state?'

'The downstairs rooms where the partying took place are in a bit of a pickle, but they don't appear to have been ransacked. I haven't checked upstairs yet so I don't know if the intruders got that far.'

'D'you reckon the housekeeper disturbed them?'

'It's possible, but like I said, she doesn't remember seeing a car or hearing any noise. She came into the kitchen, saw the door had been smashed open, panicked and ran.'

Under the staircase was a short passage, at the end of which a door stood open. Sunlight poured through a tall window and fell on a polished pine table where a stout woman with

46

large features and a plaited coronet of iron-grey hair was sitting with her hands clasped and a harassed expression on her face. Behind her, a glazed door hung from its hinges, its lock smashed and the floor around it littered with broken glass. She stared at Sukey without speaking.

'I'm from the police — a scene of crime examiner.' Sukey waved her ID, as regulations demanded, but it barely received a glance. 'I understand you're Mrs Little, the house-keeper here?'

'I've worked here for twenty years and nothing like this has ever happened before,' the woman said shakily. 'If only I'd been here at my usual time — '

'The villains might still have been here and attacked you,' Sukey pointed out. 'You could have had a lucky escape. Do you know if anything's missing?'

'We'll have to wait for the owners to tell us that,' Constable Riley interposed, as Mrs Little responded with a vague shake of the head. He glanced at his notebook. 'Mr and Mrs Maxford, you said?'

The housekeeper was trembling, obviously still affected by shock, but she appeared to be making an effort to pull herself together. 'Maxford is Madam's maiden name that she still uses, because of her business, you see,' she explained, with what Sukey felt was a hint of disapproval. 'She's actually Mrs Reynolds.'

'Ah!' Riley corrected his notes, then glanced at Sukey. 'Not related by any chance?' he asked with a grin.

'Oh sure, all my family live in places like this!' she joked back.

'So,' Riley gestured at the damage, 'you can see what Mrs Little found when she arrived here this morning, but she's still a bit shook up — how about making us all a cuppa before you get out your magnifying glass, Sukey?'

'If it isn't going to destroy evidence.' Sukey glanced round the expensively appointed kitchen, but nothing appeared to have been disturbed in the area round the sink. 'Perhaps Mrs Little will show me where everything is?'

At the suggestion the housekeeper rose, a little ponderously, to her feet, levering herself up from the table by a pair of plump, reddish hands. Plainly, the prospect of a stranger operating in her kitchen was not to be thought of. 'I'll make the tea,' she said with surprising firmness and went to fill the kettle. She began taking things from cupboards and drawers, bustling about as if nothing untoward had happened.

'Just what she needed — something to do,' whispered Riley.

Sukey went over to the door and began examining the splintered woodwork and the scattering of glass on the floor. 'I take it there's an alarm system in the house,' she commented, knowing perfectly well, from what Fergus had told her, that there was. She glanced round and located two sensors, one above the exterior door and another over the door leading into the passage. 'Was it sounding when Mrs Little arrived?'

'No. I asked her about that, but she couldn't be much help. It's normally switched off when she gets here in the morning, usually about eight o'clock. If the owners are away she has the job of setting it when she leaves the house after she finishes work, but she doesn't seem to know if they set it at night when they're at home.'

'You'd think they would, in a place like this.'

'You'd be surprised how many people don't bother.' Riley gave a resigned shrug. 'Had a case the other week when the milkman found a window of a house forced open and called us. When I arrived, the couple were still asleep in bed, their car had been nicked and they never heard a thing. If they'd had the sense to set their alarm before going to bed — ' He shook his head in exasperation at this example of human folly.

'So either this alarm wasn't set, or it had been tampered with?'

'Mrs Little says Mr Reynolds gets up early so if it is set overnight he probably switches it off. But I gather, from what she said, that no one would have been in a fit state to see to it after last night's bash,' Riley added with a wink.

Sukey grinned and gave a conspiratorial nod as if in agreement, although privately she considered it most unlikely that Paul, such a stickler for detail and routine, would overlook so important a matter as security. Unless he had been too drunk last night to think of it — but that wasn't like him either.

'So Mr Reynolds has gone to work, his wife is still in bed asleep, and neither of them heard a thing.'

'That's the way it looks.'

'What about the other staff? Surely, Mrs Little doesn't look after the house single-handed?'

'She tells me there's a Mrs Barton who comes in for a couple of hours every morning to do the housework. She also gives extra help when the folks are entertaining — like yesterday evening.'

'What time does she get here?'

'Normally at nine o'clock, but she's had to take one of her children to the dentist this morning so she won't be along until about eleven.' Riley pursed his lips and glumly shook his head. 'No witnesses at all, I'm afraid. It's all down to you to see if you can find any evidence.'

'There's not much to go on,' said Sukey, surveying the damage. 'It doesn't even look as if the intruder left the kitchen. There's hardly any sign of glass particles on the floor away from the point of entry . . . I take it that you came in by the front door?'

'That's right. Mrs Little tells me that's the way she always comes in in the morning.'

Sukey glanced at her watch; it was a quarter to ten. 'Isn't it time 'Madam' was told what's happened?' she said in a low voice.

'That's what I suggested, but the old girl seems scared rigid at the idea,' he whispered back, glancing over his shoulder to where Mrs Little was pouring boiling water into a large china pot. 'All she said was, 'She'll call me when she's ready for her tray . . . it's more than my job's worth to wake her when she wants to lie in.' I get the impression Madam's a bit of a tyrant.'

I can confirm that, Sukey thought to herself. Aloud, she said, 'Well, she'll have to know sooner or later.'

'Here's the tea,' Mrs Little announced, setting a tray on the table behind them. 'I've poured it out — help yourselves to milk and sugar.' Her voice was steadier and she seemed more composed, although Sukey noticed that her hands were still trembling.

'We've been thinking,' said Riley as he spooned sugar into his cup. 'Your employer really should be told what has happened. I know what you said about not waking her,' he went on as Mrs Little opened her mouth to object, 'but don't you think that in the circumstances she might be even more upset that you didn't inform her straight away?'

'The officer's right, you know,' said Sukey.

The housekeeper looked from one to the other, nervously biting her lip. 'I suppose so,' she agreed after a moment. 'She's going to be furious with me either way . . . might as well get it over with. I'll make her some strong coffee.' She refilled the kettle and got out another tray.

Sukey put down her cup. 'I think, if you don't mind, I'd like to check upstairs first. If the villains did get that far, they may have left some evidence. I wouldn't want it disturbed.'

There was no response from the house-keeper, who was busy measuring coffee into a cafétière. Sukey went back to the hall and climbed the stairs, keeping close to the wall and searching the heavy crimson carpet in the beam of her torch for any tell-tale fragments of glass, but finding none. Along the landing, placed at intervals between the doors that led off it, were several antique cabinets containing porcelain and crystal ornaments, while on a pier table immediately opposite the top of the stairs was a display of ivory and jade carvings. Nothing appeared to have been touched. All the doors were closed except one, which stood slightly ajar. Sukey gave a light tap, received no response, and cautiously pushed it a little further open.

The room appeared to be a bedroom, although the bed itself was invisible behind the half-open door. The high ceiling, like the one in the entrance hall, was ornamented with intricate plaster mouldings, the walls were papered in a delicate pattern of pink roses and a thick carpet the colour of alabaster covered the floor. Immediately opposite the door was a tall casement window, draped in satin curtains to match the walls, and beneath it stood an armchair, similarly upholstered, on which lay a few discarded items of women's underclothing. A pair of high-heeled silver sandals and two soft mounds of black filmy material were scattered at intervals on the carpet as though the wearer had undressed wandering across the room. The trail led from the bathroom, of which a glimpse was visible in the mirror of one of the half-open doors of a tall wardrobe on the left-hand wall, towards the middle of the room and — presumably — the bed. Sukey coughed and tapped again a little more loudly before pushing the door fully open.

She had seen death before and learned to cope with it, although the sight of a corpse, however peaceful-looking, always gave her an uncomfortable jolt. But nothing she had experienced so far had prepared her for the scene that awaited her as she stepped into the room. On the edge of a king-sized bed was the body of a woman. The head, framed in a tumbled mass of reddish-gold hair, was turned towards the door, and the greenish eyes were wide open as if petrified with the terror of imminent death. Blood from a hideous gash in the throat had poured down one arm and dripped from the fingertips on to the carpet, giving the macabre impression that the scarlet nail-varnish had somehow dissolved and mingled with the flow. The other hand was clenched round a blood-stained duvet that only partially covered the naked, mutilated body.

Sukey pressed the knuckles of both hands to her mouth to stop herself from screaming. Never, she thought in those first moments of sick horror, had she seen so much blood, so much butchery to human flesh. She turned away, drawing deep gasps of air into lungs momentarily paralysed by shock, willing herself not to throw up, not to run from the scene in a panic or do anything that would bring the people below rushing up the stairs in alarm.

Take all possible measures to preserve the scene intact, avoid contamination of evidence. Request CID attendance . . . you're in charge till they arrive. Her training came to her rescue, helped her to regain control. Carefully following the route she had taken on her way up, stumbling a little on the way downstairs as her shaking legs threatened to collapse beneath her, she returned to the kitchen. Mrs Little, a tray set with a heavy porcelain cup and saucer and a fully-charged glass cafétière on a lace cloth at her elbow, was seated at the table opposite PC Riley. When Sukey entered, she got to her feet and reached for the tray. She still appeared nervous, glancing from one to the other. 'Shall I take this up now?' she said.

'Not just for the moment,' said Sukey gently, and the woman sat down again. She appeared almost relieved at the delay. 'Kevin, could I have a word?'

'Sure.' The constable followed her back into the hall. 'Something wrong?' he asked. 'You look as if you've seen a ghost.'

'Not a ghost . . . a corpse. At least, I'm pretty sure she's dead, her throat's been cut and there are multiple stabbings.'

'Merciful Jesus!' exclaimed Riley, crossing himself. 'I'd better take a look.'

'No!' Sukey put out a restraining hand as he started for the stairs. 'No one goes up there till I've done what I can to seal the scene.'

'Oh, right, you're the specialist. What do I tell her?' He jerked his head in the direction of the kitchen.

'Say there's been an accident and we're calling a doctor.' She was jabbing buttons on her mobile phone as she spoke. 'She doesn't look the hysterical type, but you never know — ' She broke off as an officer in the control room came on the line. 'We have a suspicious death at Dearley Manor,' she said in a voice that surprised her with its steadiness. 'I need a doctor and a senior CID officer . . . and the Coroner must be informed, okay?' She signed off and put away the phone.

'Anything for me to do?' asked Riley. Far from being resentful at having to take instructions from Sukey, he appeared thankful at being relieved of responsibility. Murders, she guessed, were not exactly a daily occurrence on his patch.

'Just stay with Mrs Little until a detective arrives, and make sure she doesn't move around or touch anything else. If anyone calls, take their names but don't let them in. I'll seal off the area round the break-in in a moment. It may have nothing to do with the killing, but we can't take any chances.'

They met the housekeeper half-way along the passage. Either she had overheard their conversation, or she had already guessed from Sukey's shocked appearance that something was seriously wrong. She looked from one to the other, her eyes round with fear, her mouth working. 'Madam's dead, isn't she?' she whispered.

'We can't be certain, but she's been very badly hurt,' said Riley gently. 'It seems as if someone attacked her. My colleague has called for a doctor, but it looks pretty bad. You'd better come and sit down.' He took the housekeeper by the elbow and steered her back to the kitchen, with Sukey following.

She sank into a chair and put a hand over her eyes. 'He swore he'd do it, sooner or later. I never thought he meant it, but — '

'Who swore he'd do what?' Riley sat down facing her and reached for his notebook.

'Her husband, of course ... I heard him — he said he'd kill her — '

'You mustn't jump to conclusions — '

Sukey blurted out. Riley shot her a meaning glance that said, *You get on with your job and leave this to me.* He was right, of course; interviewing witnesses was none of her business. 'Sorry,' she mouthed and picked up her case. 'I have to fetch some stuff from the van before I start work,' she said over her shoulder as she went out.

The housekeeper's words had jerked her mind back to the reports Fergus had brought home about increasing hostility between his father and stepmother, culminating with the most recent. She recalled her son's troubled expression, heard once more the fear in his voice as he muttered, almost as if he were ashamed of entertaining the thought, *'Some-times he looks at her as if he'd like to kill her'.* Despite the assurances she had given the boy that his father was incapable of physical violence, her years of contact with the police had taught her that even the gentlest, most self-controlled of mortals has a breaking point. Was it possible that Paul had carried out that frenzied attack? The marriage had evidently been under stress for some time. Did he perhaps believe there was a lesbian relationship between his wife and the woman called Leonie? If so, it would immediately be seized on by the police as an obvious motive for the killing; either way, there was no doubt that he would be high on the list of suspects. How was she going to break the news to Fergus? There was no way of softening the horrific nature of Myrna's death . . . the effect on the boy would be devastating.

She drove her fears to the back of her mind, forcing herself to concentrate on the job in hand. With her clothes and shoes masked in a protective suit and hands encased in rubber gloves, she marked off with tape the route she had taken to the murder scene, protected the bedroom carpet with stepping boards, made notes, took photographs, sealed off with more tape the bloodstained area round the bed and the path she judged the killer would have taken on leaving. She worked quickly and methodically, with no recurrence of the wave of nausea that had all but engulfed her at the first sight of the dead woman. Satisfied that she had done all she could for the moment, she went downstairs.

In the kitchen, Riley was just putting down the telephone. 'I've been ringing round, trying to contact Mr Reynolds at his office, but he's not there,' he said. 'They tell me he came in at the usual time and went out again soon after without saying anything. According to his secretary he's supposed to be visiting a client, but he hasn't arrived yet. I left a message for him to call home.'

'Good.' Sukey set about sealing off the area round the broken door, but the realisation that in a short time she would probably come face to face with Paul switched her mind to her own position in the tragedy. She had discovered the body, she was a material witness, she might well find herself in the position of having to give evidence that could throw suspicion on her ex-husband. The prospect sickened her; she found herself wishing with all her heart that she had resisted the desire to see the trappings of wealth and luxury for which Paul had sacrificed her and their son. It would have been so easy to explain to George Barnes; he would have understood, would almost certainly have considered it preferable — even over the matter of a simple break-in — for someone with no personal connection with the victim to attend. And from this thought flowed another: What if Jim Castle was the CID officer responding to her call? He might already be on his way, could arrive at any second. She was torn between an overwhelming longing to talk to him as a friend and a lover and the knowledge that his need to remain detached and professional would demand that he treat her in exactly the same way as other witnesses.

A local GP arrived and Sukey escorted him to the scene, urging him as tactfully as possible to keep to the route she had marked out. 'You don't have to tell me the drill, it's not the first time I've attended a murder scene,' he informed her as he marched up the stairs ahead of her. His examination was brief and conclusive. 'Life declared extinct at ten-fifteen a.m.,' he said laconically, and departed.

Moments later there was another ring at the bell. That would be the CID. It would be a relief to hand over responsibility. But it wasn't a detective waiting on the doorstep; it was Paul.

5

At the sight of his ex-wife framed in his front doorway, Paul stared with his mouth open for a moment before saying sharply, 'What are the police doing here . . . and why on earth are you dressed like an astronaut?' His gaze raked her from head to foot, taking in her paper boilersuit and overshoes. 'Has there been a break-in?'

'I'm afraid so.' Sukey stood aside to let him in, closing the door behind him.

'Did they take much? Where's Myrna . . . and what's all that for?' he demanded, gesturing at the lengths of blue and white tape. He made a movement towards the stairs, but she grabbed him by the arm.

'No, Paul, you can't go up there.'

'Why not?'

They stood facing one another, Paul's expression registering anxiety, as if in anticipation of bad news, Sukey frantically searching for the right words to break it. She felt totally unprepared for the task.

'I came back for my briefcase. I forgot it — it's got my house keys in it,' he said in a sudden rush, as if he felt called upon to explain his unexpected arrival at his own home. 'That's why I had to ring the bell.'

'You aren't here in response to our message, then?'

'What message? I didn't — ' He clutched her arm, his eyes searching hers. 'You must tell me what's happened. I met the doctor's car in the lane — has there been an accident?' As if he read the truth in her expression, even before she found her voice, apprehension dawned in his eyes. 'Is it Myrna?'

'Yes, Paul, it's Myrna, but it wasn't an accident.' She felt the grip on her arm tighten as her meaning sank in.

'You mean, someone attacked her? Is she badly hurt?'

'Paul, is there somewhere we can talk privately for a moment?'

'In my study.' He led her into a small room to the right of the front door. In contrast with what she had seen of the rest of the house, the furniture was purely functional: a desk, a leather-upholstered executive chair, a filing cabinet and a bookcase. Two mullioned windows gave a view of the drive, which ran in a straight line to the gates. In the distance, Sukey saw a maroon car turn out of the lane and head for the house: DI Castle's Mondeo.

'I think you'd better sit down,' she said. 'Something dreadful's happened.'

Obediently, he lowered himself into his seat at the desk. There was one other chair in the room; Sukey removed a briefcase that lay on it, mentally noting as she did so that it must be the one he had returned to collect, and sat down to face him. Almost mechanically, he reached for a paperknife that lay there, picked it up and began twisting it between his fingers. She recalled how he had always needed something to fiddle with when he had a problem on his mind. She noticed that his hands were unsteady. 'Tell me,' he said in a dull voice.

'Myrna's dead. She's been murdered.'

Paul gave a gasp and stared at her, round-eyed and open-mouthed. His grip tightened convulsively round the onyx handle. 'My God!' he said hoarsely. 'How?'

'Someone went for her with a knife.'

'You mean, she was stabbed?'

'It's worse than that.' Sukey swallowed hard as the memory of the scene returned in all its horror. 'Her throat was cut.'

He ran his tongue over his lips, shaking his head, trying to take it in. 'Who found her?'

'I did. I was called to check the scene of the break-in, and — '

'What break-in?'

'Mrs Little found the kitchen door broken open and called the police.'

'What happened — did Myrna disturb them?'

'We don't know yet exactly what happened.' Sukey paused and took a deep breath. 'It was a frenzied attack, Paul . . . by someone with a grudge, perhaps. Can you think of anyone — ?'

He gave a short, mirthless laugh. 'I can think of plenty,' he said bitterly, unconsciously echoing Ezra Hampton's words. Her mind flashed back to the anxiety in Fergus's eyes as he said: '*He looks at her as if he'd like to kill her*'. Almost as if Paul was reading her thoughts, he added, 'And I'll be number one on the list, won't I?'

Outside, the approaching car came to a halt, doors slammed and footsteps crunched on the gravel. Sukey stood up. 'That'll be the CID,' she said. 'I'll have to go and talk to them. Are you all right?' she added anxiously as he dropped the knife, buried his face in his hands and began swaying from side to side.

Without looking up, he said in a muffled voice, 'There were plenty of times when I felt like hitting her. Times when I could have throttled her, she made me so angry . . . but I never actually laid a finger on her.' He lifted his head and looked at her beseechingly. 'I didn't kill her,' he whispered. 'You do believe me, don't you, Susan?'

She stared down at him, thinking how much he had altered in the three years since she last set eyes on him. His hair was sparser, his face thinner and his skin less healthy-looking than she remembered; new lines had appeared, emphasised now by fear as the realisation of his position sank in. At their last meeting, which she had requested in order to try to persuade him to increase the allowance he made for Fergus, his manner had been a blend of condescension and hostility, as if she was asking him to hand over a small fortune instead of the modest sum that she knew he could well afford. The encounter had been brief and acrimonious, and although he had reluctantly yielded in the end, it had left a bitter after-taste that took a long while to fade. But now, seeing his defeated attitude, drawn features and haunted expression, she felt nothing but compassion. The recent past had brought him growing humiliation and disillusionment, culminating in a ghastly tragedy. Guilty or not, a traumatising ordeal lay ahead.

An imperious ring on the front doorbell gave her a welcome excuse to avoid answering the question. 'I have to go now,' she said. 'I suggest you stay here. I'll tell the detectives where to find you.'

When she opened the door there was no

reaction from either DI Castle or DS Radcliffe apart from brief nods of recognition. 'Where's the victim?' asked Castle.

'Upstairs, sir, first room along the gallery to the right. The family GP has attended and pronounced life extinct. The local man, PC Riley, is in the kitchen with the housekeeper — she's the one who reported the break-in. There's something a bit iffy about that, by the way.'

'Done from inside, you mean?'

'No, the window was smashed from outside all right, but there's no sign of broken glass except in the immediate area.'

'Right, we'll look into that later. Where's the victim's husband?'

'In his study.' Recalling Paul's reaction to the news, Sukey found it difficult to keep her manner professional. She gestured towards the door behind her. 'He's only just been told and he's pretty shocked. I think perhaps he could do with a brandy.'

'Right. Andy, you organise that and then see what Riley and the housekeeper can tell you.'

'Yes, Guv.' Following Sukey's directions, the sergeant headed for the kitchen.

'You'd better come with me.' Carefully keeping to the common approach path that Sukey had marked out, Castle made his way upstairs with Sukey at his heels. He stopped short in the open doorway of Myrna's room. 'God, whoever did that must have gone berserk!' he muttered. She watched as his eyes raked the room. 'Did you find the weapon?'

'Not so far, but I haven't carried out a comprehensive search — I was more concerned with protecting the scene before the doctor arrived. I photographed the body from all angles, of course, both before and after his examination.'

Castle gave a nod of approval. 'Right. There's nothing more for us to do here until the forensic pathologist has done his stuff. Let's hope he isn't delayed.' He pulled out a handkerchief and put it to his nose; despite his air of detachment, his face had a sickly pallor. Myrna had gone to bed without drawing the curtains, the sun was shining on the unprotected windows and the room was becoming warmer by the minute. Sukey felt her own gorge rising as she caught the first, indescribable whiff of decay.

'Let's move out of range.' For the first time since his arrival at the house, Castle dropped his professional manner. He put an arm round her and led her a short distance along the landing, away from the grisly scene. 'Feeling okay?' he asked.

'A bit shaken, but I'll be all right.' For a brief moment, she allowed her head to lean against his shoulder before pulling away.

'Look,' he said gently, 'this is no reflection on your competence, Sook — you've done everything by the book so far and I'll be sure to mention it to the Super — but I'm taking you off the case as of this moment. I think you'll understand why.'

'Yes, I thought you would.' There was no need for him to spell it out; as Paul's former wife, her evidence was liable to be seized on by Counsel as potentially biased should he be brought to trial. In a way, the decision was a relief; she quailed at the thought that he might be convicted on evidence that she had uncovered. But he couldn't be convicted, surely, of a crime he didn't commit? Hadn't he sworn to her, only a few minutes ago, that he was innocent? Unable to contain herself, she burst out, 'He didn't do it, Jim . . . he couldn't have done. I know him, he simply isn't capable — ' She broke off, aware that her feelings were running away with her.

'I didn't hear any of that,' Castle said quietly. He waited until she was calm again before resuming his normal professional manner. 'You are to go straight back to the office and make out your report. Sergeant Radcliffe will take your statement later. Now

I'll have a word with the victim's husband. In the study, I think you said.'

'Yes, Guv,' she said meekly, and followed him downstairs. At the bottom, he punched out a number on his mobile phone. While waiting for a reply, he said over his shoulder, 'On second thoughts, better hang around in case the pathologist gets here before the relief SOCO team shows up.'

*　*　*

Paul eyed the man who entered the room and uttered a few conventional words of sympathy before drawing up a chair and sitting down to face him. So this, he thought, was the guy Susan had taken up with. He recognised the name because Fergus had mentioned a while ago that his mother was friendly with a Detective Inspector Castle, who sometimes visited their home and occasionally went along with them to football and cricket matches. He had felt many a pang of jealousy at the thought of another man establishing a degree of intimacy with his son, especially when Fergus began referring to 'Jim' instead of 'Mr Castle'. He was curious, too, about the kind of man his ex-wife would be interested in. He suspected — largely because in recent months Fergus had become cagey whenever

Jim's name was mentioned — that she was having an affair with him. He hoped she was being discreet; after all, the lad was only sixteen, too young to have to cope with a sexual relationship between his mother and another man being paraded before him.

It struck him as ironic that this man should be the one to investigate Myrna's death. He wondered if the detective knew who he was and if so, whether it would have any effect on his attitude. His own emotions were in chaos: shock at what had happened; horror at the prospect of having to identify the body; a vague awareness that he would be expected to show some sign of grief, but feeling none; above all, terror at the knowledge that sooner or later the mutual antagonism between him and his murdered wife would be dragged into the open. People would not be slow to draw the obvious conclusion. He studied the detective with a mixture of curiosity and apprehension, noting the greenish eyes with their steady, penetrating gaze, the aquiline features and the thick, glossy brown hair that made him absurdly conscious of his own balding crown.

'Mr Reynolds,' Castle was saying, 'I realise that this is a very difficult time for you, but I have to ask you some questions. It would be helpful to our investigation if we could get on with it as soon as possible, but of course, if you'd rather come down to the station and talk to us when you've had time to get over the shock — ?'

'I'm all right, Inspector.' He indicated the empty glass on the desk. 'As you can see, I've had a stiffener.'

'I'm sure you needed it.'

The other officer in the room, who had been introduced as Sergeant Radcliffe, opened his notebook and held a pen at the ready. There was a short silence before Castle put his first question.

'I understand that you and your wife were entertaining friends yesterday evening. Your housekeeper has given us a list,' he picked up a sheet of paper lying in front of him on the desk, 'and I'd be obliged if you could tell me if it's complete.' He cleared his throat and began reading. 'Mr and Mrs Ashton, Mr and Mrs Perry, Mr and Mrs Dennison, Mrs Willow, Mr Hampton and Miss Filbury.'

Paul nodded. 'Yes, that's correct.'

'Good. Now, can I take it that these are all personal friends of you and your wife?'

'Not exactly.'

'Oh?' The detective's brows lifted.

'Bradley Ashton, Sam Perry and Eric Dennison are all employed by my wife's company, Maxford Domestic Fittings,' Paul explained. 'Ashton is the Production Director, Perry is the Sales Director and Dennison is the Company Secretary.'

'I see. And the others?'

'Emily — Mrs Willow — is a tenant on the Dearley estate — '

'Which also belongs to your late wife, I understand?'

'That's right. Ezra Hampton is the Estate Manager and Leonie Filbury keeps the estate accounts.'

Castle made notes on the list and passed it to Sergeant Radcliffe. He thought for a moment and then said, 'Can I take it that this was purely a social gathering?'

'Not really.'

The detective's face was impassive as he said, 'There was some other reason, perhaps connected with the business and the estate, for inviting this particular group of people?'

'Yes.'

'And that was?'

'Another company, Headwaters plc, recently made an offer for Maxford's. My wife had decided to make the party the occasion of announcing the result of the negotiations.'

'So in a way, this was a business meeting?'

'You could call it that.'

As if trying to give the impression of a mere policeman unfamiliar with the ways of business folk, Castle asked, 'So why, I wonder, did she decide to include one of her tenants, her estate manager and an office employee? Just to make it all seem a little less formal, would you say?'

Paul read the shrewdness behind the apparently artless question and knew immediately what the detective was driving at. There was no point in beating about the bush; he might already have gleaned from Susan what manner of woman her ex-husband had married. In any case, he'd soon find out from other people how universally unpopular she was, how she had enjoyed watching other people's discomfiture. 'My wife had decided not to accept the Head-waters offer, but instead to raise the capital she needed to extend the factory by selling part of the estate to developers,' he said after a pause.

'Ah!' Castle thought for a moment before saying, 'I suppose that would be of some concern to Mrs Willow and the others?'

'It meant that Mrs Willow, and some of the estate employees, would have to move out of their homes. And I imagine that, as estate manager, Ezra Hampton would also be affected in some way.'

'You imagine.' Castle appeared to find the word significant. 'Do I take it that this was *not* one of the points your wife discussed with you?'

'She only consulted me on purely financial matters.'

'I see.' There was a brief silence, during which the detective appeared to be digesting the information Paul had given him so far. Then he said, 'So it was good news for the Maxford employees — their jobs presumably were no longer at risk — but bad news for the others?'

'In a way, it was bad news for all of them. Brad, Sam and Eric stood to lose some quite substantial perks they had been promised, and their future prospects with Headwaters would have been better than with Maxford's.'

'So perhaps the party was by way of compensation for the disappointment — a way of breaking it gently?'

'The decision had nothing to do with me.'

'You're not a director of Maxford's?'

'No. From time to time I act as their financial advisor but I have no official position within the company. I'm a partner in a firm of accountants in Cheltenham — Turner and Clark.'

'But presumably, in your capacity as financial advisor, you were involved in the negotiations?'

'My wife and I discussed the offer at

length, but I never took part in any meetings.'

'And what was your advice?'

'To accept the offer. It seemed to hold out the best prospects for the company's future.'

'But she went against your advice.' There was a brief pause, during which Castle's gaze never left Paul's face. 'This party,' he resumed. 'I take it you were present when your wife broke the news to her guests?'

'No. I left early. No one noticed — the party was getting quite noisy and they were all in a celebratory mood, thinking that they were in for a nice little windfall.' Paul became uncomfortably aware that a harsh, sarcastic note had crept into his voice. 'Myrna had even dropped hints that there'd be something for the estate people as well.'

'Do I take it that you were reluctant to, shall we say, appear to have any responsibility for what you knew was going to prove a disappointing decision?'

'That's about it.'

The detective nodded. Paul thought there was a hint of sympathy in his manner as he asked, 'So, where were you during the evening?'

'There are three holiday cottages on the estate, and one of them hasn't been let this month because some of the plumbing needs attention. I decided to spend the night there.'

'Alone?'

The question took Paul entirely by surprise. His grip tightened on the paperknife he had been fingering throughout the interview as he responded with an indignant, 'Of course! What are you suggesting?'

Castle made a conciliatory gesture. 'I'm not suggesting anything. I was wondering if anyone could confirm your story — one of the tenants of the other cottages, for example?'

Paul gave a weary shrug. 'I've no idea, I'm afraid. I didn't see anyone, but someone might have noticed a light, or seen my car.'

'We'll leave that for the moment. Tell me, Mr Reynolds, how did you feel about having your advice rejected?'

For the second time, Paul was thrown by the unexpectedness of the question. He felt his spirits sinking to a new low as he recalled the bitter argument that had followed, the poisonous atmosphere over that weekend which had soured his enjoyment of Fergus's visit, the disgusting way Myrna had flaunted her relationship with Leonie. Sooner or later, the inspector would be sure to ask why an employee in a comparatively humble position had been invited to the party. The green eyes seemed to bore into his brain as he struggled to think of some way of deflecting the inquiry from the path that, sooner or later, it was bound to follow.

There was a knock on the door; a uniformed officer entered and said apologetically, 'Sorry to interrupt, sir, but there's a young lady insists on seeing you urgently. Won't take no for an answer.'

Before the inspector could speak, the man was elbowed aside and Leonie herself burst into the room. Her eyes were wild and her face contorted with grief and fury. Ignoring everyone else, she rushed round the desk and threw herself at Paul like a wildcat, clawing at his face with both hands and screeching, 'You bastard, you killed her! I warned her you meant it but she wouldn't listen to me — ' Her words dissolved into incoherent shrieks; she began punching him, kicking his shins and tearing at his hair. It took the three of them — the inspector, the sergeant and the constable — to drag her off.

Paul sat in a daze, mechanically dabbing with a handkerchief at the blood trickling from a scratch on his cheek, while the men subdued the struggling, sobbing woman and took her out of the room. The sounds of disturbance grew fainter; somewhere in the house a door slammed and there was silence. Then DI Castle came back into the room, this time on his own, and sat down. He leaned back in his chair, lightly clasping his knees with thin, tapering fingers. To Paul's uneasy gaze he appeared like a bird of prey, but his tone was almost conversational as he said, 'Perhaps there's something else you'd care to tell me, Mr Reynolds?'

6

A little wearily, Sukey made her way back to the van, reported to the control room as DI Castle had instructed and settled down to wait. The place was swarming with police, but she paid no heed to any of them. Almost in a daze, she sat drumming her fingers on the wheel, trying to sort out the jumble of thoughts and emotions swirling round in her head. Amid the shock and revulsion, her concern for Paul in his predicament jostled with the problem of how she would break the news to Fergus and its probable effect on him. The prospect made her feel physically sick; there was no way she could soften the blow. She recalled the tremor in her son's voice and the haunted look in his eyes as he expressed the fear that his father might 'do something stupid', followed by his look of relief on hearing her confident words of reassurance. His faith in her judgment had been touching; she dreaded the thought of how he would react to the possibility that it had been shown, in such a terrible fashion, to be at fault. Her own doubts returned to torment her. Was there, after all, a darker side to Paul's nature than she had ever suspected?

The minutes ticked by. She watched in the rear-view mirror for the familiar white vans bringing the colleagues to whom she would hand over the task of searching the house for evidence that would lead to Myrna's killer, praying that the pathologist wouldn't turn up first, dreading the prospect of having to return to the death scene. Lost in thought, she was startled by a tap on the window. Sergeant Radcliffe was standing beside the van, accompanied by a wooden-faced Mrs Little.

'Sukey, would you be kind enough to give this lady a lift home?' he asked. 'I could send one of our chaps, but if you're leaving anyway — ?'

'I have to wait until more SOCOs get here, but they shouldn't be long — ah, I think I see them now. If Mrs Little doesn't mind waiting while I have a quick word?'

Without speaking, the housekeeper climbed into the passenger seat, giving no indication as to whether she minded waiting or not. She sat clutching her handbag and staring straight ahead with a blank expression. When Sukey got back into the van after a brief handover to her colleagues and enquired where she lived, she replied, 'In Dearley village, it's not far,' without turning her head.

Sukey drove slowly towards the gate, where a uniformed constable had been posted. He had stopped a small red sports car and was speaking to the woman driver, indicating with gestures that she was not allowed to enter. As if complying with his instructions, she reversed the car a few feet, but instead of driving away she wrenched the wheel hard round and shot forward. In the nick of time, he leapt aside and the car came charging like a bullet up the drive towards the house. As Sukey hastily put two wheels onto the grass to avoid it, she had a brief glimpse of a pale, strained face and boyishly short fair hair.

At the gate, the shaken constable was speaking on his radio. 'Did you see that?' he demanded indignantly as Sukey pulled up. 'Started arguing, seemed to change her mind and then — pow!'

'Whoever is she?' Sukey asked.

'Leonie Filbury,' said Mrs Little before he had a chance to reply. The incident seemed to have brought her to life. As if she had been holding her breath, she exhaled noisily and added, with a note of grim pleasure in her voice, 'She's in for a nasty shock when she finds out what's happened to her darling.'

'She'd get more than a shock if I had my way!' muttered the aggrieved officer. If he read any significance into the housekeeper's words, he gave no sign of it.

'Is Ms Filbury a friend of Mrs Reynolds?' Sukey enquired casually as she turned out of the gate and drove slowly along the narrow winding lane leading to Dearley village.

'You could call it that, I suppose!' There was no mistaking the sarcasm in the housekeeper's voice.

'Have they known one another long?'

'About six months, since Leonie — Leo, she likes to be called, can't think why — came to work in the estate office. Soon became thick as thieves, they did.' Mrs Little gave a sardonic chuckle. 'Used to make Mr R as mad as a hatter. Not that there was anything new about that,' she added darkly. 'I've seen him many a time looking as if he'd like to stick a knife in her, and now he's done it, hasn't he?' Before Sukey had an opportunity to reply the housekeeper said, in an abrupt change of tone, 'Stop here, this is where I live.' She clambered out of the van the moment Sukey pulled up, slammed the door and pushed open a wooden gate on which the words 'Pear Tree Cottage' were painted in faded white letters.

'Thanks so much for the lift,' Sukey muttered waspishly after the retreating figure. Driving on for a short distance looking for a convenient place to turn round, she came to the church. It was set well back from the road, which widened on either side of the gateway for several yards affording parking space for half a dozen or so cars. A little further along on the opposite side was the village shop.

It was almost midday and the temperature had been climbing steadily. Sukey had brought sandwiches and a flask of coffee for her lunch, but at that moment a long cool drink, or maybe an ice-cream, had more appeal. She parked in a free space, locked the van and crossed over the road. As she did so, she noticed a Land Rover parked a few spaces further on. Over the tailboard, Ezra Hampton's dog watched her curiously as she passed.

She pushed open the shop door and an old-fashioned bell tinkled a welcome. In contrast to the heat outside, the interior was pleasantly cool. It was larger than she expected from the size of the frontage and the stack of plastic baskets just inside indicated that it was run as a mini-supermarket. Several customers were at the counter and from the way they were clustered in a group rather than waiting in line to pay for their purchases, she got the impression they were engaged in conversation. As she glanced round in search of the drinks cabinet, she heard a man's voice say, 'Here's someone who can tell us. This lady's from the police.' It was Ezra.

The last thing Sukey wanted was to be subjected to a cross-examination on the events of the past few hours. Naturally, there would soon be an official statement about Myrna's death, but it was always up to the officer in charge of the investigation how much detail of any incident was revealed. She would have to be careful what she said. 'I do work for the police, yes,' she admitted, on finding herself the focus of everyone's attention, 'but I'm not — '

'She's a scene of crime examiner,' Ezra explained without giving her a chance to finish. 'Came early this morning to look into the barn fire. Bet she knows what's been going on at the Manor.'

The word 'crime' had the effect of opening the floodgates and Sukey was bombarded with questions. 'Has there been a burglary?', 'Miss Evans says she saw the doctor's car — has someone been hurt?', 'Why is there a policeman on the gate?'

'There has been rather a nasty incident, but I'm afraid I can't — ' Sukey began, but she was interrupted by a tiny, frail-looking woman with white hair who stepped forward, put a hand on her arm and looked up at her with pale blue eyes that burned with a fanatical light.

'I knew there was evil brewing,' she declared. She spoke with a local accent in a theatrical tone that was almost comic. 'Didn't I say so, only last week?' she went on, glancing round at the others as if seeking confirmation. Their only response was a succession of resigned shrugs, indulgent smiles and eyes rolled heavenwards. Over the woman's shoulder Sukey caught the eye of the proprietor, a man of about sixty with a thin face and crinkly grey hair. He gave a slight shake of the head and tapped his forehead with a yellow forefinger.

The woman turned back to Sukey, her grip tightened and she thrust her face forward until it was only a few inches away. 'I saw death in the cards,' she said earnestly, 'and there is unease on the other side . . . spirits of the departed unable to rest. Didn't I tell you, only this very morning, Mr Hadlow, how last night I saw silent figures, one bearing a shroud?'

'You did indeed, Mrs Willow, but I'm sure these good people have work to do,' interrupted the man behind the counter. 'So if you'd just like to pay for these — ' He reached across the counter, gently but firmly detached a basket containing a handful of grocery items from the woman's gnarled fingers, placed it on the counter and rang up the contents on the till. 'That's four pounds ten pence, please,' he said, holding out his hand for the money.

He waited with barely concealed impatience while she fumbled in her purse, put away her change and stowed her purchases in a dilapidated shopping bag, all the time mumbling under her breath. With evident relief, the others stood aside as she made for the door. Suddenly, she turned and raised her free hand in a gesture that struck Sukey as almost threatening. 'I saw death in the cards!' she repeated, her voice raised as if she was addressing an audience in the village hall instead of a handful of customers in its little shop. 'And mark my words, there is more evil yet to come.' She wrenched the door open and slammed it behind her, setting the bell jangling.

'Poor old Pussy!' said one woman as they all exchanged glances.

'Never been the same since Albert died,' Mr Hadlow agreed, reaching for the next basket.

A few more questions about the morning's events were directed at Sukey while everyone was being served, but she turned them all aside, insisting that they would have to wait for an official statement. Having reluctantly accepted there was no point pressing her further, the other customers departed. When at last Sukey left the shop with her can of Coca Cola, she found Ezra waiting for her.

'Just a word,' he said quietly. 'I understand why you didn't say anything to set those old gossips prattling around the village, but just between ourselves, is it Mrs Maxford who's been hurt? Or should I say, Mrs Reynolds?'

For a brief, panic-stricken moment it occurred to Sukey that, never having actually set eyes on Myrna in life, she might have mistaken the victim's identity. If the house-keeper's directions had been accurate — and there was no reason to think otherwise — the corpse had certainly been lying in Myrna's bed, and Myrna's photograph had appeared in the local papers often enough for her to be instantly recognisable, despite the ghastly wounds. All the same . . .

'I was called to the house to deal with a break-in,' she said, playing for time. 'While I was there, it became clear that a woman had been hurt, so I called for police assistance and a doctor. My job there was finished, so I came away. That's really all I can tell you.'

She made to cross the road to where her van was parked, but Ezra put a hand on her arm. His ruddy face registered acute anxiety.

'I heard they sent for Mrs Maxford's husband,' he said. 'They wouldn't do that if it wasn't serious.'

'I understand he came home to fetch something he'd forgotten,' Sukey interrupted. 'Now, if you'll please excuse me, I do have another job to go to.'

'I'm sorry to have bothered you . . . it's just that there's some estate business I have to discuss with Mrs Maxford. I need a decision from her . . . it's quite urgent.'

'Perhaps you'd better have a word with her husband. He's probably still up at the house.'

'Talking to the police, I suppose?' A change came over Ezra's expression. 'I suppose he's the one who attacked her,' he muttered, almost to himself.

'What makes you think she was attacked?'

'Just a hunch. It's common knowledge that she gives him a hard time.' When Sukey did not reply, he said, 'Sorry, mustn't keep you. By the way,' he added in another change of mood, 'I'd better put you in the picture about poor old Pussy Willow. She never could accept that Albert's gone and she started going to a medium. Trying to get in touch with him, that sort of thing. The woman's convinced her she's psychic, hence all that rubbish about ghostly figures and seeing death in the cards.' Ezra sighed and shook his head. 'Been through a lot, poor old lady. I hope there'll be no need for the police to go troubling her.'

'Isn't it possible she might have seen something?'

'She's always seeing things, especially after dark. She often goes to the churchyard at night and stands by his grave. If anyone comes along, she makes out she's looking for her cat.'

'How sad. Well, thanks for the information, Mr Hampton. Now, I really must go.'

'Of course. Good-day to you.'

Sukey went back to the van feeling thoroughly depressed as she wondered how many other people who had regular contact with Paul and Myrna would also be jumping to the conclusion that his was the hand that had wielded the knife.

7

'I told her he meant it, but she only laughed.'

Apart from giving her name, it was the first time Leonie Filbury had spoken since being handcuffed and pushed, still screaming and struggling, into the back of a police car. Once there, her resistance had collapsed and she slumped against the officer sitting next to her like a clockwork doll whose mechanism has run down. She remembered nothing of the short drive to Dearley village police station, nothing of the formalities on arrival. Her one conscious thought was that the person whom she loved best in all the world was dead. They wouldn't say how, wouldn't answer any of her questions. All they seemed concerned with was the fact that she, Leonie Filbury, had attacked Paul Reynolds. That was why she was here, in this cramped, bare room, staring into a mug of tea which a woman police officer, who introduced herself as Jennie, put in front of her. An image seemed to form in its steaming surface — an image of Myrna, gazing back up at her, the beloved features distorted almost beyond recognition. She covered her eyes with her hands to blot out the horror; convulsive sobs constricted her throat and all but choked her.

Jennie pushed a box of paper tissues towards her. 'Come along, dry your eyes and drink your tea,' she said gently, but the note of sympathy in the young woman's voice only made the tears fall faster.

At last, after several minutes of passionate weeping, she became calmer. She groped for the box of tissues, pulled out a handful, scrubbed her wet cheeks and swollen eyes and took several gulps from the cooling tea. 'Sorry,' she muttered, running her fingers through her cropped hair. 'Made a bit of a fool of myself, didn't I? Shock, I suppose.' She gave the officer a searching look. 'You have arrested him, haven't you?'

'Arrested who?'

'Her husband, of course — who else?'

'What makes you so sure he did it?' The voice was still gentle, but cool and detached now.

'Of course he did it. I told you . . . I told the others . . . I told *her* — ' Leonie felt her voice cracking at the memory of how urgently she had pleaded with Myrna to take the threats seriously and how lightly her warnings had been brushed aside.

'Now, come along, you've cried enough.' The officer's voice was brisk now with a touch of impatience, as if she was dealing with a child making too much fuss over a hurt knee. A feeling of hopelessness compounded Leonie's misery as she realised that this woman, with her crisp white shirt, her scrubbed hands and her mouse-coloured hair in its prim little bun, would never understand that what she was suffering was more painful than a thousand hurt knees. It was the love of a lifetime, snatched away forever when it had barely begun. 'Sorry,' she repeated hopelessly.

'So tell me, exactly what did Mr Reynolds say or do to make you so certain he's the one who killed her?'

'He said he was going to.'

'When?'

'I don't know. Several times. Myrna told me it was just talk, but I saw the look on his face when he said it.'

'Let me get this clear. You were present and heard him threaten his wife on a number of occasions?'

'No, I was only there the once,' Leonie said reluctantly, as if the admission somehow weakened her case. 'But I know there were other times, she told me so. She used to say he'd never touch her — said he didn't have the balls.'

'All right, tell me about this one occasion. What made him so angry?'

'They'd been having a row. I didn't hear what it was about, I wasn't in the room when it started.'

'When was this?'

'One day last week — I don't remember which.'

'And where did this row take place?'

'In her office in the house. She'd asked me to see her with some figures from the estate accounts and I could hear them arguing as I went up the stairs. I couldn't make out what they were saying until I got close because the door was shut — it's quite a heavy door — and then I heard him shout, 'One of these days, Myrna, so help me God, I'll take you by your beautiful neck and throttle the life out of you!' And now he's done it, hasn't he?'

The policewoman was writing in her notebook. 'Those were his exact words?' she said.

'Yes.'

'You're prepared to swear to that?'

'On my life. I'll never forget them, nor the anger in his voice.' Leonie bit her lip and took a deep breath to check the further outbreak of weeping that threatened to engulf her.

'Did he say anything else after that?'

Caught off guard, Leonie hesitated for a fraction of a second before saying, 'No. Isn't that enough?'

'It's important that you tell me everything you heard.'

This time, Leonie did not hesitate. 'I have,' she said firmly.

'All right. What happened next?'

'I didn't know what to do. I didn't like to go in, so I waited for a moment. It all seemed to go quiet so I decided to knock on the door. Myrna called out 'Come in' and I did. Paul — Mr Reynolds — was standing at the window with his back to me. His hands were clenched and I could see he was shaking. Then he turned round and I'll never forget the look on his face. He was white as a sheet and his eyes were staring . . . and he gave Myrna one blinding look of sheer hatred before he pushed past me and went out of the room.' At the memory, Leonie felt another wave of emotion welling up inside her, but this time it was anger, not grief. In that moment she too would willingly have committed murder.

If the policewoman noticed her agitation, she gave no sign. 'And how did Mrs Reynolds look? Did she seem agitated?' she asked.

'Not a bit. She invited me to sit beside her at her desk while we went through the figures.'

'She said nothing about the scene with her husband?'

'No. I was the one who raised it. I tried to warn her to take it seriously, to lock her bedroom door at night, to try not to anger him — '

'And what was her reaction?'

'She just laughed and told me not to fuss. Then she kissed me on the cheek and — ' Leonie put her fingers to the spot where Myrna's lips had brushed her face. This time, the memory was too much to bear.

When she had pulled herself together, Jennie stood up and said, 'Well, thank you Ms Filbury, that's very helpful.'

'Can I go home now?'

'We'll have to see about that. There's that little matter of the assault on Mr Reynolds — we don't know yet whether he'll want to press charges.'

Leonie stared in bewilderment. 'Press charges — against *me*? After he killed Myrna?'

'We don't know that it was he who killed her, but we do know you attacked him and caused actual bodily harm,' Jennie said drily. 'So I'm afraid we'll have to keep you here for a while.'

They put her in a tiny cell and locked the door. An eternity seemed to pass before they came and told her she could go.

★ ★ ★

At the same time as DI Castle finished interviewing Paul Reynolds, Eric Dennison, Company Secretary of Maxford Domestic Fittings Limited, was eating a sandwich lunch in his Swindon office. A normally even-tempered and good-natured man, he was seething with resentment as he mulled over the events of the previous evening. A pleasantly convivial occasion — perhaps a little too convivial on the part of certain members of the party — had turned into a shambles as Myrna Maxford, Company Chairman, almost casually pulled the plug on their dreams and expectations. Eric reflected with mounting fury on the hours of discussion and paperwork that he, his fellow directors and their secretaries, to say nothing of their opposite numbers at Headwaters, had put into ensuring that the takeover went ahead smoothly — all now consigned to the dustbin.

At least, the new extension to the factory would go ahead just the same. Myrna had gone out of her way to reassure her fellow directors on this point, her clear, penetrating voice cutting through the exclamations of shock and disappointment as they and their wives absorbed the significance of her decision. Eric knew from Irene, his wife, that a lot of eagerly planned changes in lifestyle, based on the anticipated benefits from the takeover, would have to be thrown out of the window. Protests had at first been muted — Myrna's capacity for making life uncomfortable for those who challenged or tried to thwart her decisions was well known. It was June, Bradley Ashton's wife, who had lost control, picked up a bottle and charged at Myrna, screaming abuse. Poor old Brad, looking even more devastated by his wife's loss of control than by the change of plans, had gabbled apologies and dragged her out of the room; in the stunned silence that followed she could be heard throwing up in the hall.

After that, the party came to an abrupt end, with the remaining guests forcing themselves to take their leave and thank their hostess as if nothing untoward had happened. *We know which side our bread's buttered*, Eric remembered thinking as they collected their coats and went silently out into the night. The thought was immediately followed by another: *Why do we all let the bitch get away with playing cat and mouse with us? Why the hell don't we stand up to her?* Futile questions both, to which he well knew the answer.

Being of a prudent and cautious nature, he

had never been in the habit of considering plans for spending money until it was safely in his pocket, and he had applied the same philosophy to the anticipated windfall. 'Never count your chickens before they're hatched', and 'There's many a slip 'twixt cup and lip', he had counselled Irene every time she came home with a new brochure advertising world cruises, elaborate conservatories or indoor swimming pools. Poor Irene! He recalled her look of disbelief as she learned that it had all come to nothing.

He could still see the almost feline smile of satisfaction with which Myrna had dropped her bombshell. For a moment he wondered whether after all the whole exercise might have been a malicious hoax. Had she been stringing everyone along, raising hopes and expectations while anticipating the moment when she would dash them to several pieces? Having worked for her for several years he knew she was capable of anything, but he dismissed the thought almost immediately. She was far too shrewd a businesswoman to deliberately waste her company's time and money on a practical joke. Just the same, there was no doubt that she had derived a certain sadistic pleasure from the dismay and disappointment her change of heart had caused.

The buzz of the telephone on his desk interrupted his musings. The middle-aged receptionist, who had worked for the company since leaving school, was calling to say that Mr Reynolds wanted to speak to him urgently. 'I think he might be ill, he sounds a bit strange,' she confided. 'I said it was your lunch-break and couldn't it wait and I thought he was going to cry.'

'All right, put him through.'

There was a click and a silence of several moments before Paul said, in a hoarse, unsteady voice, 'Eric? Is anyone with you?'

'No, no one. Is something wrong?'

'Have the police been in touch . . . are they there?'

'The police? What are you talking about? Why should they — '

'They've been here . . . at the Manor . . . questioning me . . . they think I killed her — ' The words jerked out in spasms, punctuated by snuffling gasps as if the speaker was being starved of air.

'Killed — killed who? For God's sake, Paul, what are you saying? What's happened?'

'Myrna . . . she's dead and they think I did it . . . they'll want to question everyone — '

'When did this happen?'

'Some time during the night. I told them I

wasn't there, but I know they don't believe me, not after Leonie — '

'What's Leonie got to do with it?'

'She went for me, told them I'd threatened Myrna. Eric, you've got to tell them — '

'Are you saying you've been arrested?'

'No, they let me go, but I know they'll be — '

'So where are you?'

'At one of Myrna's cottages. I spent the night here.'

After the initial shock, Dennison's analytical brain clicked into gear. 'I noticed you left the party early,' he said. 'Why was that?'

'I had to. I knew what the bitch was planning and I didn't want — '

'You *knew*?' A fresh surge of anger blotted out for a second the shock of the news. 'And you never tipped us off? You let her string us along, watched us all make fools of ourselves — '

'I'm sorry, Eric. I should have warned you . . . I wanted to, but she . . . you know what she's . . . what she was like.'

'Of course, don't we all?' *A tigress who could purr like a domestic kitten one minute and tear your throat out the next. A witch who had all of us — Brad, Sam and me — by the balls.*

'Eric?' Paul's voice, pleading and urgent,

101

dragged him back to the present. 'Are you still there?'

'Yes, I'm here, I'm trying to think. Did you go back to the house after we all left?'

'No, of course I didn't. I didn't go anywhere near the place. That's what I keep telling the police, but they — '

'I take it you've given them the names of everyone who was there?'

'Yes, that's why I'm phoning. They'll be at your place soon, asking questions. You must talk to the others, make sure they tell them I wasn't there . . . Eric, please — '

Dennison was by now only half listening to the near-hysterical babbling. His mind was busy with problems closer to home. He must get hold of the others, make sure they all told the same story — but first he had to get rid of Reynolds. 'Listen, old chap,' he said soothingly, 'you stay where you are and try not to worry. Leave it with me. Have you got your mobile with you?'

'Yes.'

'Right. Stay with it. I'll be in touch.'

★ ★ ★

'This is how we play it,' said Dennison to his fellow directors, Bradley Ashton and Sam Perry, after putting them in the picture. 'It

102

was a nice, friendly gesture on Myrna's part to throw that party — a kind of consolation prize for the disappointment she knew we must all have been feeling. We quite understood and accepted her reasons for pulling out of the takeover. There was no ill-feeling; it all went off quite amicably. She was perfectly all right when we left, all together, at around midnight. Obviously, the police will want to talk to everyone who was there so we must get on to the girls and make sure they know what to say. We let it be known that there's been bad blood for a long time between Myrna and Reynolds — we can all quote our own observations on that score. Incidentally, you'll have noticed I haven't asked the obvious question. If either of you did it, I don't want to know.'

'Whoever did it, did us all a favour,' muttered Ashton. No one disagreed.

'D'you reckon Reynolds knows about our, er, little secrets?' asked Perry.

Dennison considered the question with pursed lips. 'Most unlikely,' he said after a pause. 'She played most things close to her chest as a matter of principle, never let one hand know what the other was up to if she could help it.'

'I hope you're right.' Perry uncrossed his legs and then recrossed them, flicking an imaginary speak of dust from his carefully pressed trousers as he did so.

'It's a chance we have to take.' Dennison regarded him with ill-concealed distate; Sam Perry's 'little secret' was a particularly repellent one. 'Anyway, he left the party early so he's in no position to contradict our story.'

'Which is?' asked Ashton.

'Haven't you been listening? So far as the police are concerned, the line we stick to is this: She ran a tight ship, but she was a good employer; her business judgement was sound and we all respected it. We worked as a team, none of us has any conceivable motive for killing her and we're all very shocked. Got that?' The others nodded. 'Brad, you'll make sure June — '

'Stays sober?' Ashton interposed with a harsh, mirthless laugh. 'I'll do my best.'

'What about Hampton and Filbury?' said Perry. 'How will you deal with them?'

'Leonie loathes Paul Reynolds and she'll be more than happy to see him go down for killing Myrna, whether he did it or not. Hampton could be a problem, though.' Dennison frowned and thought for a moment, then his brow cleared. 'Come to think of it, I don't believe he was even there when the balloon went up. I heard him say something to Myrna about having to see to a sick animal, so maybe he left early. I'll check.' Dennison made a note alongside the elaborate doodle he had been scribbling on his desk pad, then said, 'The weak link, as I see it, is that old woman, Mrs Willow. She struck me as being a bit gaga.'

'She is a bit gaga, according to Hampton,' said Ashton. 'Hears voices and sees ghosts. I noticed her a couple of times during the evening, staring into space and talking to herself. I doubt if she understood half of what was going on around her — but if she did, she could be dangerous.' The others nodded in agreement.

'We can make sure the police understand — without labouring the point — that she's not to be regarded as a reliable witness,' said Dennison. 'I imagine anyone in the village would support that. But of course, there are times when she appears perfectly rational. We don't want her throwing a spanner into the works, do we?'

'What do you suggest we do?' asked Perry.

With a gesture that held a hint of finality, Dennison scored a thick line under his doodle and put down his pencil. 'I think maybe I'll go and have a quiet word with her,' he said.

8

Sukey found a convenient place to turn the van and set off on her journey back to Gloucester. She had driven only a couple of hundred yards when she spotted the slight figure of Mrs Willow, weighed down with her shopping bag, walking slowly ahead of her. On impulse, she pulled over, wound down the window and called, 'That looks heavy. Would you care for a lift?'

The face that turned in response to the offer was lit up by a smile of mingled surprise and pleasure. 'How very kind. Thank you!' The little woman slid nimbly into the van and planted her shopping bag between her feet. She was obviously used to being in a car; she clipped on the safety belt and settled back without any hesitation or fumbling.

'I live in Dearley's Acres Lane,' she said briskly. 'Straight on and the first turning on the left. It isn't very far really, but it seems a long way when I've got a load of shopping.'

Sukey gave a sympathetic chuckle. 'Gets heavier with every step, doesn't it?'

Mrs Willow uttered a faint, inarticulate sound. Thinking that she was probably a little

106

hard of hearing, Sukey repeated the remark, glancing at her passenger as she did so. To her consternation, the old woman was staring at the road ahead with a glazed expression, a faint smile playing round her colourless mouth. 'That's what you always say, isn't it, Albert?' she mumbled in a faraway voice, as if she was talking in her sleep. 'Every time you take me shopping, when you carry the bags back to the car. 'Gets heavier with every step', you grumble.'

Sukey felt a prickle of gooseflesh and her mind went back to the scene in the shop, Mr Hadlow's significant gesture and Ezra Hampton's explanation for the widow's eccentric behaviour. It was clear that the death of her husband had seriously affected her mental state. She appeared to have fallen into a light trance; her eyes were vacant and her lips continued to move, but no sound emerged.

There was nothing that Sukey could do but drive on, hoping the spasm would soon pass. A little over half a mile further on they came to some substantial farm buildings, set well back on the right hand side of the road. A tractor with its engine running stood in the concrete yard, which was surrounded on three sides by stone barns. A painted board proclaimed that this was the home farm and office of Dearley Manor Estate and another warned would-be intruders that the premises were protected by a security system. Next door, approached by a short gravelled drive and surrounded by a well-tended garden, was an attractive Cotswold farmhouse. Ezra's Land Rover was parked by the front door; through the bars of a heavy wooden gate his dog watched with pricked ears as Sukey drove slowly past, looking for some indication that she was near her destination.

At last she spotted a rough wooden sign bearing the words 'Dearley's Acres Lane' hanging from a post a short distance beyond the farm. As she signalled and slowed down, a voice at her elbow said, 'That's it, go left here.' A little startled, she gave her passenger a quick glance and found her looking perfectly relaxed and wide awake and plainly remembering nothing of her strange behaviour of a few minutes ago. As they bumped along the narrow, rutted lane she pointed first left and then right with a blue-veined hand, keeping up a commentary on the weather, the nature of the crops and the state of the harvest. 'Always get a good yield from Dearley's Acres, they do,' she said with a note of pride in her voice.

'Where did the name Dearley's Acres come from?' asked Sukey.

'Ah, that's an interesting story. The fields

on either side of this lane were what Mr Walter Dearley started with when he settled here about three hundred years ago.' Her manner became suddenly animated. 'They say he inherited money from his father who was a rich wool merchant, but all he wanted to do was farming. So he bought a few acres of land and he and his son built a house here. By all accounts they did well from the outset, grew very rich and bought a lot more land. The original fields had become known as Dearley's Acres and the name stuck long after the family died out. The last Mr Dearley was killed in the Great War and the estate was sold . . . to *that woman's* grandfather.'

The venom in the last phrase, accompanied by a tightening of the speaker's jaw and a spontaneous clenching of the hands that held the shopping bag, made Sukey shudder. She had no doubt that it was Myrna who had aroused such bitter feelings. All she could think of to say was, 'Have you lived here long?'

'All my married life.' They were approaching a row of cottages, slightly dilapidated in appearance in contrast to the well-maintained properties in the village. 'The second one along has been my home for over fifty years. Though for how much longer, who knows?'

'What do you mean?' Even as she asked the

question, Sukey remembered what Fergus had told her of Myrna's plans and the answer came as no surprise.

'*She*,' the word, accompanied by a savage jerk of the silvery-white head, was like an angry hiss, 'is planning to sell Dearley's Acres for houses, hundreds of them. Says she needs the money and we've all got to move out.'

'That's dreadful!' Sukey stopped the van and sat for a moment, taking in the panorama of fields and woodland that rolled away to the horizon. In the middle distance, the chimneys of the Manor were just visible above a stand of tall trees. 'It would be a terrible shame to spoil this lovely countryside with a housing estate. Surely, Mrs Maxford wouldn't want that on her own doorstep!' For a moment, dismay at the prospective desecration of yet another beauty spot made her forget that the owner of Dearley Manor was no longer in a position to be affected by anything.

'Maxford!' The word was almost a snarl. 'Reynolds was her proper married name. Didn't even have enough respect for the poor man to acknowledge him as her husband.' The old woman turned her head aside and her voice fell to a low mumble as she added, 'Perhaps it was he who brought about her death!'

'Who said anything about her being dead?'

'Didn't I say I saw death in the cards?' There was a strange, almost wild look in Mrs Willow's eyes and a throbbing intensity in her voice that sent another wave of gooseflesh rippling along Sukey's skin. 'And I've seen other signs — mark my words, there's more evil yet to come.'

Ignoring Sukey's exclamation, Mrs Willow almost sprang out of the van, slammed the door and marched up to her cottage gate without a word of farewell or a backward glance. Feeling utterly bemused, and more uneasy than ever on Paul's behalf, Sukey backed the van into a field entrance, turned and resumed her interrupted journey. As she passed the gates of Dearley Manor she noticed a car waiting to leave. The driver was a woman she recognised as a reporter from a local radio station, which meant the news had reached the media. Her first thought was for Fergus. He would still be at the supermarket, but his shift ended at four and he often reached home before she did. Invariably, almost his first action was to switch on the radio and she found herself praying that today she would get there first so that she could be the one to break the dreadful news.

It was not to be. By the time she had written out her statement as DI Castle instructed and afterwards attended the scene of a burglary in Cheltenham, it was nearly halfpast four before she left the station and the home-going traffic was beginning to build up. When at last she turned on to her drive she found the garage open and Fergus's bicycle propped against the wall; a slight movement behind the curtains told her that he had been looking out for her. His face as he opened the front door was white and strained and he grabbed her by the arm before she got a foot inside.

'Mum, I've just heard on the radio!' he burst out, his voice cracking with fear. 'A woman's been found dead at Dearley Manor — do you know anything about it? Is it Myrna?'

'Yes, Gus, I'm afraid it is.'

'Was she — ?' He seemed unable to utter the word 'murdered', but she read it in his eyes.

Gently, she closed the door and led him to the kitchen. 'Let's have a cup of tea while I tell you what happened. I'm feeling pretty whacked.'

He appeared almost relieved at putting off the moment of truth. 'I'll make it. The kettle's just boiled.'

'Good lad.'

The radio was still playing. The news bulletin was over; pop music filled the house and Fergus switched it off without being asked. He made the tea and poured it into two mugs he had put out in readiness. It was their normal afternoon ritual when she was on the eight to four shift; after their day's work they would relax together at the kitchen table, drinking their tea, eating biscuits, exchanging news and gossip. Today, they sat in silence for several minutes; she seeking a way of minimising the fear and shock, he never taking his eyes from her face while mutely asking the question he was afraid to put into words.

At last she said, 'This is going to be hard for you, Gus — hard for us both. As you've probably guessed, Myrna was murdered — stabbed. As a matter of fact, I found her.'

'Oh, Mum, how awful for you!'

'It was, rather,' she admitted. Her voice trembled as the hideous memory resurfaced.

He reached across the table and grasped her free hand. She felt a lump in her throat as she looked down at the bony wrist jutting out from the sleeve of his baggy sweatshirt. She worried at times that he was too thin for his height, but the doctor assured her it was normal for a lad his age and he'd start to fill out once he'd finished growing. A gush of tears took her by surprise and he got up and put an arm round her shoulders while she fished out a hanky and scrubbed her eyes, swallowing and breathing hard in her efforts not to upset him further by breaking down.

'She'd been stabbed,' she said when she felt able to speak, 'and there was rather a lot of blood.'

'How come it was you who found her? And who do they think — ?' This time, it was Fergus's voice that wavered and failed.

'The police have only just begun their inquiries, but I'm afraid a lot of people are going to jump to the same conclusion.'

'You mean, that Dad — ?' He sat down again and gripped his mother's hand, this time seeking rather than giving comfort. At last, he was coming face to face with the horror. 'He wouldn't kill anyone, you know that. You must tell them, he couldn't have done it! *Mum*,' he pleaded as she remained silent, trying to think of some words of reassurance. 'You don't think he did it, do you? Have you seen him? What did he say?'

'Yes, I've seen him and he swore to me that he didn't kill Myrna.'

'And you believe him, don't you?'

Wearily, she ran her fingers through her hair. 'I want to believe him. I told you a few days ago, I don't think he's capable of violence, but several people seem to think that it must have been him.' Ezra's words, and

Mrs Little's and Mrs Willow's, came back with a rush. How many more times — and by how many others — would those insinuations be repeated?

'What people?' She hesitated for a moment and he repeated the question, urgently, staring into her face. 'What have you heard?'

'It seems to be common knowledge that things between Dad and Myrna had gone pretty sour,' she said at last.

'Who says so?'

She could only spare him so much. 'Look, I'd better tell you the whole story, but you must promise to keep it to yourself?'

'I promise.'

As gently as she could, avoiding the worst of the dreadful details, Sukey explained how she came to find Myrna's body, the events that followed the discovery and the various comments she'd heard from people who had known her. 'There's no doubt she had a lot of enemies,' she finished, 'but we have to accept that Dad is going to be under suspicion. Everything I've heard — and no doubt a lot more besides — is going to come out and it won't help him. Of course, forensics may find evidence that points directly to someone else, in which case — '

'But supposing they don't?' Fergus broke in. 'What if whoever did it didn't leave any clues — or supposing they left a false trail, something to throw suspicion on Dad because everybody knew how things were between him and Myrna?' His voice rose to a panic-stricken squeak and he almost leapt out of his chair. 'Mum, you must do something!'

'Now you're just being silly. Sit down and listen to me.' Various thoughts that had been buzzing round Sukey's head began to settle into some sort of order. 'The more I think about it, the more I'm inclined to believe Dad didn't kill Myrna,' she said as Fergus sank back into his chair. 'He might have lost his temper with her, grabbed her, even hit her without meaning to if she really drove him so wild at times, but I don't believe he would ever have — ' Just in time, remembering she had spared her son the agony of knowing exactly how his stepmother died, she ended, ' — gone for her with a knife.' Desperately casting around for something to boost the argument and counter the doubts in her own mind, she went on, 'Especially as she was killed in her bedroom, which seems to suggest that it was premeditated.'

Fergus seized on the notion as if it were a lifeline. 'That's it, don't you see?' he said eagerly. 'They hadn't shared a room for ages — Mrs Little can testify to that. He wouldn't have been there, she was probably having an affair with someone else and it went wrong. Maybe she was being as bitchy to the other man as she'd been to Dad and he wouldn't take it.'

'There are any number of possibilities. It's pretty clear she had enemies, and selling that land for development was going to upset a lot of people.'

'That's right. Dad would know. Where is he now? You said you'd seen him.'

'He was waiting to be interviewed.'

'Does that mean — ?' Fergus's eager expression changed back to one of apprehension. 'He hasn't been arrested, has he? Have you told me everything?'

'Now don't get wound up again. The police will have to question loads of people — everyone who was at last night's party, for a start. The inquiry has only just begun. I've had to make a statement as well because I found the body, but I'm out of it now because of my connection with the family.' Sukey heard the note of irony that crept into her own voice. 'Jim was the first CID officer on the scene and he was in charge when I left, but I shouldn't be surprised if they give the case to someone else for the same reason.'

'So we won't know what's going on?'

'Not officially. I might be able to worm a bit more information out of Jim than is officially released, but — '

The telephone rang as she spoke. For a few moments the pair of them were transfixed, staring first at the instrument and then at one another as if afraid of what they might hear. Then Sukey picked it up and said, 'Hello.'

'Susan?' It was Paul's voice and he sounded distraught. 'Susan, I need your help . . . I must see you.'

9

'Where are you?'

'At the cottage.'

'What cottage?'

'One of Myrna's holiday cottages. I spent last night here. Your people left it in a terrible state — ' A trace of peevish indignation overlaid the fear and anxiety in Paul's voice. 'They practically tore the place apart. What were they looking for, for God's sake?'

'A weapon, bloodstained clothing — ' As she spoke, Sukey caught Fergus's eye and read the mute question. 'Dad', she mouthed at him.

He reached out a hand. 'Let me speak to him, please!'

'In a moment. Paul?'

'Yes?'

'Why do you want to see me? What's happened?'

'Nothing so far — I mean, I haven't been arrested, but I've been asked so many questions and I don't think that detective friend of yours believes half what I told him. Can I come and see you?'

'No!' The last thing she wanted was for Paul to be at the house if Jim should call round. She was half prepared for him to start arguing, but he seemed unsurprised by her refusal.

'Then, will you come here? Susan, I must talk to you . . . you're the only person who can — '

'Where is this cottage?'

'There's a turning to the right about half a mile past the main gate to the Manor — Dearley's Acres Lane.'

'Where Pussy Willow lives?'

'That's right — how did you know?'

'I gave her a lift home this afternoon.'

'I see.' Paul sounded taken aback by the information, but made no further comment. 'Okay, a mile or so past her cottage there's another turning to the left with a sign pointing to Dearley Holiday Homes — they're barn conversions a couple of hundred yards or so along and mine's the one on the left as you drive in. It's a first floor flat actually, with parking space underneath — you'll see my car there. What time can you get here?'

'Hang on a minute, I haven't said I'm coming yet.' The stress of the day was beginning to take its toll. More than anything, Sukey wanted an early supper, a

120

relaxing bath and bed. 'Why can't we talk over the phone?'

'It's not the same . . . please, Susan.'

Touched by the desolation in his voice, she relented. 'All right, I'll be along later. Have you had anything to eat?'

'Not yet.'

'Neither have we. I'll come over after we've had our meal. Why don't you pop out to a pub somewhere and get a bite in the meantime?'

'I thought of doing that, but I couldn't face it, everyone would be looking at me.'

'Why should they? You can go to a place where no one knows you.'

'I told you, I can't face people, not yet.'

'Isn't there any food in the cottage?'

'Only a tin of baked beans and a packet of biscuits the last tenant left behind. I don't suppose you — ?'

She knew from experience that the way he left the question unfinished was quite deliberate. Remembering how in times gone by he had expected her to understand and sympathise with his predicament over his passion for Myrna, with hardly a thought for her own hurt, she hardened her heart and said briskly, 'Well, that'll keep you from starvation if you really can't face going out. Fergus and I haven't had our meal yet so it'll be an hour or so before I'm free to leave. He'd like a word with you, by the way.'

She held out the receiver to Fergus; he grabbed it and began gabbling in a voice hoarse and unsteady with emotion. 'Dad, I don't care what the police think, I believe in you, I'll never believe you killed Myrna.' There was a short pause and then he said, 'Dad? Dad, are you there?' Slowly he replaced the instrument and looked at his mother in hurt bewilderment.

'What did he say?' she asked.

The boy's eyes were clouded with tears and a sob almost choked him as he replied, 'He just said, 'Thanks, son', and hung up.'

*   *   *

A large rock, painted white with the words 'Dearley Holiday Homes' picked out in black, was embedded in a sloping grassy bank alongside the entrance to a paved courtyard and a cluster of stone buildings that had once been the busy heart of a working farm. It was obvious that no expense had been spared in turning the ancient barns into modern dwellings; there were genuine Cotswold tiles on the roofs, the walls had been skilfully cleaned and repointed and the doors and window-frames were of solid timber. Two of the units were single storey cottages that had probably once housed sheep; now, they sported chintzy curtains behind leaded windows and hanging baskets full of geraniums. Tourists' cars, one bearing a foreign numberplate, stood outside the varnished front doors.

Sukey parked her elderly Astra beside Paul's showroom-bright Jaguar in a covered space which, long ago, would have sheltered carts and agricultural implements. Overhead, some original oak beams had been retained and incorporated into the structure of a first floor apartment which was entered by a door in the far corner. As she got out of the car, a swallow flashed past her head and vanished into the shadows. Peering upwards, she made out several of the mud nests clinging to the walls and felt a twinge of pleasure that modern development had not driven the birds from their ancestral home.

The door opened. Paul appeared and beckoned her into a tiny hallway. With one hand on the latch, he peered out into the gathering dusk.

'Are you expecting anyone else?' she asked.

'Not expecting. Dreading.' He closed the door, dropped the safety catch and switched on the light. His face was grey and drawn and there was a livid scratch running from just below his right eye to the corner of his mouth.

'Whatever happened to your face?' she asked.

'Oh, that!' He gave a grim smile and touched the wound for a second with an unsteady hand before climbing the narrow staircase with Sukey at his heels. At the top was a square landing with three doors leading off it. He opened one and gestured to her to enter. 'That hell-cat Leonie,' he said. 'She went for me in front of Inspector Castle, accusing me of killing Myrna, 'like you said you would', she kept screeching. Needless to say, the Inspector found that very interesting,' Paul finished bitterly. 'His manner changed after that and I'm sure he suspects me, especially after the business with the keys.'

'What keys?'

'My keys to the house. You remember, I had to ring the bell because I'd left them in my briefcase? That is, I thought I'd left them. I told the Inspector they must be in there and he made me open the case and look.'

'And they weren't there?'

'No, they were here all the time, on the floor under the bed. One of the policemen found them when the place was being searched. They must have fallen out of my pocket when I undressed and I suppose I kicked them out of sight without noticing — '

'Paul, where's all this leading?' Sukey interrupted.

'Don't you see — they think I hid them, that I was only pretending I couldn't get into the house. I was giving myself an alibi — '

'You mustn't read too much into it.' She did her best to sound reassuring. 'Husbands and lovers are always suspect at the start of an investigation, but it doesn't mean the police don't look any further. 'If you didn't kill Myrna — '

'*If* I didn't kill her! You mean, you think I could have — ?' His voice quavered and faded, the voice of a man at the end of his tether.

'I didn't say that, I simply meant that if you know you're innocent you've nothing to worry about.'

'How can you be so sure? People do get convicted for things they don't do, you read about it all the time — '

'Not very often and I'm sure it won't happen this time, so why don't we sit down and talk about it over some coffee? I've brought milk and a jar of instant, and I picked up a few other provisions on the way.' She handed him the plastic supermarket carrier she had brought with her and he accepted it mechanically, dumbly staring as if

125

it were some strange object. They were standing in a comfortably furnished sitting-room with windows overlooking the courtyard. 'Isn't this cosy!' she went on, wondering if Myrna had personally supervised the furnishings, which were of good quality and obviously chosen by someone with flair.

'You should have seen it earlier, after your people had been through it,' Paul said, with a grimace. 'They didn't find anything, of course — apart from those wretched keys — but they took my fingerprints,' he added resentfully. He put the shopping on a chair and closed the curtains before switching on the light. She had the impression that he did not want to be seen by anyone outside, that he had been surreptitiously looking out for her.

'That was for elimination purposes,' she told him. 'You live in the house where the body was found, so your prints must be all over the place.'

'That's what they told me.'

'There you are, then. Now, where's the kitchen?'

'Through there.' He pointed to a glazed door at the far end of the room.

'Right. Let's get the kettle on.'

After Paul had drunk two mugs of hot coffee and wolfed down a quantity of cheese and ham sandwiches — he had eaten nothing, having failed to locate a tin-opener for the baked beans — Sukey said, 'Now, what's this urgent matter that couldn't be discussed on the phone? And please, Paul, don't take too long over it. I know you've had a stressful day, but it's been pretty gruelling for me as well. I was the one who found her, remember?'

'Yes, of course, that must have been rotten for you. But I had to go to the mortuary and identify her,' he pointed out, 'and after all, she is . . . was . . . my wife.'

'Yes, I know.' Sukey leaned back in her chair and shut her eyes for a moment at the thought of that once lovely body, cold and still on the mortuary slab. At least, she would have been cleaned and tidied up before Paul saw her; he would not have to live with that awful scene in the bedroom. She opened her eyes again. 'Right, what's this about?'

Paul stared into his empty mug as if reluctant to look at her. 'It's a bit embarrassing,' he mumbled, 'but the fact is, like I told you, I stayed here last night. I left the party before it ended — I couldn't bear being around to watch Myrna spring her nasty little surprise on everyone and have them think I was a party to her schemes.'

'Who's 'everyone'?'

Paul began ticking names off on his fingers.

'She'd invited three executives of Maxford Domestic Fittings and their wives, plus Ezra Hampton, Pussy Willow and Leonie Filbury, for drinks. She'd led them on to believe that it was a kind of celebration of the takeover by a big company called Headwaters — maybe you've heard about that?'

'Yes, it's been in the local paper.'

'Well, they were all excited, talking about the goodies it would mean for them and swopping plans for spending the extra moolah.'

'All of them? What were Ezra and the others expecting to get out of it?'

'I've no idea what their expectations were, if any. Maybe they just assumed it was a social invitation. But they — especially Pussy, at any rate — were going to be affected by the change of plan, and that was why she'd invited them. She knew how upset they were going to be and she wanted to enjoy their reaction. She was a spiteful, sadistic bitch.'

He almost spat out the final words and the flash of hatred in his eyes was frightening, but Sukey managed to keep her voice cool and level as she replied, 'So I've gathered. This change of plan — I take it you're speaking of her decision to sell Dearley's Acres?'

'That's right.' Paul looked at Sukey with a strange, almost guarded expression. 'How did

128

you know about that?'

'Mrs Willow told me. She was in the village shop when I went to buy a can of Coke and she had a lot of heavy shopping so I offered her a lift.'

'What did she say?'

'Part of the time she was babbling a lot of stuff about seeing restless spirits wandering around carrying shrouds and how there was more evil yet to come.'

'You didn't take any notice of that, did you? She's been off her rocker since her husband died, poor old thing.'

'So Ezra Hampton told me, but in between she seemed rational enough. She told me about Myrna's plans to sell the land and she was upset, to put it mildly.'

Paul ran restless fingers through his thinning hair. 'I don't understand . . . how come you met Ezra as well? What did he — ?'

'Never mind that now.' Sukey was beginning to feel impatient. 'Get on with what you were saying. You stayed here last night — I assume you told the police that?'

'Of course. Inspector Castle immediately asked if I was on my own and I said I was.'

'And were you?'

'Yes.' He began fidgeting with the mug, his eyes once more avoiding hers. 'That's the trouble, you see. I've no alibi, no one to back up my story. They said Myrna was killed around two o'clock in the morning and I knew they were thinking I could easily have sneaked back to the Manor once everyone had gone home . . . but if someone had been with me all night and could say I'd been here until eight o'clock, when I left for the office — ' At last, he lifted his eyes and looked at her with a pleading, hang-dog expression that sickened her. 'I couldn't ask anyone else, you're the only one I can trust — '

'I don't believe I'm hearing this!' Sukey exploded. 'Are you asking me to perjure myself and put my job on the line just to get you out of a hole?' *To say nothing of destroying my relationship with Jim Castle,* she added mentally.

'Please, Susan, just think about it, don't say no straight away — '

'I *am* saying no and I don't have to think about it. Who's going to believe it anyway? And if I spent the night here with you, how are we going to explain how I was at home having breakfast with Fergus soon after seven this morning? And don't tell me that you expect your son to lie for you as well?'

'We could say your car wouldn't start, the battery was flat and I charged it up for you so that you could get away at first light.'

'And what am I supposed to have been doing here in the first place?'

'Everyone knows my marriage to Myrna was on the rocks — we could say I was going to ask her for a divorce, that you and I were talking about making a fresh start. I could say I didn't tell the police at the time that you were with me because I didn't want to compromise you.'

He leaned forward, reaching out to take her hand, but she snatched it out of his reach. 'I'm sure they'd think that was very gallant of you,' she said coldly. 'Now, if that's all you have to say to me — '

'You won't do it, then?'

A whining note crept into his voice. He looked abject, defeated, a shadow of the confident, handsome, talented man she had once loved. Was this what marriage to a ruthless, manipulative woman had done to him? Pity took the hard edge off her anger and she said gently, 'No, Paul, I won't. It wouldn't work anyway, it's a crazy idea.'

His sigh of despair was almost a groan. 'I suppose so. I feel so desperate, so helpless. I know everyone will think I killed Myrna because of the way things were between us.'

'You're not the only one with a motive and everyone will be thoroughly investigated, I promise you.'

'You won't say anything to Fergus about this?'

'Certainly not. I'd hate for him to know that his father could even think of such a half-baked idea — and speaking of Fergus,' she went on, suddenly remembering the stricken look in the boy's eyes as he stood with the telephone receiver in his hand, 'he was really upset that you hung up on him like that with hardly a word. You could at least have talked to him for a couple of minutes, given him some reassurance.'

'I didn't mean to upset the kid. Give him my love and tell him I'm sorry . . . and please, tell him his father isn't a murderer.'

'I don't have to say that — he believes in you completely. He still looks up to you in spite of everything and I just hope he isn't going to be let down. My advice to you is, stop hiding in your bolt-hole like a guilty man, carry on with your job and go out and about as normally as possible. Oh, one thing more. This Leonie woman — was there a lesbian relationship with Myrna, do you think?'

Wearily, Paul shook his head. 'I've no idea what went on between them when I wasn't around. It's obvious that Leo was besotted with Myrna, and Myrna seemed to play along with her when I was around, but that could

132

just have been to get up my nose.'

'I see. Well, one way or the other, there would seem to be plenty of people who won't be sorry Myrna's out of the way.' Sukey stood up and went over to the door. 'I'm going home now, I need some sleep and so do you. There's no need to come down, I can see myself out.'

It was nearly nine o'clock, her head ached, she was almost dropping with fatigue and her one thought was to get indoors, have a bath and crawl into bed. Fergus would be waiting, anxious to hear what was happening. She would have to think up some story to satisfy him, but for the moment she had to concentrate on her driving, on reaching home safely. She backed the car slowly across the courtyard and turned out into the lane, where a man out walking his dog stood on the verge to let her pass. The drive back to the junction took longer than she expected, but she reached it at last, thankful that she had not had to cope with the added stress of manoeuvring past another vehicle in the narrow lane, and sat waiting until it was clear for her to turn onto the main road. There was no traffic approaching from the left; to the right, a single car began to signal and slow down, preparing to turn towards Dearley. She was momentarily caught in its headlights as she pulled out and headed for home.

★ ★ ★

The minute Sukey's car was out of sight, Paul put on a dark jacket and rubber-soled shoes, found a torch and left the flat. As he closed the door softly behind him, he lingered for a moment in the shadows to make sure there was no one about, that he could slip unobserved out of the courtyard and into the darkness of the lane. All was quiet; nothing stirred. In the cottages, lights glowed through curtained windows. He imagined the occupants, relaxing after a day of fine weather, probably congratulating themselves on having chosen such a good week for their late summer break in the country. He wondered if any of them knew of the drama that had occurred so close to their idyllic rural retreat. It was possible they had not; many people preferred to detach themselves from everyday affairs while they were on vacation and they might not have seen a newspaper or bothered to turn on the radio or watch the television news. In either event, it was unlikely that they knew who he was or that he was the chief suspect in a murder inquiry. Still, he preferred not to

134

come face to face with any of them.

His mind slipped back to carefree holidays with Susan and Fergus, before he met Myrna and fell under her destructive spell. A wave of anger was building up inside him, as much at the thought of what he had thrown away as for the disillusionment and humiliation he had — after the first euphoric months of their marriage — endured at her hands. He had no regrets over her death, only that he had let her get away with making his life a misery for so long. She was an evil bitch and she'd got what she deserved. But he was still not free of her malign influence; in death even more than in life she cast a blight over his future, taunting him with the prospect of arrest and imprisonment.

Satisfied there was no one about, he walked along the lane until he came to a stile, climbed over and followed the public footpath running along the edge of a patch of woodland towards the village. A short distance further on, he came to another stile where a second path led through the wood towards Dearley's Acres Lane.

The moon was up and almost full. The trees cast black shadows across a landscape bleached to a pale silvery grey. After the warmth of the day, the temperature had dropped sharply and Paul turned up his collar before clambering over the stile. As he landed on the other side his foot slipped on a stone and he almost fell. Trembling, he stopped for a moment to steady himself before plunging onward. The dense foliage overhead almost blacked out the moon; he listened, holding his breath, before switching on the torch. The heavy metal case felt suddenly icy cold in his hand and he fumbled in his pocket for a pair of gloves, holding the torch under one arm while he put them on.

He had never before walked in the woods at night and only seldom in daylight. The air seemed to be full of strange stirrings and rustlings; he had an uneasy sensation of being observed by invisible, hostile creatures. He was tempted to turn back; he began trying to convince himself that there was no need for this, that it was unlikely that old Pussy Willow had really seen anything, that even if she had, no one would believe her. But he had to be sure. A man in his situation couldn't afford to leave anything to chance.

10

After the forensic pathologist had examined Myrna's body and authorised its removal to the morgue, Castle organised the setting up of an incident room, ordered an intensive search of the house and grounds and gave instructions for the preliminary interviewing of witnesses. In the midst of the activity, the media — having somehow got wind of the murder — turned up in force and pressed for a statement, which he delivered on the front steps of the Manor to waving microphones and clicking cameras. At about six o'clock he left DS Radcliffe in charge of operations on the ground and returned to headquarters to make his initial report, physically and mentally drained and conscious that he had eaten nothing all day but a sandwich from a pub in the village.

A police cadet brought him a cup of coffee and a ham roll from the canteen. He had just taken the first bite when he received a telephone call to say that he was wanted in the Superintendent's office. 'Immediately,' the secretary added, prompted by an impatient voice in the background. Muttering under his breath, he swallowed a mouthful of coffee, covered the cup with a saucer and wrapped the remains of the roll in a paper tissue before obeying the summons.

Superintendent Sladden was a portly man with a high, balding crown, plump white hands and a well-fed appearance that made Castle more than ever conscious of his own neglected stomach. He appeared to be in a benevolent mood; he gave a gracious smile and waved his Inspector to a chair.

'Right, Jim, tell me all about the Dearley Manor killing. It sounds nasty,' he added with a certain relish.

'Nasty is the word, sir.' Castle quickly outlined the circumstances of the discovery of Myrna's body, the cause of death and the action taken so far. The Superintendent listened intently until the end of the formal report, then sat without speaking for several moments as if digesting what he had just heard, never taking his eyes from Castle's face. At last he said, 'Something else you want to tell me, I think?'

'Er, yes there is, sir. I'm glad to have this opportunity of speaking to you about it personally, because I have a bit of a problem with this one.'

'I rather thought as much. I hear from Sergeant Barnes that it was one of his

SOCOs who found the body and that you've taken her off the case. He didn't seem to know why.'

'She happens to be the ex-wife of the victim's husband and it seemed advisable in the circumstances — '

'Absolutely,' the Superintendent interposed. He showed no surprise, merely reinforcing his approval with a grave nod. 'You did exactly the right thing. Is that all?'

'No, sir. It isn't generally known, or at least, I hope it isn't, that Sukey — Mrs Reynolds — and I are, well — ' Castle found himself floundering like an embarrassed schoolboy.

'An item?'

Castle looked at his senior officer in surprise, partly at hearing such a colloquial expression from a man not noted for his informality and partly at the unfamiliar twinkle in the prominent eyes.

'Yes, in a manner of speaking,' he admitted. 'It's early days yet, but if things turn out the way I, that is, we hope — '

'I see. Well, I'm sure you understand that I'll have to assign another officer to the case from now on?'

'Naturally, sir — it's what I expected you to say. There mustn't be any suggestion of personal involvement on anyone's part in a case like this.'

'Quite so. We can't be too careful.' Sladden resumed his normal air of ponderous gravity. 'We bring what looks like a watertight case to court, defence counsel gets wind of the fact that some of the evidence has been collected by someone who might have an axe to grind and before we know where we are it all goes pear-shaped and the jury acquits another villain.'

'Exactly, sir.'

'From what you've told me, I think we can be reasonably sure the husband's the killer; it usually is in these cases,' Sladden went on. It was a favourite theme of his: in ninety per cent of murders, the partner turns out to be the guilty party. His satisfaction when he was proved correct, especially when expensive police time had been spent examining strong but ultimately misleading evidence to the contrary, could be almost insufferable.

Castle nodded in respectful agreement. 'It certainly looks that way. There's that business of the keys — he had access to the house throughout the night, despite claiming otherwise — and the smashed kitchen door seems like a clumsy attempt to make it appear an outside job. And there's the Filbury woman's testimony that he'd threatened his wife on more than one occasion and the housekeeper said something to that effect to the local chap. We've made a start on interviewing the guests at the party, but there were eight of them so it'll take time to see them all and sift through their statements — '

'Quite, quite, it's early days yet and we have to explore every possibility,' Sladden conceded. 'I'll put DCI Lord in charge — you'll give him a thorough briefing, of course.'

'Of course, sir.'

'Right, that'll be all for now.' Castle had just reached the door when the Superintendent cleared his throat and said gruffly, 'I hope things work out for you and your lady friend, Jim.'

'Oh . . . thank you, sir.'

Bemusedly shaking his head at the realisation that the old boy was human after all, Castle returned to his tepid coffee and half-eaten roll. By the time he finished writing his report it was almost nine o'clock. Wearily, he put down his pen, took off his reading glasses and reached for the telephone.

Fergus answered. His mother, he said, was out, she'd had a phone call that sounded urgent and she hadn't said when she'd be back. He seemed evasive, which wasn't like him. Castle was curious but didn't press him, reminding himself that he had no right to insist on knowing Sukey's every movement except when she was on duty. So he asked

Fergus to be sure and tell her when she got back that he'd like a word with her. He tried DCI Lord's number and received no reply. No doubt Lord, like anyone in his right mind, had gone home hours ago. He'd see him first thing in the morning; at the moment, his priority was to get a drink and something more substantial to eat than a canteen ham roll. He put on his jacket and headed for his favourite watering hole, which also happened to serve hot suppers until ten o'clock.

The Bear Inn, one of Gloucester's most historic hostelries, was tucked away in an alley a short distance from the police station. Towards the end of the week it would be noisy and crowded at this time of the evening, but today was Monday and apart from a few regulars it was comparatively quiet. Round one of the tables Castle recognised a small group of off-duty police officers in civilian clothes and he gave them a friendly wave as he passed. Normally, he would have been happy to join them, but tonight he felt the need to be on his own. He felt frustrated at not having been able to talk to Sukey; he had thought of her several times during the day, wondering if she was all right and not suffering too much delayed shock after her gruesome discovery. By the time he returned to the station she had been off duty for over two hours and there had been so much to do that he had not had a spare moment to get in touch with her. He wondered what it was that had been so urgent it couldn't wait and felt a stab of resentment against the unknown caller. There had been enough pressure on the poor girl for one day; she should have been left in peace to unwind and get an early night. He patted his pocket to make sure he had his mobile phone with him, hoping she'd give him a quick call before turning in.

He was half-way through his steak and chips when he spotted DS Radcliffe leaning against the bar with a tankard of ale in his hand. Castle caught his eye and beckoned; here was someone whose company was always welcome. The two men had been friends since they joined the Force. Andy Radcliffe was the less ambitious of the two; having been made a sergeant, he had no inclination to seek further promotion while Castle, after a spell of service in London during which he had been married and divorced, had come back to Gloucester with the rank of Detective Inspector. The difference in rank had done nothing to damage their friendship, although they instinctively observed the formalities whilst on duty or when discussing their work.

Radcliffe sat down at Castle's table and a

waiter put a generous portion of shepherd's pie in front of him. 'Am I ready for this!' he exclaimed, plunging his fork into the food.

'Have you only just got back from Dearley?'

Radcliffe nodded with his mouth full. 'Handed over to DS Jackson an hour ago,' he said when he was free to speak. 'Security's been a bit of a problem at the Manor, as you know. So many places where anyone could sneak in, but I think we're okay — we've got a round-the-clock dog patrol and plenty of lighting.'

'Fine. Any sign of the weapon?'

'Nothing definite. Forensics took some knives from the kitchen for a routine check, although there was nothing immediately suspicious about them. We'll have to wait for a detailed report and meanwhile carry on with the fingertip search in the morning. We'll press ahead with the witness statements, of course, although everything points to the husband. Needless to say, he's still denying it and there's no evidence so far.'

Castle laid down his knife and fork and said, 'The Super's taken me off the case.'

Radcliffe's bushy eyebrows lifted, but all he said was, 'Who's he putting in charge?'

'DCI Lord.' Castle hesitated for a moment before adding, 'I imagine people will be asking themselves why.'

Radcliffe thought for a moment and drank deeply from his tankard before replying, 'Prominent local business-woman . . . lot of influential friends . . . case calls for a senior investigating officer. I wouldn't have been surprised if Mr Sladden had taken personal command.' He set the tankard down, carefully placing it on one of the cork mats bearing the name of a local brand of ale before adding, 'I wouldn't think it was personal, Jim, and I hope no one else will jump to that sort of conclusion.'

Castle had a feeling it was an oblique reference to his relationship with Sukey. Although he was pretty certain Andy had guessed how things were between them — not that he had ever made the slightest allusion to it — he liked to believe it wasn't generally known. The two of them had always been careful to appear strictly professional during working hours and keep their private life exactly that, but one could never be sure. People weren't slow to pick up the odd, inadvertent word or glance that might give the game away.

Radcliffe's next remark took him by surprise. 'I was surprised to hear that Sukey Reynolds was back on the case — I understood you'd taken her off it,' he said.

'I did. What makes you think she's back?'

'Jackson says she was turning out of the lane to Dearley as he was on his way to the Manor to relieve me.'

Castle frowned. 'She wasn't on official business, that's for sure.'

'Ah . . . maybe she's got a friend living somewhere near there.'

'She's never mentioned it. Maybe Jackson was mistaken.'

Radcliffe shrugged. 'Possibly, but he seemed pretty sure it was her.' He finished his drink, pushed back his empty plate, yawned and stood up. 'I'm going home to get some sleep, it's been quite a day,' he said. 'If you don't mind my saying so, Guv, you look as if you need some as well.' Imperceptibly, the relationship had ceased to be between old friends and become professional again.

'You're right.' Castle pushed back his chair and stood up. The two men made their way back to the station car park without speaking, except to exchange good-nights.

★ ★ ★

Sukey had left a message on the answering machine at Castle's flat in the Tewkesbury Road. She sounded exhausted. 'It's nine-forty-five and I'm off to bed, I'm bushed,' her

146

recorded voice informed him. 'I've swapped shifts with Nigel Warren so I won't be on till four tomorrow. Give me a call when you've got a moment — but not tonight.' There was a pause before she said, in a warmer tone that made him long to be able to reach out and touch her, 'Sleep well, Jim.'

He glanced at his watch. Almost ten-thirty; she was probably already asleep. He'd have to wait till tomorrow to find out what she had been doing in the neighbourhood of Dearley Manor earlier. Not, he reminded himself, that he had any right to question her about where she went in her free time. Their relationship hadn't reached that stage yet. Still, it was an odd coincidence. As he told Andy, she'd never mentioned knowing anyone in that neck of the woods — apart from her ex, of course, but she'd hardly have been paying him a social visit, especially in the present circumstances.

He reset the machine and began to get ready for bed. He felt pretty bushed himself.

11

DI Castle slept soundly, awoke at his usual time without the aid of an alarm, showered, breakfasted and was at his desk by eight o'clock the following morning. Almost immediately, his telephone rang: DCI Philip Lord, arriving a few minutes earlier, had been greeted with the news that he was to take over the inquiry into the death at Dearley Manor.

'Any idea what's behind the switch?' asked Lord.

'Yes, but I'd rather not talk about it here,' said Castle. 'You'll want a thorough briefing, of course. Why don't I meet you there, say in an hour's time?'

'Fine.'

Castle put down the phone, picked it up again and called Sukey's number. It rang several times before she answered and when at last she came on the line her voice was heavy with sleep. 'Oh, Jim,' she said, yawning. 'Sorry I couldn't stay up to talk to you last night, I was out on my feet when I got home.'

'I can imagine. It can't have been much fun, having to go out again, after such a gruelling day.' He waited, half expecting her to tell him where she had been, but all he heard was her quiet breathing. After a moment, he said, 'I'm sorry if I woke you. Are you feeling rested?'

'Yes, I'm fine, thanks.' A series of soft grunts and a rustling sound came over the wire, as if she was shifting her position in bed. She would be sitting up, or maybe propped on one elbow, her short dark curls ruffled and her sharp features relaxed and rosy from sleep, the covers sliding from her shoulders, the pillow dented where her head had been resting. He could amost feel the warmth of her body, inhale its scent, touch her smooth flesh . . .

'What time is it?' she asked and the picture faded as he glanced at the clock on his office wall.

'Ten past eight. I wanted a word with you, to find out how you are, and I don't know what the score's going to be today.'

'What do you mean?'

'I'm handing over the Dearley Manor inquiry to DCI Lord on the Super's instructions. I have to go there to brief him and I'm not sure what time I'll be back. It depends what the day brings, but I hope to be around when you come on duty at four.'

'Right.' There was a pause before she said, 'I take it you had to let Mr Sladden know about us — is that why he's taken you off the case?'

'Of course. It's in both our interests — yours and mine, I mean. You know how lawyers pounce on these things, twist them around to suit their arguments — '

'Yes, we've already agreed on that.'

This wasn't getting them anywhere. He had the feeling that she was holding something back; normally, if she was out when he phoned, she would tell him where she had been without being asked. She hadn't asked any questions about how the inquiry was progressing either, although he knew how concerned she was on Reynolds' behalf. He was tempted to tackle her about it, but decided not to. Not now, not over the telephone, not when it might lead to misunderstandings. And he had to leave in five minutes to keep his appointment with DCI Lord. It would have to wait.

'Well, take care. See you later,' he said and rang off.

★　★　★

'It certainly looks as if Reynolds is our man,' said Lord, sitting back in his chair and clasping his hands behind his head. He was a short, dapper man in his fifties, stockily built with dark hair and a small moustache that gave him a slightly Chaplinesque appearance.

'It does look that way,' said Castle. 'Sladden agrees,' he added wryly, and the two men exchanged amused glances at this restatement of the Superintendent's many times expressed views. They were sitting at a table in the first floor sitting-room of Dearley Rectory, a rambling Victorian mansion on the edge of the village. The incumbent, a widower who on the recent death of his wife had retreated to a small suite of rooms on the ground floor, had placed the rest of the house at the disposal of the police for use as an incident room. At the Manor, the search of the grounds was continuing, while further afield officers were pursuing house to house enquiries.

'There doesn't seem to have been much love lost between him and his wife,' Lord went on, tapping the file containing Castle's report, 'and he had plenty of opportunity — all he had to do was wait till everyone had gone home after the party and sneak back into the house. That yarn about not having the keys sounds pretty thin to me.'

'And to me,' agreed Castle. 'I have to say, though, he put up a very convincing show at being shocked and horrified at his wife's death — and he stuck to his story even after the Filbury woman went for him, although he was obviously shaken. Up to then, he'd been insisting that his relationship with his wife was perfectly normal.'

'All well-rehearsed, no doubt. It won't surprise me if he offers to appear on the box, pleading for help in finding the killer while knowing bloody well he's done it himself.'

Castle nodded. 'It wouldn't be the first time that's happened, either.'

'He must have been heavily bloodstained after the attack, though no sign of the clothes so far, I see?'

'No, and speaking of blood, there's one odd feature,' said Castle. 'You've probably already noticed from the SOCOs' reports that there was no trace of it outside the room where the killing took place, and no shoeprints. You'd expect him to have trodden some of it about, but — '

'Yes, that had occurred to me. Of course, the two were husband and wife, weren't they? Maybe he wasn't wearing any clothes — there's no reference to any prints of bare feet either, but he could have kept his socks on and then taken them off straight away and disposed of them. They'd be easy to hide, or simply wash out and dry before the body was discovered.' Lord made a note on a pad. 'I'll have a check made in the bathroom — both in the main house and the cottage where he's holed up.'

'They didn't share a room,' Castle pointed out. 'They hadn't for some time, according to the housekeeper and the Filbury woman.'

'Nothing to stop him stripping off in his own room and sneaking along to hers,' Lord pointed out. 'He could have pretended he was there for a bit of the other and then — ' He made slashing movements through the air with his pen. 'Which suggests a certain degree of premeditation. Made a thorough job of it, didn't he?' he went on, gesturing at the photographs lying on the table. 'Not a nice thing for Sukey to find.'

'She was pretty shaken.'

'I can imagine.' Lord sat for a moment with his mouth bunched up as if he was sucking a non-existent sweet, a habit he had when thinking. Then he said, 'You took her off the case more or less right away. Ex-wife of the suspect, I understand?'

'That's right.'

'And you and she — ?'

'We do have — a relationship,' Castle admitted. 'We don't want it trumpeted around, though.'

'Sure, no problem. The official line is that the remaining directors of the deceased's company have demanded a senior officer to

153

handle the inquiry. The Super's instructions.'

'That's decent of him. He did seem quite sympathetic — it's nice to know he has a human side.'

'Oh, he has his good points. Now, back to business. Let's see where we are with witness statements.' Lord picked up another file and began reading the list of contents. 'I see Radcliffe has been to the Maxford head office and talked to the company secretary.'

'Eric Dennison. That's right,' said Castle. 'He already knew about the murder — Reynolds got on to him as soon as I'd finished with him. Radcliffe says he appeared very shocked, which is only natural. He expressed concern for the future of the company without Mrs Maxford's hand at the helm, paid tribute to her business acumen and so on. He confirmed the names of the people present at the party as given by Reynolds, admitted to some disappointment at the outcome, but claimed everyone accepted their MD's reasons for her decision and the evening ended amicably about midnight.'

'What about the others — do they tell the same story?'

'Radcliffe wasn't able to see anyone else from the company yesterday — the other two directors were out so he's going back today. And there's the wives to see and the estate manager — Hampton — to catch up with as well, and that old lady who lives on the estate, Mrs Willow.'

Lord nodded, still studying the list. 'Who's Mr Ernest Clark of Turner and Clark?'

'The senior partner of Reynolds' firm of chartered accountants. Radcliffe says he was very upset to hear of the trouble Reynolds is in. He's a fatherly old boy who thinks highly of him, both professionally and personally. He seems to have tried to act as a kind of counsellor when the first marriage broke up — even warned Reynolds against Myrna Maxford, said he knew her by reputation as a man-eater — but Reynolds was quite besotted and refused to hear a word against her. I gather relations between the two men were pretty frosty for quite a while after the divorce.'

'Has Mr Clark noticed any recent change in Reynolds' behaviour?'

'He did say that he's shown signs of being under stress and wondered if the marriage was in trouble. He thought of tackling him about it, but decided against it . . . said something about 'making his bed and having to lie on it'.'

Lord put the file aside. 'Okay, I'll go over Radcliffe's reports in detail later. What about the housekeeper — Mrs Little?'

'We took a preliminary statement about how she found the supposed break-in and then sent her home. My intention was to send a WPC round to see her today.'

'Right, I'll see to that.' Lord made more notes. 'Do I understand that Dennison confirmed Reynolds' claim that he left early and put it down to differences between him and his wife?'

'That's right. As you say, sir, it seems to be the general opinion, in spite of his claim to be on what he calls 'normal terms' with her.'

'And I see from your report on the interview with Reynolds that he had pushed strongly for the takeover. Any idea if he stood to gain anything from it?'

'Not in terms of material advantage — or if he did, it didn't come out at the interview. I got the impression he was pretty miffed at having his advice rejected. It probably meant a certain loss of face.'

'Hm. Not a motive for murder in itself, perhaps, but if there was bad blood already — ' Lord broke off as a young woman officer knocked and entered with a sheet of paper in her hand. 'Yes, Yvonne, what is it?'

'Fax from forensics, sir. They think they may have identified the murder weapon.'

Lord scanned the message, reporting the gist of its contents aloud. 'Traces of blood on a knife removed from the kitchen . . . sample sent for DNA testing . . . and guess whose prints are on the handle?'

'Reynolds?'

'The same. Let's hear what he has to say about that.' Lord got up and reached for his jacket. 'Thanks for your help, Jim. I'll let you know how things go — I dare say you're still interested?'

'I'd appreciate that, thank you, sir.'

* * *

At about the time that two senior detectives were discussing the investigation into the murder of his wife, Paul Reynolds was aroused from an uneasy, whisky-induced slumber by the shrilling of his mobile phone. Ernest Clark was on the line.

'Ah, good-morning, Reynolds. I hope I didn't disturb you?' he said in his precise, measured tones.

'Oh, er, not at all, sir.' Paul glanced at his watch. 'Oh, Lord, I must have overslept — I'm sorry, I'm going to be very late — '

'Don't worry about it, my boy.' The voice became positively paternal. 'As a matter of fact, I was hardly expecting you to arrive on the dot after your tragic loss. Have the police made any progress with their inquiries?'

157

'Not that I know of, sir . . . very kind of you to ask,' Paul mumbled, still only half awake.

'Shocking business, shocking,' Mr Clark went on. 'In view of the grief and distress you are undoubtedly suffering, I should like to make it clear that we — Mr Turner and I — do not expect you to return to the office until you feel able to do so.'

'That's very kind of you, sir, but I've been advised to carry on with my normal life — as far as possible, that is.'

'That sounds like sensible advice, but I want to emphasise that we are not putting any pressure on you.'

'I appreciate that, sir, I really do.'

'Now, have you any appointments today that you would like Miss Deacon to reschedule for you?'

'Just a moment, I'll check.' Dragging his wits together, Paul got up and stumbled across the room. He picked up his jacket, which lay on the floor where he had thrown it, with the rest of his clothes, before falling into bed, took out his personal organiser and stabbed at the keys. 'Nothing this morning, but I've arranged to take Mr Barrington out to lunch. He's an important client, I really should keep the appointment.'

'Ah yes, the racehorse trainer. You're quite

right, we must do our best to keep him sweet or he'll take his account elsewhere. If you're sure you feel up to it — '

'I'll be fine after I've had a shower and some breakfast. Thank you very much for calling.'

'Not at all, my boy. Just wanted you to know that we're all behind you.'

Mr Clark rang off and Paul put down the phone. His head was spinning; he sat on the edge of the bed for several minutes trying to clear his thoughts. What was it Susan had said last night? *Stop hiding in your bolt-hole like a guilty man.* And the senior partner had endorsed that advice. Well, it was up to him to act on it. He got up, showered and shaved, put on his clothes and went into the kitchen to forage among the remains of the provisions that his ex-wife had brought. He spooned instant coffee into a mug, made a sandwich with the rest of the ham and settled down to eat it while waiting for the kettle to boil. Something strange seemed to be going on in his head; he felt as if he were standing outside himself, watching his physical body performing the routine tasks as if they were outside his control, while his mind struggled to make sense of the harrowing events of the past thirty-six hours. It was almost as if they had happened to somebody else. He asked himself what he was doing here, why he wasn't in his own home, eating in his own kitchen the breakfast that Mrs Little normally prepared for him. Then the thought occurred to him that it had never been his own home. Like everything else, it had belonged to Myrna. She had thought of him as her property as well, to do as she liked with. But not any more. Whatever lay ahead, at least he was free of her.

An insistent ringing at the doorbell jerked him back to reality. He put down his half-eaten sandwich and went to answer it.

'Ah, good-morning, Mr Reynolds.' The grey-haired man with the bushy eyebrows who had taken notes during that terrifying interview with DI Castle the previous day was standing at the door, holding up an identity card. 'I dare say you remember me, sir — Detective Sergeant Radcliffe. This is Detective Constable Hill. May we come in for a moment?'

'Yes, of course.' Paul stood aside, closed the door behind them and led the way upstairs. 'Please, sit down. Is there any news?'

'There have been certain developments, sir,' replied Radcliffe. The two men perched on two of the dining chairs, their attitude suggesting that they were not intending to stay long. A stab of fear turned the partially-eaten sandwich to lead in Paul's stomach. Was he about to be arrested?

'We've found what we think may be the murder weapon,' the sergeant went on.

'Oh?' Paul felt his knees buckle and he pulled out a third chair and sat down facing them.

Radcliffe gestured to his younger colleague, who opened a briefcase and took out a transparent plastic envelope, which he laid on the table. The blade of the knife it contained glinted in the sunlight slanting through the window. 'Ever seen this before, sir?'

Paul felt his gorge rising. He swallowed hard and said, 'It looks like one of a set that Mrs Little keeps in a block in the kitchen.'

'That's where it was found by a scene of crime examiner, sir.' Radcliffe pushed the envelope forward, keeping his eyes on Paul's face. 'If you look closely, you'll see traces of blood round the base of the blade, where it joins the handle.'

Paul stared in horror at the tell-tale brownish stain. 'Is it . . . my wife's blood?'

'Oh, it's much too soon to say, sir. We have to wait for the result of DNA tests and they take quite a time.' Radcliffe paused for a moment before saying, 'Now, when it comes to fingerprints, we can check those much more quickly.'

'There are fingerprints on the knife?' Paul's heart was thumping. 'Have you — have you identified them?'

'Yes, sir. They appear to be yours. Perhaps you can explain that?'

'I . . . let me think.' Paul fought to control the rising nausea. He felt the eyes of both detectives boring into his and knew they were waiting for him to betray himself. He looked from one to the other, desperately searching for the right words.

'Mr Reynolds?' Radcliffe's voice held a note of impatience.

Paul took a deep breath. 'Yes,' he said slowly, in staccato, disjointed phrases at first, then more fluently as his thoughts became clearer. 'I think I can . . . explain it, I mean . . . sometimes I leave home early — before the housekeeper arrives — and then I have to get my own breakfast. Sometimes I have a grapefruit and I cut it with a knife from the block that Mrs Little keeps near the sink.'

'I see.' Radcliffe nodded gravely, while Hill scribbled in his notebook. 'Can you recall the last time you did this?' It was all too plain where the questions were leading.

'It wasn't yesterday morning because I stayed here on Sunday night . . . and it wasn't Saturday, so it must have been . . . yes, it was last Friday. That's right,' Paul went on with sudden inspiration, 'I remember now, I was in a hurry because I had an early appointment with a client in Worcester. I got a bit careless and cut myself quite badly.' He held out his left hand to show the forefinger with its shiny piece of waterproof sticking plaster. 'More haste, less speed,' he added. He forced a smile, which was not returned.

'You didn't think to wash the knife?'

'I'm sure I rinsed it . . . I usually do, but perhaps I didn't make a very good job of it.'

'And then put it back in the block?'

'I suppose so.'

'You don't seem very sure.'

'I can't remember exactly, but that's what I would normally do. Mrs Little doesn't really like anyone touching things in the kitchen.'

'It's her private domaine, eh?'

'I think that's the way she sees it.'

Radcliffe stood up and signalled to Hill to put his notebook and the knife away. 'Right, sir, that seems to have cleared that up. Now, if you wouldn't mind coming down to the station with us to sign a formal statement, and at the same time give a sample of blood — for the purpose of comparison, you understand — '

★ ★ ★

163

After Jim Castle rang off, Sukey got out of bed and put on her dressing gown. On the bedside table was the mug of tea that Fergus had brought her before leaving for his job at the supermarket. It was stone cold. She remembered thanking him for it, listening to his footsteps clattering downstairs and the slam of the front door behind him while summoning the energy to sit up and drink it. She must have fallen asleep again.

Her head felt heavy. Despite being mentally and physically exhausted, she had lain awake for a long time reliving the events of the previous day. Fergus had waited up for her, frantic for news of his father, and she had done what she could to reassure him. 'If he didn't do it, they can't prove he did', she had said repeatedly until the words seemed to lose all meaning while Fergus, like Paul, had seized on the word 'if' as though it was somehow a betrayal on her part, an acknowledgement that there was room for doubt.

She went to the bathroom, poured the tea down the washbasin, splashed cold water over her face and went downstairs. In the kitchen, she switched on the radio and caught the local news: '*Police investigating the murder of Mrs Myrna Maxford, the well-known local businesswoman, have taken away a number* of items from the house for forensic examination. A police spokeswoman is quoted as saying. 'We are following up several leads, but our inquiries are at an early stage'. The next news bulletin is at — ' Sukey switched off with a sense of partial relief; at least, Paul hadn't been arrested. She wondered if he had slept, whether there had been any further visits from the detectives.

She made some fresh tea and put two slices of bread in the toaster. For some reason, she found herself thinking of old Mrs Willow — 'Pussy' Willow, Ezra Hampton had called her. It had been a kindly thought on his part to try and protect the old lady from being needlessly worried by the police, but since she had been among the last people to see Myrna alive they were certain to want to interview her. Not that they were likely to be impressed by tales of having read death in the cards or predictions of 'more evil to come'. Like Ezra, as well as the proprietor of the shop and his customers — and probably the entire population of Dearley — they would take any such assertions with a large pinch of salt. And yet . . . was it feasible that, if she had been wandering around the village after the party, she *had* spotted someone — a real person, possibly the murderer — who to her disordered imagination might have taken on the appearance of a ghostly apparition? Paul insisted that he had remained all night in the flat where he had taken refuge and Sukey was sure — well, almost sure — that he was telling the truth. The police would be taking a less charitable view, especially after the business of the keys. Sukey found herself wishing that she had made more of an effort to talk to Mrs Willow, to find out what her movements were after leaving the Manor. Someone — probably Ezra — must have given her a lift home. Ezra had mentioned that she sometimes went out late at night looking for her cat. It would be worth having a word with Jim, asking him to drop a hint to DCI Lord that dismissing the old woman's claims out of hand might mean a vital clue was overlooked.

Sukey drank her tea, ate her toast and went upstairs. The next few hours were her own and there were plenty of household chores to catch up with. Resolutely putting the murder inquiry from her mind, she showered, got dressed, loaded the washing machine and went round the house with the vacuum cleaner. While working, she began planning the evening meal. Being on a later shift meant that it could be after ten o'clock before she got home; a chilli con carne would be easy to reheat and Fergus could have his earlier if he wanted it. She could hardly expect him to wait; at his age, he was permanently hungry. She was beginning to regret agreeing to the change as it meant that he would have to eat supper on his own. Normally, it wouldn't be a problem, but in his present state of anxiety for his father he needed company. Still, he would probably invite Anita round. For teenagers, their relationship was holding remarkably firm.

While the chilli was cooking she made a cheese sandwich for her lunch and was just about to eat it when she heard the sound of a key in the front door. She looked up in surprise as Fergus entered the kitchen; although the supermarket was only ten minutes' cycle ride away, he normally took a packed lunch to work. He went straight to the radio and switched it on. Pop music blared out and he turned the volume down before saying, 'I wanted to hear the news.'

'It's not on till one o'clock.'

He slumped into a chair and opened his packet of sandwiches, but made no attempt to eat them. His young face was drawn and there were violet smudges under his eyes. Sukey's heart went out to him. 'You look worn out — didn't you sleep?' she asked.

'Not much.' He bit his lip, struggling with his emotions. 'I'm so worried about Dad.'

'I know.' She got up to give him a hug, and he clung to her like the child he had so recently been. She could feel his body trembling against hers.

'He must be feeling so awful,' he said, his voice half muffled against her shoulder, 'stuck in that flat on his own. Couldn't he come here and stay with us?'

'I explained last night, it's difficult on account of my job. I'm off the case and strictly speaking, I shouldn't have gone to see him. I made him promise not to mention my visit to the police'

'Yes, I know, I just thought — '

She gave him a squeeze and released him. 'Come on, eat your sarnies and I'll make some tea — or would you prefer coffee?'

'Tea's fine.' Normally, he would have offered to make it, but today he sat glumly staring in front of him, half-heartedly chewing his food. On the radio, the music ended and a woman read the weather forecast. Next came an extract from a new comedy series due to begin that evening, weak jokes punctuated with gales of inane laughter from a studio audience, followed by a series of traffic announcements which seemed to go on indefinitely, while the minute hand of the kitchen clock dragged itself towards the hour and Sukey and Fergus sat silently facing one another across their kitchen table with their half-eaten sandwiches and two untouched mugs of tea between them.

The time signal for one o'clock came at last and Fergus reached out to turn up the volume again as the announcer began reading the headlines: a parliamentary spat between the Prime Minister and the Leader of the Opposition over monetary union; a military coup in an African state; a hurricane heading for the Gulf of Mexico and a prominent athlete accused of drug-taking. Only the final item was of any interest to the two tense listeners: *'A man has been helping the police with inquiries into the murder of business-woman Myrna Maxford.'*

12

'They didn't say it was Dad, did they? Maybe it's one of the other men who were at the party ... it could be any one of them, couldn't it, or maybe someone we don't even know about?' Fergus's voice was hoarse and unsteady; he reached across the table and clutched his mother's hand, his eyes pleading for the reassurance they both knew she could not give.

Sukey put her free hand over his. 'I think we have to assume that it is Dad,' she said gently. 'That business with the keys would have made the police suspicious — '

'But you said he'd explained to them about that. It was a natural mistake, he must have been in a fearful state after hearing about Myrna — '

'On its own, I wouldn't have thought it was enough for them to take him in for questioning; they must have found some other evidence.'

'What sort of evidence?'

The words brought back Paul's anguished question of the previous evening, 'What were they looking for?' and her response,

'Bloodstained clothing . . . a weapon.' *At least, they hadn't found anything like that — not then anyway. But that was yesterday. Supposing — ?* Aloud, she said, 'I don't know, Gus, but there must have been some development that we haven't been told about.'

'Mum, you're not saying you think he did it?' Fergus all but choked on the final words.

'No, of course I'm not, but there may be some circumstantial evidence that needs explaining. You heard what the announcer said — he hasn't been arrested, just helping with inquiries.'

'But supposing he can't explain, supposing they charge him — Mum — ' The grip on Sukey's hand tightened so violently that she flinched and he released it with a mumbled word of apology. 'Mum,' he repeated, 'you've got to *do* something!'

'Oh, Fergus!' The sight of his distress brought tears to her own eyes. 'What can I do? I'm off the case, and for all I know Jim is too — I explained that last night. Other SOCOs are working on it now. I know them all, you can trust them — '

'They don't know Dad like we do. We know he couldn't possibly kill anyone — '

'Gus, they deal with evidence, that's all. They hand it over to forensics, and then it's

171

passed back with reports to the investigating officers — '

'Yes, I know all that, but surely there's nothing to stop you asking around, talking to the people you met?'

'What do you suppose the police are doing?'

'They might not ask the right questions — or talk to the right people. That old lady you told me about, the one they say's a bit gaga, suppose she did see the real killer and could describe him?'

'I'm sure the police will be talking to her — if they haven't already — but she really is very strange and I doubt if they'll take her stories of spooks and death in the cards very seriously.'

'But she could be a vital witness. You were kind to her, you gave her a lift . . . maybe she'd talk to you, tell you things she wouldn't tell the police — ' He was distraught, grasping at straws, on the verge of breaking down altogether. 'Mum, you could at least go and see her, it's worth a try . . . *please!*'

She was already half persuaded; at odd times during the morning, despite her efforts to concentrate on other things, similar thoughts had been passing through her head. Mrs Willow might be confused and subject to occasional delusions, but she was by no means senile. If she had caught a glimpse of a strange figure moving stealthily around in the moonlight, she would have been more likely to identify it as one of the 'uneasy spirits' she claimed to have seen; but it was still possible that, if handled with tact and patience, she could give a recognisable description. Ezra Hampton had hinted that to be questioned by a uniformed police officer was liable to upset her, but . . .

Fergus tugged impatiently at her hand. His eyes were feverish. 'Please, Mum!' he implored. 'You've got plenty of time, you're not on duty till four.'

It was a plea she could no longer resist. 'All right, I'll try and have a word with her,' she promised, and for the first time since he learned of Myrna's death something like a smile passed briefly over his face. It brought home to Sukey, almost more than his frantic pleading, the strain he was under. 'But not a word to Jim or anyone else, d'you hear?' she insisted and he nodded, gratitude shining through the tears that he brushed away with the back of his hand. 'Right, you get back to work now or you'll be in the doghouse. I've made a chilli for supper.'

'Fine. See you later. Thank you, Mum!' He gave her a bear-hug, kissed her on the cheek and hurried from the house, leaving an untouched mug of tea and a half-eaten sandwich on the table.

★ ★ ★

August had given way to September and the weather had changed with the month. A cool wind from the south-west swept over the Cotswolds bringing ragged clouds and a fine drizzle that drifted like mist over the land. Ignoring the first road into Dearley, which would have taken her past the Manor and possibly in sight of police officers who would recognise her, Sukey drove on a further couple of miles before turning into the narrow lane which brought her to Dearley's Acres Lane without the need to go near the village.

In the field opposite Pussy Willow's cottage, the stubble faded now to a dull greyish yellow where yesterday it had shone golden in the sunshine, a tractor drawing a plough was clanking to and fro, pursued by a flock of gulls and a scattering of rooks that hovered and swooped as they hunted for food in the widening band of freshly turned earth. Sukey pulled onto the verge, got out of the car and pushed open the wooden gate that bore the legend, 'Holly Cottage', a name obviously inspired by the hedge separating the little front garden from the road. A tabby cat appeared from behind the cottage and ran to her, gazing up at her with huge green eyes and miaowing, then turning to run ahead of her along a brick path leading up to the front door. This had an unused appearance, having no bell-push, knocker or letter-box. It occurred to Sukey that, like many country folk, Mrs Willow probably used the back door for her comings and goings. As if in confirmation, the cat, which had momentarily vanished, re-emerged from behind the cottage and began winding itself round her legs, still miaowing piteously, before running back again. Sukey followed and found it standing in front of a green painted door with a fox's head knocker, an old-fashioned round door-knob and a letter box, all of well-polished brass. She gave a brisk rat-tat-tat and waited.

There was no sound from inside the cottage. She knocked again, a little more loudly, and rattled the flap of the letter-box. The cat continued its protestations, switching its attention between the door, which it obviously expected to be opened at any minute, and two empty earthenware bowls which stood on the ground alongside an ancient iron bootscraper. 'What's up, Puss?' said Sukey. 'Did your missis forget your breakfast?' In response, the cat rubbed itself against her legs and gave an optimistic purr as she stooped to stroke it. She began to be concerned; it was one thing for Mrs Willow to be out, but she had a feeling that to leave her cat without food or water was something she would not normally do.

She was about to bend down and call through the letter-box when she heard a heavy step on the path behind her. A man's voice said, 'Are you looking for Mrs Willow?' Sukey jumped and swung round to see Ezra Hampton. 'Oh, it's you,' he said before she had a chance to speak. 'I saw the car and thought I'd better see who it was. She gets flustered if strangers come to the house; she's got this fear of being turned out, you see — '

'I've knocked a couple of times, but she doesn't answer,' said Sukey. Her momentary alarm at Ezra's unexpected arrival turned to relief at having someone with whom to share the problem. 'The cat doesn't seem to have been fed, either. Do you suppose she's ill or something?'

Ezra frowned. 'I haven't seen her about today, come to think of it,' he said. He pounded on the door with his fist and shouted, 'Mrs Willow, are you there? It's Ezra.' When there was still no response, he grabbed the doorknob and twisted it. The door swung open. 'Funny,' he muttered uneasily, 'she's usually so fussy about locking up if she goes out.' He raised his voice and called again, 'Pussy, are you all right?'

There was no reply. 'Do you think we should go in?' Sukey suggested. 'Maybe she's been taken ill, or had a fall.'

Ezra nodded. They stepped into the neat kitchen, where everything appeared to be in place. The cat had rushed in ahead of them and disappeared through a door in the far corner. 'We'll try the back room, that's where she usually sits,' said Ezra. On the other side of the tiny hallway were two more doors, one of which stood ajar. He pushed it wide open and gave an exclamation of alarm. 'She's here ... it looks as if ... I don't like the look of her — ' He stood still, pointing, seemingly reluctant to enter the room.

Sukey caught a glimpse over his shoulder of the figure on the floor and pushed past him. 'Let me see,' she said urgently.

Mrs Willow lay on her back on the empty hearth with her head resting on the edge of a cast-iron fire basket. She was fully dressed and there was no visible sign of injury, but at the sight of the wide-open eyes gazing up at the ceiling in a fixed, glassy stare Sukey knew instinctively, even before her fingers touched the marble-cold flesh in a fruitless search for a pulse, that the old woman was beyond help.

Her first thought was, *No one will ever know now whether what you saw on the night of Myrna's death was her killer or a figment of your imagination*, and the second, *If this was an accident, it could be very convenient for someone.*

'Is she dead?'

It was Ezra, bringing her mind back to the immediate problem. She got to her feet and said, 'I'm pretty sure she is, but we must get hold of a doctor right away to be sure. Do you happen to know — ?'

'She goes to the surgery at Barcomb.' His voice was a dull monotone. He seemed dazed, unable to take it in.

'Do you know the number?'

He fumbled in his pocket and pulled out a grubby note-book, found a place and held it out to her. 'There's no telephone in the cottage,' he said.

'My mobile's in the car. Leave it to me.'

★   ★   ★

'Two stiffs in the same village in two days — that's quite a score,' said Mandy Parfitt. She put a mug of tea in front of Sukey, dragged a chair from an adjoining desk and sat down opposite her. For the moment, the two civilian SOCOs were alone in the office.

'And you found both of them. Are you going to make it three in a row for the bonus point?'

'Oh, shut up!' Sukey gave a watery grin and sipped gratefully at the tea. 'It is turning out to be quite a week,' she said wearily. *And you don't know the half of it*, she added mentally. *I'm going to have to explain what I was doing at Pussy Willow's cottage, and there'll be no bonus points for that.*

'At least, it doesn't sound as if this death is suspicious,' Mandy went on. 'What did the doctor say?'

'Not a lot, really, except to confirm that she was dead, had been for some hours. She didn't have a history of heart trouble, but then heart attacks and strokes often happen without warning and it could have been one or the other that made her fall. He said that whatever the cause, hitting her head on that iron grate was probably enough to finish her off, but of course he'll have to inform the coroner and there may be an autopsy.'

'Presumably he'll have informed our people as well?' Mandy pointed out.

'Yes, of course.' Sukey stared down into her mug to avoid meeting her colleague's eye. At least one difficult interview lay ahead.

Mandy put down her empty mug and thought for a moment before saying, 'I hear Inspector Castle's taken you off the Maxford case. I thought it was very considerate of him.'

'Yes, wasn't it?' The remark could mean one of two things: either it had not occurred to Mandy that Castle's decision had been prompted by anything other than a recognition of the trauma Sukey was presumed to have suffered, or she knew the real reason but was tactful enough not to say so. What was more to the point, the subtext of her comment was almost certainly, *So what were you doing in Dearley this afternoon when you weren't even on duty?*

'Of course, he's off it himself now, or didn't you know?' Mandy went on.

It was what he had warned her might happen, but Sukey pretended to appear surprised. 'No, I hadn't heard. Any idea why?'

Mandy shrugged. 'Something to do with protocol, according to George Barnes. He says the victim's business associates wanted a more senior officer to take charge, so the Super's given the case to DCI Lord. Bit of a cheek, if you ask me.' To Sukey's relief, she appeared to regard the explanation as perfectly reasonable.

There was a silence, interrupted by the appearance in the doorway of Castle himself. 'Ah, Sukey, could I have a word?' He stood holding the door open, indicating that the conversation was to be in private.

'Of course, sir.'

She followed him along the corridor to his office. 'Close the door, please,' he said, still in his slightly brusque official manner. He sat down behind his desk and waved her to a chair facing him. She sat in some trepidation, waiting for him to speak. Uncharacteristically, he concentrated for several seconds on the brass paperweight he was fingering instead of looking directly at her. At last he raised his head. 'This is going to be upsetting for you, I know,' he began, and her stomach gave a lurch.

'Paul's been arrested, hasn't he?' She could hear the catch in her own voice as her throat contracted with a surge of emotion.

'Not arrested. He came to the station voluntarily this morning to help with the inquiries.' Sukey gave a wry smile at the non-committal formula she had heard so often. 'He wasn't detained, but he's still very much in the frame. I thought it would be easier for you if I told you privately,' Castle added gently.

'Thank you.' She felt sympathy for Paul, but for the moment her aching concern for Fergus almost drove everything else from her mind.

'The SOCOs found a knife in the kitchen

with traces of blood and Reynolds' finger-prints on it,' the detective went on. 'We have to wait for the result of tests on the blood, but there's no doubt about the prints.' He spoke as if the case was all but wound up, as if no further inquiries would be necessary.

'But that needn't mean a thing!' Sukey burst out. 'He lives in the house, he's entitled to go into the kitchen and use a knife. He could have had an accident and cut himself — maybe it's his own blood?'

'Funnily enough, that's what he's claiming. He showed us a cut on his hand, but doesn't seem all that certain when he did it or when was the last time he used a kitchen knife. He says he often prepares a grapefruit for his breakfast — he has to get his own as the housekeeper doesn't always arrive in time to do it before he leaves in the morning.'

And his wife wasn't likely to do it, was she? Sukey thought waspishly. Aloud, she said, 'Well, there you are then. You've admitted it wasn't enough to justify arresting him.'

'Yes.' There was a pause and Sukey felt her pulse rate increase. Something about Castle's demeanour told her that there was worse to come. His next words confirmed it. 'There's something else you have to know,' he said. Beneath his cool, detached manner she detected a genuine understanding of her

182

predicament. 'I had a call from DCI Lord a few minutes ago to say another body has turned up in Dearley and he's pretty certain there's a link.'

'You mean old Mrs Willow?' There was no point in pretending she didn't know, even though the news of her involvement had obviously not reached him.

His brows shot up and his eyes bored into hers. 'Who told you?' he demanded.

'No one. Ezra Hampton and I found her.'

'I hope you had a good reason to be there,' he said angrily. 'I'd like to remind you that you're a SOCO, not a detective, and that I expressly took you off the Maxford case.' There was no hint of gentleness in his manner now.

Sukey felt her confidence ebbing away as she tried to justify herself. 'Ezra told me yesterday that she's . . . was . . . very nervous about strangers coming to the house,' she explained. 'It sounded as if she might have seen something or someone prowling around that night after everyone had gone home. I thought she might have important evidence, but not be willing to talk to the police — that perhaps she'd be more comfortable with me, seeing we'd already met and had a chat.'

'Oh? How did that come about?' His tone was glacial.

Feeling like a suspect under questioning, Sukey explained how, after driving Mrs Little to her cottage at Sergeant Radcliffe's request, she had encountered Ezra, Pussy Willow and several other people in the village shop. 'She was going on about there being death in the cards, more evil to come and an uneasy spirit in a shroud prowling around on the night of the murder. The other people in the shop obviously thought she was completely out of her tree, but I wondered . . . anyway, I happened to overtake her walking home a few minutes later so I offered her a lift.'

'You were supposed to be coming straight back here to make your report, not go driving around the countryside with deranged old women.'

'I was on my way to do that, but she was going in my direction and she was struggling with a heavy load of shopping. I couldn't just drive past her — '

For a moment, she detected a flicker of sympathy in Castle's expression. 'We'll let that go for now,' he said. 'Go on.'

'She does — did — have irrational moments, but she wasn't deranged, not by a long chalk,' Sukey insisted, more confidently now. At least, he hadn't scoffed at her; his intent expression told her he was interested.

'She was talking quite sensibly most of the time, telling me about the history of the village, but she was so sad, and missing her husband so terribly — ' She broke off and swallowed hard to check another wave of emotion. This, she reminded herself, was not professional behaviour. She pulled herself together and said, 'Please, do you mind telling me what evidence there is that Paul had anything to do with her death? The doctor seemed to think she might have had some sort of seizure and fallen.'

'DCI Lord called in the forensic pathologist, who isn't convinced that the wound on the head was caused by her falling on the iron grate. In other words, he's regarding the death as suspicious. If he's right, then I think we must assume that Mrs Willow did see something or someone, and that whoever killed Mrs Maxford wasn't going to take a chance on her story being taken seriously.'

'If that's true, then her murder was premeditated and the killer went to a lot of trouble to make it look like an accident.' Impulsively, Sukey leaned across the desk. Forgetting for a moment that this was an interview between a senior police officer and a civilian employee who had stepped out of line, not a heart-to-heart discussion between lovers, she put a hand on his arm. 'Paul's no angel, Jim, but he could never do that, not in a million years,' she said earnestly. 'You must believe me — '

'Let's stick to facts, shall we?' His voice was cold as he withdrew his arm; the rebuff was deliberate. 'This morning's house to house inquiries revealed that he was seen by the tenant of one of the cottages soon after nine o'clock last night, leaving the flat where he's been staying since Sunday. Another man who was out walking his dog remembers seeing him come back an hour or so later. No particular importance was attached to it at the time, but in the circumstances he's got some explaining to do.'

Sukey stared at him in bewilderment. 'I don't understand. He had no reason to go out again.' This unexpected development found her completely unprepared. 'It must have been immediately after I — '

'After you left him, yes. That's where you were when I phoned, wasn't it?' Dumbly, she nodded. 'Radcliffe said an officer reported seeing you driving away,' he went on, 'but he thought he must have been mistaken. What's got into you? You know the form — you have no right to speak to anyone connected with the case, let alone a suspect. Well?' he snapped as she still remained silent. 'Haven't you anything to say?'

'Paul is a human being, he's someone I once loved and he's the father of my son,' she said at last. It was a struggle to keep back the tears. 'He rang me yesterday evening, desperate for someone to talk to. He wanted to come to my house, but I wouldn't let him because I didn't want a scene in front of Fergus. He was scared out of his wits that he was going to be arrested and I tried to reassure him — '

'On what grounds?'

'On the grounds that I believe him when he tells me he didn't kill Myrna.'

'So you have already told me.' Castle got up from his desk and began pacing to and fro, tossing a bunch of keys in the air and catching them, a habit of his when disturbed or baffled over a difficult case. Sukey watched him, wondering what was going through his head. Suddenly, he swung on his heel, returned to his desk and sat down. 'You will write out a full statement for DCI Lord of what passed between you and Reynolds,' he said curtly. 'And from now on, you will stay out of this case completely, do you understand? Completely,' he repeated. 'That's all. You can go.'

Sukey got to her feet and met his steely gaze with a hint of defiance. 'I'll include everything in my statement that's relevant, but part of our conversation was personal,' she said. 'Sir,' she added as an afterthought. For a split second, before she turned and left the room, something in his expression told her she had got past his guard.

13

The young doctor explained, as she slid a needle into a vein in Paul's arm, that the purpose of the test was to establish what group he was in. He nodded, turning his head away to avoid the sight of his blood flowing into the glass phial. 'It's just the first step in the process of elimination,' she explained chattily as she withdrew the needle and pressed a square of dressing onto the wound. 'You're looking a bit shaky,' she went on, scrutinising him with a professional eye. 'I advise you to wait for ten minutes or so before you leave. I'll ask one of the officers to fetch you a cup of tea.'

'No thanks, I'll be all right,' he assured her. The last thing he wanted was to remain in the police station for a moment longer than was necessary. 'I have an important appointment — I mustn't be late for it.'

'I'm sure a few minutes won't hurt.' It was almost as if she was trying to delay his departure. He wondered what other nasty surprises lay in store for him that day. He rolled down his sleeve, his fingers fumbling with the button on the cuff. She was right, he was a bit shaky and it might give the wrong impression if he appeared too eager to get away. He put on his jacket and followed her outside; she had a quick word with a policewoman who nodded, showed him into a small room off the reception area and returned a few minutes later with a polystyrene cup of scalding tea. He sat there, turning it between his hands, trying to imagine what would happen next. He wasn't under arrest, he told himself, just 'helping with inquiries'. As soon as he'd drunk his tea, he was free to go. It tasted better than he expected and he had to admit the doctor had been right; by the time he finished it he felt a whole lot steadier. He put down the empty cup, opened the door and peered out. The desk sergeant, who was dealing patiently with an elderly woman's vociferous complaint about a neighbour's dog, took no notice of him as he walked past on his way to the exit. It was a relief to be out in the street again.

The lunch with Edward Barrington did a great deal to lift his spirits; the popular trainer was a genial, extrovert character with a hearty appetite for good food and drink and an inexhaustible fund of anecdotes from the world of horse-racing. More importantly, apart from the sporting pages, he seldom read a newspaper or showed interest in anything that did not directly concern his own affairs. If he had heard of the murder it was plain that it meant nothing to him. When Paul drove him home after a prolonged and lavish lunch at an exclusive country restaurant — when it came to keeping on the right side of important and wealthy clients, Turner and Clark were generous in the matter of expense accounts — Barrington had insisted on taking him on a tour of the stableyard and introducing him to his head lad, who proudly showed off the horses under his care, reciting from memory their pedigrees and track records with frequent interruptions from the proprietor, by that time in an almost unstoppably expansive mood. When Paul got back to his office it was almost five o'clock.

It came as no surprise when the reception-ist informed him that the senior partner wanted to see him, but her next words sent a shiver down his spine. 'He's got two men with him, police detectives, arrived a few minutes ago. Maybe they've got some news.' Her manner was sympathetic.

'Thanks, Carrie, tell him I'll be with him in a minute.' It might be something to do with the blood test, he thought, then remembered that Radcliffe had told him a DNA test could take weeks and wondered uneasily what else the inquiries might have turned up. He left his briefcase in his own office and went to the toilet. As he was drying his hands, he caught a glimpse of himself in a mirror. He'd slept badly and it showed, but a good lunch had put some colour into his cheeks. He straightened his tie, smoothed his hair and went along to obey the summons.

Ernest Clark, silver-haired, dapper and bespectacled, greeted him in his usual affable manner as he entered. 'Ah, there you are, Reynolds,' he said. 'Did the meeting with your client go well?'

'Very well, thank you, sir. I'm afraid it went on a little longer than I anticipated — '

'Never mind, never mind, you can tell me all about it later. Now, I think you've met these two gentlemen.' He indicated DS Radcliffe and DC Hill, who had risen to their feet as Paul entered. 'They'd like a few words with you and you can talk in here if you like. It's quite all right, my boy,' he went on as Paul murmured something inarticulate, 'I want a word with Turner and we can just as easily talk in his office as in mine, so take your time.' The old man paused at the door to say with a chuckle, 'We've had a nice little chat — you'll be pleased to know I've given you a good character reference.'

'Thank you, sir,' said Paul, trying to muster a smile.

'Nice old gentleman,' observed DC Hill as the door closed behind him. 'One of the old school.'

Paul nodded. There was a pause, during which the detectives sat down again and indicated with a gesture that he should do the same. 'Well,' he asked impatiently, 'is there any news?'

'We haven't made an arrest yet,' said Radcliffe, 'but there have been developments.'

'What developments?'

The detective ignored the question. 'Would you mind telling us where you were between nine o'clock and mid-night yesterday?' he asked.

Taken by surprise, Paul began to flounder. 'I — I was in the flat where you saw me this morning, I spent the night there,' he said nervously. 'Why do you ask?'

'You didn't go out at all?'

He was on the point of denying it, then remembered the man with the dog he'd met on the way back. 'I needed a breath of air, I went for a short walk, that's all,' he said after a pause.

'Can you remember where you went?'

'Through the woods behind the cottage — there's a path leading to the village.'

'In the dark? That was bit unusual, wasn't it? Most people stick to the roads if they go walking at night.'

'I had a torch — and I knew my way.'

'Perhaps you were going somewhere in particular? To see Mrs Willow, for example?'

'Why would I go and see her?'

'You tell me.' Radcliffe leaned forward, his eyes locked on to Paul's. 'Did you see her?'

'No!' he almost shouted. 'What are you driving at? Has something happened to her?'

'Did you go to her cottage?'

Paul ran a tongue over lips that felt as dry as paper. 'No,' he repeated.

Radcliffe glanced at Hill, who consulted his notebook and said, 'We have a witness who claims to have seen you returning from the direction of Mrs Willow's cottage between nine-thirty and nine forty-five yesterday evening.'

'I didn't see anyone — and I didn't see Mrs Willow, she was out,' Paul said desperately.

'So you admit going to her cottage?'

'All right, I did. I wanted to talk to her.'

'What about?'

'I heard she'd been saying she saw someone prowling about the night my wife was killed. She's known to suffer from hallucinations and I thought, even if she did see someone, no one would believe her, but I wanted to make sure. I thought it was possible she might have — '

194

'Might have seen a real person, maybe recognised them?' said Radcliffe as Paul hesitated. 'Maybe she saw the killer,' he said softly. 'Is that what you thought?'

'Well, yes, I suppose so. She's a nervous old lady, but she knows me and I thought, maybe it might help the investigation, maybe she'll be more willing to talk to me than to the police.'

'And did you see her?'

'I've already told you, she was out, or maybe she was in bed asleep.' Paul could feel his agitation rising by the minute and knew it must be showing. 'I knocked, but there was no answer,' he insisted. 'Look, will you please tell me — '

'Mrs Emily Willow was found dead at her home this afternoon, and we are treating the circumstances as suspicious,' said Radcliffe. There was a short silence, during which Paul looked in terror from one detective to the other, reading accusation in their eyes. Then came the words that he had been dreading. 'Paul Reynolds, I'm arresting you on suspicion of being implicated in the death of Emily Willow. You do not have to say anything . . .'

He sat in a bemused silence, listening to the formal caution. When it was finished he said, 'I want to talk to a solicitor, please.'

The same evening — the second after the horrific death at Dearley Manor — June Ashton, wife of Bradley Ashton, Production Director at Maxford Domestic Fittings Limited, was drinking vodka and tonic and nibbling crisps in the sitting-room of their comfortable, if a trifle down-at-heel, detached four-bedroomed home. The television was showing a news bulletin, but a threatened strike of airline pilots, squabbles over the progress of European monetary union and the fate of the English football team were of no interest to June and she allowed her mind to wander over her plans for improvements to the house — plans which had initially been thrown on the junk heap by the volte-face on the part of 'that bloody woman', but which might, with any luck, become a reality now the treacherous cow was out of the way. The savage nature of Myrna's death caused June no disquiet; on the contrary, her first reaction had been that it was no more than she deserved. 'I'd have done it myself if I'd thought of it,' she told Bradley when he arrived home on Monday with the news.

Still hung-over from the previous evening, she had been taken aback at the mixture of anger and alarm in his expression as he retorted, 'For God's sake, don't let anyone else hear you say that, especially after the exhibition you made of yourself last night.'

She recalled with a twinge of self-disgust her own behaviour on hearing Myrna Maxford's announcement. She had made a fool of herself, no doubt about it, yelling hysterically, charging at the bitch and threatening her with a bottle, then losing all dignity by throwing up in the hall as Bradley dragged her out of the room. She'd passed out as soon as they got back home and she was still asleep when he left for the office the following morning. The memory, when she came to about midday, had added to the misery of the hangover and she'd been prepared for Bradley to have a real go at her when he came home.

Instead, having broken the news of the murder, he had gone on at length about how he and the others — Eric Dennison and Sam Perry — had agreed that nothing was to be said about how upset and disappointed they all were that the takeover wasn't going ahead. If anyone asked, she was to say that it had been a pleasant evening and that they all understood the reasons for Myrna's decision. It wouldn't look good, he said, if the police found out how angry and upset they'd all been, and he'd finished up by saying, rather nastily, that she'd better stay off the booze in case she opened her big mouth once too often. That didn't mean, she told herself as she slowly sipped her drink, that she couldn't have just a small one — or maybe two — now and again. It wasn't as if she had a serious problem.

She heard an approaching car and turned down the volume on the TV to listen; yes, that was Brad arriving home. There followed the familiar series of sounds: the metallic creak and click of the up-and-over garage door, the brief revving up of the engine as the car was driven inside, the clang as the door closed behind it. She wondered what sort of mood he was in. Although there had been no further direct reference to the episode with the bottle, the atmosphere between them had been on the cool side for the past forty-eight hours. She took another fortifying mouthful as the sitting-room door opened and he came in.

His first words were not encouraging. He made no response to her standard greeting of, 'Hullo darling, had a good day?' but said curtly, his eyes on her glass, 'I see you're at the booze again. I thought we agreed — '

'It's only a small one,' she assured him. It was perfectly true, but she could see he had his doubts. 'I promised I'd cut it down and I have. It's the first one today, truly.'

He gave a nod of approval, apparently convinced. 'Well done, keep it up,' he said. He even gave a brief smile. It was his smile that had bowled her over the first time she met him. His voice had fascinated her as well, faintly husky but with a touch of resonance. She used to boast to her friends, after she began dating him, of his 'devastating' smile and his 'dark brown' voice. Now and again she recalled those days, when old Grant Maxford was running the company and their lives were on an upward curve. Then, it seemed, things could only get better. That was before the old man's death and his daughter took over. And before Bradley took a mistress.

She watched as he went over to a side-table where they kept the tray of drinks. He poured a tot of whisky and settled down on the sofa beside her. At fifty, he was still good-looking, his thatch of brown hair only lightly flecked with grey, his waistline trim from regular exercise, his skin healthy and comparatively unlined. He was, she had to admit, wearing better than she was. That morning after her shower she had taken a good look at herself in the full-length bedroom mirror and made a resolution — not the first, by any means, but this one she really intended to keep — to go on a crash diet, cut down the drink and tone up her figure with some regular exercise. It was important to get her act together, not lose her self-control again. She had made a start that very morning by signing on at a fitness centre; her muscles ached a bit after her first workout so she had allowed herself this one drink. Thank God, she hadn't got to the stage where she needed professional help.

'So what's new in the world this evening?' Bradley asked, sipping his scotch with his eyes on the screen, where the announcer was reading the closing headlines.

'Nothing much.'

'Anything about the investigation?'

'Not yet.'

He picked up the remote control and turned up the volume. A petite blonde with a toothy grin gave the weather forecast, promising heavy overnight rain and making stabbing gestures at a map of the British Isles drowning under a computerised deluge. 'Driving conditions are likely to be difficult, so please take care,' she admonished them with a cheery wave before signing off.

'Wonder if they've caught Myrna's killer,' said Bradley as they sat through the commercials, waiting for the local news to begin.

'Whoever it was did the world a service,'

muttered June, then added, 'Just kidding,' on seeing his frown of disapproval. She wondered how he would react when she dropped her bombshell. She allowed herself to savour it for a moment before the first headline had them gasping and exchanging glances of disbelief: 'A second suspicious death in Dearley village'.

'My God, whatever's going on?' she exclaimed as the other items were read out, ignored by them both.

He made an impatient gesture. 'Be quiet and listen,' he said.

The scene switched to an isolated cottage, cordoned off by blue and white tape and surrounded by police, one with a dog. A woman reporter described how the body of Mrs Emily Willow had been discovered by two callers at the cottage early that afternoon. 'There was no sign of forced entry and the first indications seemed to suggest that the death could have been accidental,' she said. 'However, it now seems clear that police are treating it as suspicious, although they refuse to comment on a possible connection with the brutal murder two days ago of local businesswoman Myrna Maxford. They have, however, confirmed that a man has been helping with inquiries into that killing; his name hasn't been revealed, but he is widely believed to be the first victim's husband, Paul Reynolds.'

'They can't think he killed her!' June exclaimed. 'I only met them a few times, but he seemed devoted to her.'

'Relationships aren't always what they seem,' said Bradley.

'Too right,' June agreed softly. This seemed a good moment. The camera cut to the next item, a strike at a local factory where workers were waving banners and shouting slogans in support of a sacked colleague. She turned the volume down again and said, 'So many people have guilty secrets, don't they? Shall we talk about yours, Bradley?'

He gave a start that sent the remains of his drink slopping to and fro in his glass and turned to look at her with a mixture of irritation and unease in his expression. 'What the hell's that supposed to mean?' he snapped.

She settled herself more comfortably against the cushions and brushed an imaginary crumb from her skirt. *Take your time, play it cool and watch him squirm*, she told herself.

'How's Glenda Yates these days?' she asked, keeping her tone deliberately casual, her head tilted on one side and her eyebrows lifted, the way she'd practised in the mirror. 'Your bit on the side,' she added as he gaped at her in dismay. He looked quite ridiculous; it was all she could do not to laugh aloud.

From incredulity, his expression turned to fury. 'The bitch, she swore she'd keep quiet if I — ' He broke off, tossed back the remains of his drink and got up to pour another, a stiff one this time.

'If you went on dancing to her tune?'

He took a gulp from his glass; his hand was shaking. 'When did she tell you?' he demanded.

'When did who tell me?' June knew exactly who he was talking about, but she wasn't going to make it easy for him.

'Myrna of course, who else?'

'What would have been her motive in telling me? She'd have risked losing her hold over you if I knew — although of course, it's your parents you're really worried about, isn't it? Your tight-wad, puritanical Mummy and Daddy would change their minds about leaving their money to their one and only blue-eyed boy if — '

'Shut up!' He swung round and glared at her. 'How do you know all this if Myrna didn't tell you? Glenda wouldn't — '

'Oh, so you're not denying it then?' She was really enjoying herself now; it was good to see him suffer a taste of what she had gone through for so long. 'Tell me, how did Myrna find out — about Glenda, I mean?'

He sat down again and stared despondently into his empty glass. His shoulders slumped. 'God knows,' he muttered. 'She had her methods; she'd got Dennison and Perry screwed down as well.'

'Really?' She wasn't entirely surprised; they had all apparently accepted the brake on their careers without protest. 'This gets more interesting by the minute. I think I can manage another drink — no, don't bother, I'll get it myself.'

'You're not going to get pissed again?' he said urgently. 'I told you — '

'Oh no, don't worry, I'm not going to rock the boat. Besides, I want to stay sober so I can understand everything that's been going on.'

'Tell me first, how *did* you find out about Glenda?'

June burst out laughing. It really was rather funny, she thought as she settled down with her second vodka and tonic and the dish of crisps. The diet could wait. 'Men are so stupid,' she told him. 'D'you think I don't know what my own perfume smells like, or the colour of my own hair? I guessed right from the start, although of course I didn't know at first who the lucky woman was.'

'So how — '

'Does it matter? It wasn't difficult, but whether it was your former secretary or the Queen of Sheba wasn't the point. I wasn't going to risk our marriage falling apart — not until Alice was older — and you were still behaving reasonably towards us so I soldiered on, pretending everything was fine, keeping the home nice, showing an interest in your old fart of a father's terminally boring army stories, putting up with your toffee-nosed harpy of a mother and her constant hints that her son married beneath him — ' Her tone grew increasingly bitter at the recollection of the veiled insults she had suffered in silence over the years.

'There's no need to be rude about my parents, and I don't remember hearing any complaints from you,' he said sulkily. 'We've always been comfortable, haven't we? You could have done a lot worse — '

'Oh yes, we've been reasonably comfortable. And things were going to get even better, weren't they? Old Grant Maxford was going to give you a real stake in the company, you and Eric and Sam, instead of just a nominal shareholding. It was in recognition of all that the three of you had done to make the company prosperous, he said. There were going to be salary increases, an annual bonus — and then what happened? He died before he could put it all into effect, his bloody, scheming, avaricious daughter took over and it all came to nothing.'

'You can't blame me for that,' said Bradley when she paused for breath. He had sat in silence during her tirade; now he straightened up and looked her full in the face, seizing the chance to say something in his defence. 'She knew how hard it is for men of our age to get jobs, she had us over a barrel — '

'Bullshit! If the three of you had stuck together and stood up to her, you'd have had *her* over a barrel. How d'you suppose she could have run the company without your co-operation? But of course, it wasn't as simple as that. She was blackmailing all three of you, wasn't she?'

He made a helpless gesture. 'That's about the size of it,' he muttered.

'So what did she have on Eric and Sam? I imagine it's something more serious than an affair. Neither of them has a wealthy vampire for a mother-in-law.'

This time, he let the insult pass. 'It is, much more serious and if it comes out there'll be hell to pay. As things stand, there's no reason why the Headwaters takeover shouldn't go ahead once everything's settled, and then things will start to look up for all of us. Otherwise — ' He turned and took her by the hand. 'Look, June, I know I've been a bit of a shit in some ways, but we have to stick together until this is over. We all know — you and I, Eric and Sam, Nicola and Irene — what an unspeakable she-devil Myrna was. We all hated her, but we have to keep our feelings to ourselves or the police might get the idea that one of us could have killed her. That's why we're all going to say, if anyone asks, that the party went fine, we all respected Myrna's judgement and understood her reasons for rejecting the takeover.'

'Yes, you told me all that last night.'

'I'm glad you remember,' he said caustically. 'The state you were in — '

'Don't let's go into all that again. Brad, you don't really believe Paul Reynolds killed her, do you?'

'You heard what was said.'

'Helping with inquiries, that's all.'

'It makes no difference as far as we're concerned. We stick to our story, if and when we're asked.'

'What about the other people at the party? They saw what happened.'

'We thought of that. Eric's going to have a word with Hampton — the estate manager — and ask him not to mention your little outburst. If we assure him we're hoping that

207

once the legal side of things is sorted out the takeover by Headwaters will go through and there'll be no question of selling the land, we can see no reason why he shouldn't back us up. Leonie Filbury will be quite happy to say anything that will help throw suspicion on Paul.'

'What a sweet bunch you all are!' June exclaimed. 'Only thinking of your own skins and never mind if an innocent man gets charged. But there's someone you've forgotten, isn't there? That old duck Myrna introduced to everyone as Pussy — she might not be so easy to persuade. I can't imagine she's got anything to hide.'

'Eric said he'd have a word with her as well. He was going to see her yesterday evening . . . oh, my God!'

'What is it?'

Bradley's face was ashen. 'Mrs Willow — Pussy *Willow*,' he said hoarsely.

'The old lady whose body they found this afternoon?' said June in astonishment. 'You mean — ' It took a second for the full implication to sink in. 'Oh, no! You said Eric went to see her, and now she's dead and you think — '

'It doesn't mean . . . he might not have gone, he could have changed his mind or maybe they just had a chat and he left before . . . let's hope no one saw him.' He took her by the shoulders and said urgently, 'We have to keep calm, June. This'll complicate things, but I'm sure it'll be all right. I'll have a word with Eric on the phone, he may not have heard the news — '

'Are you saying we have to stick to that fairy-story you've concocted?'

'Have you got a better idea?' He gave her a shake. 'Just get this into your head: if it all goes wrong, if the police start probing, we could all be out of a job, or worse.'

'You think one of them might have killed Myrna, don't you?'

He let go of her and turned away. 'I didn't say so,' he muttered.

'Come to that, *they* might think *you* did it,' she taunted him. 'I wonder which of you had the strongest motive?'

14

To Sukey, Wednesday seemed interminable. Every case that she attended turned out to be so minor that she began to wonder whether a hint might have been dropped in the ear of Sergeant George Barnes: *Give her the most boring assignments for a day or two; that'll teach her to keep her mind on her own job and stop kidding herself she's a detective.* When at last she completed her final report and was free to leave, she decided that a workout followed by a spell in the sauna at her health club might help to dispel the aggravations of the day.

She called Fergus to let him know she would be home later than usual, but received no reply. She tried Anita's house, with the same result. There was nothing odd about that; the two often went to a café to meet friends after they finished work but, remembering how distressed Fergus had been over last night's arrest, she was more than usually concerned for him. Having vainly tried to contact Paul, she had called Jim, begging him to say whether or not it was her ex-husband who had been taken into custody, but he refused to be drawn. His manner was curt and dismissive, as if she was a persistent journalist trying to get an off-the-record statement. She was both bewildered and angry at being kept at arm's length at a time when both she and her son most needed his support. Then she recalled a comment that Fergus, with surprising insight, had made the previous evening: 'He's probably jealous that you're so concerned about Dad'. It was a possible explanation, but it only increased her frustration.

The club was almost deserted when she arrived, which was a relief; idle gossip was the last thing she needed. She changed into her exercise gear and began her workout, putting more energy than usual into each part of her programme in the hope that physical effort would — if only for a short time — release her mind from the twin problems she now faced: how to help Paul, and how to mend her fences with Jim. She had been prepared for the official reprimand, but not for the damage to their personal relationship.

She finished her routine with a ten-minute jog on the treadmill, stripped off in the changing room, swathed herself in a towel and climbed into the sauna. The solitary occupant, a slightly overweight blonde, appeared to be asleep. Sukey sat down on the slatted wooden bench, leaned back and closed her eyes. It was bliss to feel the warmth soaking into her body; already, some of the tension and irritation was slipping away. She relaxed, drifted, dozed . . . then jerked awake again as a voice said, 'Excuse me, but aren't you Susan Fowler?'

'Er, no, I'm — that is, yes, I was before I got married,' Sukey replied, momentarily confused. In the subdued light she studied the other woman's features. They seemed vaguely familiar, but she could not for the moment put a name to them.

'June Brinkworth,' the woman said. 'We were in the same year at college, remember? You were doing media studies and I did business.'

'Of course!' Sukey exclaimed. The intervening years rolled away as memories of student days came flooding back. June had been the outstanding personality among their crowd, the stunning blonde whom they all envied because she could do anything with her hair, never had zits or put on weight and was always besieged for dates by the most eligible men. She had taken her diploma in business studies and gone off to a job in London which no one doubted would lead to a glittering career in the field of fashion,

212

advertising or public relations. Time had not dealt kindly with her; the golden girl of almost two decades ago was hard to recognise behind the lumpy figure and heavily made-up features.

'You've hardly changed,' June said. 'I know what you're thinking, and you're right,' she went on before Sukey had time to respond. 'Maybe if you'd been married for fifteen years to the two-timing son of Dracula's daughter you wouldn't look so good either.' Her tone was caustic, but without self-pity.

'I didn't exactly fall on my feet marriage-wise,' Sukey said. 'Mine threw me over for a rich bitch and left me with a ten-year-old kid to bring up.'

'Men are bastards, aren't they?'

'Some of them.' Sukey thought of Jim and added with a touch of spite, 'On second thoughts, most of them.'

'Tell you what, let's get showered and go for a drink. I'm nearly cooked anyway.'

'Sure, why not?'

★   ★   ★

'I'm s'posed to be giving this up!' June remarked as she gestured with her second vodka and tonic before downing half of it at one go. 'Still, when you meet an old friend

213

you're allowed to make an exception, aren't you? Cheers!'

'Cheers!' Sukey repeated, raising her first spritzer in response. She was already wondering what she had let herself in for; normally sympathetic to other folks' troubles, she felt that for the moment she had enough of her own to think about. And June was displaying all the symptoms of someone in urgent need of a confidante. For ten minutes or so, their conversation had been little more than a series of, 'Do you remember — ?' recollections, after which they lapsed into silence, Sukey trying to think of something more to say, June apparently brooding over whatever was on her mind. In an effort to set the ball rolling again. Sukey said, 'The last time we had a drink together it was your farewell bash in that pub where we used to hang out round the back of Shire Hall. You'd just landed a plum job and were headed for fame and fortune in London.'

'That's right, I was.'

'So, what brought you back?'

'Fell in love, didn't I? Married a whizz-kid engineer with a brilliant future in a local company. Only it didn't quite work out the way I expected.' June emptied her glass and held it out to the bar attendant. 'Large vodka and tonic, and don't drown it this time.' She opened her purse and took out a ten pound note. 'Have one yourself,' she added as she handed it over.

'Hang on a moment, this should be my round,' protested Sukey.

'You drink too slowly. You can get the next one.'

'I thought you said you were giving it up.'

'I said I'm *supposed* to be giving it up. And I am, I am . . . but I can make an exception now and again, can't I?' June accepted her third drink along with her change and the bartender's thanks, and slid off the bar stool. 'Let's find somewhere more comfortable to sit and you can tell me the story of your life — and I tell you what, I'm starving, didn't have much in the way of lunch, so why don't we have a bite to eat? Alice is staying at her friend's house tonight — '

'Alice?'

'My daughter. The one reason why I don't walk out on Bradley. He can whistle for his dinner tonight, eat dog-food for all I care.' June led the way to a table in a corner of the lounge, flopped into a chair and took a hefty gulp from her glass. 'Better still, he can share a trough somewhere with his fellow sinners.'

'His what?'

June sniggered. The effect of the alcohol on an empty stomach was beginning to show.

'Oh, my husband's not the only one with a dirty little secret. I don't know what the others have been up to — ' she gave an exaggeratedly furtive glance round the half-empty lounge, then leaned forward and lowered her voice before continuing, 'but that harpy knew all about it, the same as she knew about Brad's little tart. Don't ask me how, but she knew.'

'Sorry, you've lost me. Who knew all about what?'

'Myrna, of course. Myrna Maxford. The one who got carved up, and serve her bloody well right.' June took another gulp of her drink. 'Don't you read the papers?'

Sukey's pulse leapt into overdrive. 'Yes, of course, but I didn't realise — ' Keeping her tone as casual as possible, she asked, 'What's that got to do with your husband and his, er, friends?'

'Directors of the company, aren't they? Would have had a real stake in it if *she* hadn't scuppered all our hopes and dreams. As it is — ' June broke off and stared at what was left in her glass. 'Shouldn't be surprised if one of them did her in, and no one deserved it more. Shouldn't be telling you, Bradley said I was to keep my mouth shut.' She shot Sukey a look of tipsy anxiety. 'You won't say anything, will you?'

'Of course not.' Sukey felt a twinge of conscience at the lie, but this was hardly the occasion to declare her interest. She finished her own drink and said, 'You mentioned food just now. I'd like that, but I have to call my son first to see what he's doing.'

'Tell him to go for a takeaway.'

It was clear that June was desperate for company. With a little encouragement, she might be persuaded into more revelations. Just the same, Sukey was concerned for Fergus. He almost certainly needed company as well, but he could always invite Anita round, or go to her house. And he'd be the first to encourage her to go after anything that might help his father. She got out her mobile phone. 'I'll call him from outside, there's too much noise in here,' she said.

* * *

'Have you had anything to eat?' was Sukey's first question to Fergus when she got home at eight o'clock.

'Yes, thanks — Anita's Mum invited me for supper. I rang to let you know, but you were out. I found your message when I got home.'

'There wasn't any word from Jim, I suppose?'

'No.' His eyes were bright and his mouth

217

was working. 'Haven't you seen him today?'

'No. I get the feeling he's avoiding me.'

'Then you may not have heard . . . Dad hasn't been charged, but he's still being questioned and they're examining a knife they think may be — '

His voice cracked on the final words; she held out her arms and he hid his face on her shoulder. Her heart ached for him. 'No, I hadn't heard,' she said wearily.

The last couple of hours had been, to say the least, frustrating. June had insisted on taking her to a crowded and noisy Italian restaurant where the service was slow and the food, when it arrived, indifferent. To make matters worse, she had learned nothing further of any value; as if aware that she had already said too much, June had brushed aside any mention of Myrna's death and its probable effect on her husband's career. 'Don't let's talk about that shit, tell me about yourself', she had said more than once and Sukey, as determined to conceal her own interest in the case as June was to avoid further reference to it, had given up the attempt and steered the conversation to their respective children. It had been a relief when June, by that time considerably the worse for wear, announced that it was time she was going home and ordered the waiter to ring for a taxi. 'Been smashing to see you, we must do it again', she had mumbled, before staggering out without leaving an address.

'Let's go in the kitchen. I could murder a cup of tea,' Sukey suggested.

Fergus drew away from her, brushed a hand over his eyes and gave a thin smile. 'I'll put the kettle on,' he said.

'Good lad.'

'So, who's the old friend you met up with?' he asked as he reached into a cupboard for the teapot. There was a note of reproach in his tone, as if he suspected her of having put his father's plight to the back of her mind in favour of some trivial social encounter.

'Not exactly a friend, just one of a crowd I used to go round with at college. We got chatting in the sauna and after we'd showered and changed we went for what was meant to be a quick drink. And guess what, she got tight and let drop that her husband's a director of Maxford's — and hinted that Myrna was blackmailing him.'

'No kidding!' A spoonful of tea missed the pot and scattered over the table.

'And possibly some of his colleagues as well,' Sukey added. She went on to repeat June's somewhat garbled remarks, while Fergus listened with his eyes and his mouth stretched to their limits, the kettle steaming unheeded behind him until Sukey took charge and switched it off. She made the tea and poured it out while he peppered her with questions.

'This could help Dad, couldn't it?' he said eagerly. 'You must tell Jim right away.'

'I've been thinking about that on the way home, trying to decide what to do. You know I've been told in no uncertain terms to keep my nose out of the case. Jim made it clear last night he wasn't prepared to discuss it with me, and he's been taken off it anyway.'

'Yes, but this is important new evidence.'

'It isn't evidence, it's hearsay — and from a total lush who'll almost certainly deny having told me anything, even if she remembers, which is doubtful. She said she'd been warned to keep her mouth shut, remember. I just wish I'd managed to worm a bit more out of her. I don't even know her married name, or the names of the other directors she mentioned.'

'Why didn't you ask?'

'I'd have had to tell her mine. She might have recognised it and I didn't want that.'

'Mm, I see your point.' Fergus thought for a moment, then said, 'Dad will know.'

'That's not much help at the moment, is it?'

220

Fergus's shoulders, which had straightened in excitement over his mother's news, slumped again. 'No,' he muttered. After a moment he said, 'They'll be in Myrna's files, though . . . their names, I mean.' He spoke thoughtfully, as if an idea had struck him.

Sukey looked at him curiously, but he avoided her eye. 'Sure they will, but that's no use to us,' she pointed out. 'We can hardly go banging on Maxford's door demanding to see them.'

'Her files aren't at Maxford's.'

'What?'

'They're at the Manor. She worked from home — she had a fantastic office there, with a computer and everything. Dad took me into it once, when she was away. I had to promise not to let on, or she'd have been furious. He was only supposed to go there when she sent for him.' He spoke rapidly, between mouthfuls of tea, still not looking directly at his mother.

'That's very interesting, but I don't see how it helps. We can't get into the Manor, and even if we could, the files are probably all locked away.'

'They're most likely on the computer. I might be able to access them.'

Something in her son's manner told Sukey

he was about to suggest something preposterous. 'Gus, if you're thinking of breaking in, forget it!' she said.

'No need for that,' he said smugly. 'I've got a key.'

15

'Hang on, I'll go and get it.' Fergus dashed upstairs and returned with a single key dangling from a brass ring.

Sukey stared at it in astonishment. 'Where on earth — ?' she began.

'It's the back door key,' he explained. 'A spare one. Dad gave it to me when I was staying at the Manor during half-term and Myrna was away on some business trip. He'd taken the week off, but he got a call from his office one day, something about a problem over a client's account that he had to go and sort out. He offered to take me into town so we could meet for lunch, but I didn't fancy that so I decided to stay behind and get on with some school work. He gave me the key in case I wanted to go out for anything.'

'Wasn't Mrs Little there?'

'No. Her sister was ill and she had the day off to visit.'

'How come you've still got it?'

'Dad said I might as well hang on to it. I wasn't to let Myrna know, of course, she'd have gone bananas,' Fergus added with a hint of malicious glee. 'I think he enjoyed feeling he'd put one over on her now and again. Well?' he went on as Sukey remained silent, 'how about it? The police must have finished there — they'll probably be gone by tomorrow.'

'You could be right about that,' she admitted.

'They might even have left the place already. Why don't we go now and suss it out? It's only nine o'clock.'

'No, Gus, I'm not going to let you rush me into doing something daft. I want time to think — and anyway, we're both tired.' Sukey felt herself being torn in two directions. If what June had hinted was true, it meant that Myrna could have been blackmailing up to three people, every one of whom would have a motive for killing her. She had gone on to suggest that there was a conspiracy of silence, to which she had been made a party. But what store would the police set by a second hand report of the maunderings of a jealous, alcoholic wife, especially when it came from someone known to have a personal interest in their prime suspect? Yet, if Fergus was right and there was incriminating information about Myrna's employees stored away in her computer, it might put a whole new slant on the case. Whoever brought it to light would deserve Brownie points . . . but on the other hand, if she allowed him to persuade her to go along with his scheme and they were caught in the act . . . the situation bristled with complications.

'Even if the cops are still there, it's perfectly legit,' Fergus went on, as if reading her thoughts. 'We can always say I've come back to collect some stuff I left last time I stayed at the Manor.'

'You don't imagine they'd let you go poking around in Myrna's office, do you?'

'It's worth a try,' he begged. 'Mum, you promised you'd do what you could to help Dad.'

'All right, I'll think about it, but we're not going tonight, that's for sure. If we go at all, it has to be in daylight. No, be reasonable,' she went on as he started to protest. 'We can't work in the dark, and if the place is supposed to be empty and someone sees all the lights on — '

'You've got a point there,' he admitted grudgingly. Then another thought struck him. 'Those people you mentioned — the ones you think Myrna might be blackmailing — they could be after the files as well. They might have already got at them and destroyed them.' Enthusiasm gave way to gloom.

'They'd have to find some way of getting into the Manor,' she pointed out. 'I don't

225

suppose anyone dished out keys to them.'

He brightened again. 'That's true. And they wouldn't know how to get past the security system.'

'Do you?' For a moment, Sukey detected an escape route, but Fergus firmly closed it.

'Of course,' he said complacently. 'Dad showed me.'

★ ★ ★

Thursday was marginally more productive in terms of information than Wednesday had been. For the second day running, Sukey had no direct contact with Jim Castle; although he greeted her pleasantly enough when he came into the office to speak to George Barnes, he made no attempt to seek her out or speak to her personally. It was Mandy Parfitt who told her that the death of Emily Willow was now officially being treated as murder. 'She was felled by a single blow from a chopper,' Mandy informed her as they drank the mugs of tea with which the SOCOs habitually began their day. 'It was found outside her own back door, next to a pile of logs. We're assuming it belonged to her; there were smudgy prints on the handle and they all seem to be hers, so the killer must have worn gloves.'

'Do they reckon it was Myrna's killer who did it?'

'It looks very much like it — there was no sign of forced entry. Her TV is missing, but it could have been taken to make it look like robbery.'

'The back door wasn't locked when I got there,' Sukey recalled. 'I suppose whoever it was just knocked and she opened up and let him in.' *And Paul was seen coming away from the cottage at about the right time . . . it does look black for him. But I simply can't believe . . .*

Mandy broke into her thoughts. 'She quite likely knew him,' she pointed out. 'I suppose the poor old thing must have seen something that could have helped identify him. A different MO, of course, so I doubt if it was premeditated.' She paused for a moment and glanced across at George, who was speaking on the phone, before saying quietly, 'The grieving widower's still in custody — I guess you know that.'

'Yes.' Sukey kept her voice level and tried to appear unconcerned, but she found Mandy's direct gaze disconcerting and switched the conversation to the day's assignments.

When she returned to the office at the end of the afternoon, she found it temporarily

227

deserted. She settled down at her desk to process the samples and photographs from the day's cases: a series of break-ins, apparently related, and a stolen car found abandoned and partially cannibalised. She was just sealing up the final envelope when the door opened and Jim Castle looked in. 'Any idea where George is?' he said.

'I'm afraid not, sir. I haven't seen him since I got back half an hour ago. He finishes at four and he hasn't cleared his desk, so he can't be far away.'

'I see. Thanks.'

He was about to leave when she said quickly, 'Jim, can we have a word?'

With evident reluctance he came into the room and closed the door. 'I thought I'd made it clear — ' he began.

'You made it clear you were angry with me for going to Dearley on Tuesday, but I took that as an official reprimand,' she said. 'Does it have to mean we're no longer friends as well?' She tried to sound matter-of-fact, but she could hear her voice wobbling.

He looked uncomfortable. 'In the circumstances, until this case is wrapped up, I think it's advisable that we keep our personal relationship on ice,' he said. His manner was stiff; it sounded as if he had rehearsed the speech for just such a moment as this.

'You don't want to risk being suspected of colluding with a potential witness for the defence, is that it?' Sukey said. She felt suddenly desolate; she had hoped and believed that their estrangement was a temporary one, borne out of their confrontation of two days ago.

He seemed to read her feelings and his manner became marginally more conciliatory. 'You have to understand the position I'm in — '

'Oh, I understand *your* position all right,' she snapped in a quick burst of resentment. 'You're worried about your career prospects. Just for a moment, try and understand mine. My son's father is being held on suspicion of murder, and I'm convinced of his innocence, but DCI Lord thinks he's got the case sewn up so I have to keep quiet and not rock the boat or do anything to upset his precious theories — '

'That's enough!' He spoke in a low voice, one eye on the door. 'Do you want the whole section to hear you?'

'I'm sorry.' She knew she had overstepped the mark; so far from healing the breach between them, she had made matters worse.

'When all this is over, we can have a proper talk about it,' he said.

'Presumably, by 'it' you mean 'us'?'

'What else?'

She choked back the lump that was rapidly forming in her throat. 'There might not be anything to talk about,' she said through her teeth, and deliberately turned her back on him.

Without another word, he went out and closed the door.

★ ★ ★

When Sukey and Fergus arrived at Dearley Manor soon after five o'clock, they were relieved to find the gates standing open and no sign of a police presence. Just the same, she made a point of driving round the back of the house and parking the Astra well out of sight of the road to avoid the risk of some curious villager noticing the car and deciding to investigate.

'Mrs Little's not here either,' Fergus commented as he turned the key in the back door. The broken panel had been replaced with a piece of wood, but the lock was intact. 'There's no sign of her bike.'

'It never occurred to me that she might be,' said Sukey. 'I suppose she's still officially employed here. I wonder what'll happen to the house — did Myrna have any relations, do you know?'

'Dad said something once about cousins in Australia, but surely, won't it go to him? I thought — '

'It depends whether she left a will, or the property might be entailed in some way.' *He certainly won't inherit if he's convicted of her murder*, she added mentally but, knowing how much the thought would upset Fergus, she kept it to herself.

He opened the door to the accompaniment of a succession of loud bleeps and they hastily stepped inside. 'Keep your fingers crossed,' he said as he stabbed a series of buttons on the control panel. The bleeping ceased and he grinned in triumph. 'Stage one accomplished.'

'Better lock it again,' she suggested and he complied before returning the key to his pocket.

'Good thinking,' he said. 'Right, I'll lead the way.' He strode out of the kitchen; for the moment, he had taken charge. She followed him along the passage, across the entrance hall and up the stairs. On all sides were the traces of the police investigation: surfaces liberally dusted with aluminium powder, gaps on the floor where rugs and the stair carpet had been removed for forensic examination. 'Gosh, what a mess!' he exclaimed. 'I suppose poor Mrs Little will have the job of getting this lot cleaned up.'

'I hope she's got over the shock,' Sukey commented. 'She took it pretty badly.'

'She might be out of a job. I hope someone will look after her.' They had reached the landing and he turned to give his mother a sly grin. 'I think Ezra fancies her — or maybe it's just her cooking.'

'Let's get on with what we came for, shall we?' They were standing a few feet from Myrna's bedroom and the memory of what she had found there was like a punch in the stomach. She had a sudden desire to get away, out of this cold, silent house where that dreadful deed had been committed and into the fresh air. For two pins she would have turned tail and left, but it was obvious that Fergus had no such inhibitions.

'Right, this way.' He set off along the landing and tried the handle on a door at the far end. For a moment Sukey found herself praying that it would be locked, that they would have no alternative but to give up this crazy enterprise she had allowed herself to be talked into. Her heart sank as he pushed open the door and beckoned to her. 'Come on!' he said and reluctantly she obeyed. 'It doesn't look as if this room's been searched,' he remarked.

'I've no doubt the police came in here to

have a look round, but if nothing had been disturbed there'd have been no need to dust for prints.' Sukey glanced round at the well-appointed office with its elegant furniture and commanding view. 'Myrna certainly knew how to make herself comfortable,' she commented.

Fergus made no reply. He went straight over to the computer, sat down and switched it on. 'Wish me luck,' he said. They watched in silence as a series of symbols came and went on the screen. He pressed keys and after a second the single word *'Password?'* appeared. 'Thought so,' he said. 'Have to see if I can find it. I'll start with the company's name.' He tried keying in 'Maxford', 'Domestic' and 'Fittings', then various combinations based on the words, but with no success.

'What about trademarks?' Sukey suggested. 'Don't they call their products Maxi something? Maxiflow, Maxispray — '

'Good idea.' He keyed the names in, then gave a little groan of frustration as yet again the message, *'Not recognised, try again'* flashed up on the screen. 'Guess I'll never make a hacker,' he said disconsolately.

'Never mind, it was worth a try.' A stab of acute disappointment made Sukey realised how much she too had been pinning on this enterprise, despite her earlier reservations.

At that moment, the telephone on Myrna's desk rang and they both jumped. 'What do we do?' asked Fergus.

'Nothing. Leave it. We're not supposed to be here.' They waited as the ringing went on, then stopped as the answering machine clicked into life and a woman's recorded voice invited the caller to leave a message.

'That's Myrna,' said Fergus shakily. He had gone very pale. 'Creepy, isn't it.'

'Shush, listen.'

'Hi gorgeous, this is your very own favourite sleuth, just got back from my week in little old LA.' It was a man, speaking with an American accent that Sukey had a feeling was assumed. 'I spent the flight dreaming about that wonderful body of yours, so how about a little moving and shaking this evening?' the caller went on, confirming her suspicion as it gradually reverted to an English pronunciation. 'I'm here in the office until around six, then I'll be at home . . . and all yours.' The final words were spoken in a lascivious growl; there was a further click and the message ended.

'The filthy cow, I had a feeling she was cheating on Dad!' Fergus exclaimed, his expression a mixture of indignation and disgust that quickly turned to alarm. 'If the

234

police find out, they'll use it against him, say he knew about it and that's why — '

'Let's not panic.' Sukey tried to sound reassuring, but the same thought had occurred to her. 'For a start, let's see if we can check where that call came from.' She reached for a pencil and a notepad that were lying on Myrna's desk, picked up the phone and tapped out 1471. She was half expecting to hear that the caller's number had been withheld, but luck was on their side. Her pulse-rate quickened as she jotted down the figures and then pressed the callback button.

After only two rings the voice they had heard moments before came on the line and said, 'Glevum Investigations, Doug Brown speaking.'

'I'm so sorry, I must have called the wrong number,' said Sukey politely and hung up. She turned to Fergus and repeated what she had just heard. 'We haven't wasted our time after all,' she said. Her heart was thumping harder than ever.

'I don't see that it helps all that much,' he said. 'So Myrna had a boyfriend, but he couldn't have killed her if he was out of the country — and anyway, he doesn't even know she's dead.'

'Oh, come on Gus, wake up. 'Glevum Investigations, your favourite sleuth' — this guy's a private detective. Remember what June told me? Myrna had some dirt on her husband and his colleagues, but she didn't know how she came by it.'

'Of course!' His eyes lit up again. 'She employed this guy to investigate them. Mum, you'll have to go and talk to him.'

'You don't suppose he'd tell me anything, do you?'

'Why not?'

'Client confidentiality and all that. Besides, the last thing he'd want would be to get mixed up in a murder case, especially if he's been having an affair with the victim.'

'But if you tell the police, they'll find out he's been carrying on with Myrna. They already think Dad killed her, they'll say that was his motive — '

'If I tell the police, I'll be dropping myself in it,' she reminded him. 'What excuse do I offer for this little adventure? I'm in enough trouble already.'

'We can't just let it go.'

'No, of course not, but — '

At that moment their attention was distracted by the sound of a car. They exchanged apprehensive glances; Fergus moved to the window, peered cautiously out and said, 'It's Leonie. What the hell's she doing here?'

236

'Maybe the same as we are. Come to collect some of her stuff, remember?'

'Oh, right.' Fergus patted his pocket containing the computer game he had brought along by way of an excuse for being there. 'What d'you reckon we should do?'

'Switch that off, for a start.' She nodded towards the computer. 'We don't want anyone knowing we've been trying to hack into Myrna's files.'

'She may not come up here.'

Sukey's brain was working at top speed, considering and rejecting possible courses of action. 'When she sees our car out there she may take fright and leave,' she began, but Fergus interrupted.

'She's not leaving, she's parking the car . . . she's got a key in her hand, she's coming in — '

'Then we'd better show ourselves before she gets suspicious and calls the police.'

16

'Who's there?' Leonie's voice, harsh and apprehensive, floated up from the hallway as Fergus reached the head of the stairs with Sukey a short distance behind him.

'Hullo, Leo,' he said coolly. 'What are you doing here?'

Leonie glared at him. With her stocky build, blunt features and pugnacious stance, she reminded Sukey of an aggressive bulldog. 'What the hell are *you* doing here?' she retorted as the pair of them slowly descended the stairs. 'And who's *she*?' She jerked her head in Sukey's direction.

'This is my mother. Mum, this is Leo.'

'Nice to meet you,' said Sukey, with a friendly smile that was not returned. 'I'm sorry if we startled you. We came to collect something Fergus left behind.'

'Oh yeah?' The tone was scornful, the blue-grey eyes suspicious. 'What was that?'

'Just one of my computer games — I left it in my room,' said Fergus, in the soothing tone Sukey was accustomed to hear from him when he assured her that he had done all his homework before going out.

238

'It needed two of you?'

Sukey sensed that the girl was instinctively guarding the territory of her late employer. 'Fergus wanted to show me where he used to sleep when he stayed here with his father,' she explained.

The reference to Paul only increased Leonie's hostility. 'I'm surprised you had the nerve to come near the place, after what he did,' she snarled.

Fergus flushed and took a sharp breath. Sensing that he was about to explode, Sukey said quickly, 'I know how upset you must be feeling over Myrna's death, but it's not fair to take it out on Fergus.'

'What do you mean, you know?' At the mention of Myrna's name, the belligerent manner all but collapsed; the girl was close to tears. '*Nobody* knows how I feel . . . nobody but me really understood her or knew how sweet and good she really was — '

Once more, Sukey moved in to forestall an indignant contradiction from her son. 'Fergus has told me how close you were to her,' she said gently.

'He has?' The statement appeared to take Leonie by surprise and her manner seemed to soften. 'We loved each other,' she said. Her tone was defensive, as if she expected some signal of disapproval.

'So I understand,' Sukey said quietly. She did not for one moment share the infatuated girl's confidence in Myrna's fundamental goodness, or her belief that her love was returned. It was more likely that the dead woman had been stringing her along, either to amuse herself or as part of some deep and devious game of her own, but it was possible that Leonie, having obviously spent a lot of time in her company, might have picked up some valuable information that could, with a little tact and patience, be uncovered. Fergus had mentioned that she was employed in the estate office and not in the headquarters of Maxford Domestic Fittings, but she might at least know the names of the company directors and even have some inkling of what — if anything — they had to hide. Since the attempt to break into Myrna's computer files had failed, anything was worth a try.

'It's natural to feel upset when someone you care about suffers such a dreadful death,' Sukey said, 'but really, you shouldn't jump to conclusions. You don't know that Paul killed her.'

'No?' The girl's tone hardened again. 'Why have they arrested him, then?' she demanded. 'Of course he did it. He threatened her — I heard him — '

'He didn't mean it, not really, he couldn't

have!' Fergus shouted. 'She made him angry and he lost his temper, that's all. Anyone would, the way she — ' He was scarlet with rage at the attack on his father. Leonie was bridling like a young cockerel spoiling for a fight and Sukey knew instinctively that if a slanging match were to break out, the opportunity to gain her confidence would be irretrievably lost.

'Gus, will you please be quiet!' she said, raising her voice. It was a long time since she had spoken to him so sharply and he gaped at her in shocked astonishment. The hurt and dismay in his expression, the unshed tears that glittered in his eyes, reminded her of how as a child he used to look at her after she had scolded him. Knowing how much he was hurting already, she felt a stab of remorse at the thought of adding to his pain, but now was not the time for explanations.

'Go and wait in the car,' she commanded. 'At once!' she almost shouted, sensing that he was about to argue. 'I want to talk to Leonie alone.'

He glowered at her resentfully, but did as he was told. When he had gone, Sukey took Leonie by the arm. 'Why don't I make you a cup of tea?' she suggested. She half expected a rebuff, but the girl allowed herself to be led into the kitchen where she sat down, covered her face with her hands and began softly weeping. The blaze of anger had died out, drowned in a wave of misery that went straight to Sukey's heart. It would, she knew, be cruel to destroy her tender memories of Myrna, but if there was any chance that she might, without realising it, know something that would help to clear Paul and lead to the real killer, then sooner or later she would have to be made to face up to the truth: that the woman she had idolised was a ruthless, power-hungry monster. There was no way of sparing her the anguish, but at least it could be broken to her gently — and in private.

But first, some common ground had to be established. Sukey left her to her grief while she filled the kettle and rooted in cupboards for everything else she needed. She made tea, filled two mugs, put them on the table and sat down. 'I'm afraid there's no fresh milk, but I found a carton of UHT in one of the cupboards, I hope that's all right,' she said. Leonie made no reply, but she wiped her eyes, stuffed her handkerchief into her pocket and picked up one of the mugs. 'Why do we have to put up with men?' Sukey went on chattily. 'They're such a load of shits, aren't they?'

It was a shot in the dark, but it found its target. Leonie stared at her in evident surprise and said, 'You think so too?'

'I've every reason to, haven't I? My ex threw me up for another woman and left me alone with a ten-year-old kid.'

'What an arsehole! When was that?' For the moment, Leonie appeared to have forgotten that they were speaking about the man she held responsible for Myrna's death.

'Nearly six years ago — when he met Myrna.'

'Oh, him!' Leonie gave a contemptuous snort and Sukey sensed the dawn of kinship between them. 'Myrna's told me about the way he used to bad-mouth you!'

'It doesn't surprise me. Whenever we had a row, he always managed to twist things round to make me feel it was my fault.' Sukey waited for a moment before asking casually, 'When did he say all this?'

'When he first met Myrna. She used to tell me how he made a dead set at her as soon as he met her. She knew he was married, of course, so she did everything she could to discourage him, but he gave her all this sob stuff about how unhappy he was and how much he needed her. You had no time for him, you cared more about your career than about him —'

'It's not true!' Sukey declared indignantly. 'I gave up work when Fergus was born and I did my best to be a good wife and mother.'

'I believe you.' Leonie put out a hand and touched her on the arm. 'It must have been tough for you — but it has been for Myrna as well. She didn't see through him until it was too late. She never even knew he had a child, not until after they were married.'

'So why didn't she divorce him?'

'She was dependent on him, don't you see? She'd put all her financial affairs into his hands — and of course it was her money he was after all along.'

'The bloody toe-rag, he swore blind her money had nothing to do with it! He kept going on about how madly in love he was, how crazy she was for him, how drop-dead gorgeous she was.' Sukey had become so carried away in her rôle as confidante that she had almost begun to share the girl's belief in the lies Myrna had fed her. Just the same, the bitterness that crept into her voice brought an immediate response.

'That was her trouble, don't you see? Being rich and beautiful — every fortune-hunting rat was after her.' Leonie's eyes were glaring and her voice was harsh with hatred and resentment. 'She told me she'd always believed Paul was different, that he only wanted to love and take care of her, and look after the business for her — but he was just like all the rest.'

'Are you saying she handed over control of the company?'

'Of course. No one else knew, it was a private arrangement between the two of them. She trusted him implicitly.'

Knowing for a fact that Myrna had done nothing of the kind, Sukey found it an effort not to betray herself as she remarked, 'I always had the impression that she was a very astute businesswoman.'

'That was just a big act.' Leonie's manner, which exuded venom when speaking of Paul, melted into tenderness. 'When her father died and she found herself in charge of Maxford's, she didn't know which way to turn. She understood a little about running the estate, and of course she had Ezra to look after that for her, but she didn't know the first thing about managing a company. She was at the mercy of Dennison, Perry and Ashton, and they just carried on the way they wanted to and only told her what they wanted her to know.'

'I'm sorry — who are Dennison, Perry and Ashton?'

'The Maxford directors.' Sukey mentally chalked up her first piece of solid information. 'Old man Maxford trusted them,' Leonie went on, 'but they were just waiting for him to pop off so they could run things to their own advantage. After a while she began to suspect that they were up to no good, but she couldn't prove anything; she was putty in their hands. Paul promised to get them sorted, he said he'd take care of everything for her . . . but he was as bad as all the others and now he's killed her. Well, at least he'll never get his filthy hands on her money. He'll rot in jail for the rest of his life and serve him right!' She fished a tissue from the pocket of her baggy denim jacket to mop away a fresh flood of tears. 'It was all going to be so different,' she gulped pathetically when she could speak again. 'She'd had enough of men . . . I was going to look after her . . . we had it all planned — '

'Just a moment,' Sukey said. 'You said Paul was as bad as all the others. Were you talking about the other directors, or did Myrna have lovers?'

'Lovers!' The tear-stained features registered horror at the suggestion. 'Of course she didn't have lovers. I told you, she was sick of men. She confided in me soon after I began working for her how disgusting she found them.'

'How long ago was that?'

Leonie scrubbed at her eyes and made a valiant effort to control yet another outburst of weeping. 'Only six months,' she said brokenly. 'They were the best six months of my life. Knowing her changed everything. It was going to be so wonderful, and now — '

She was a pathetic figure, sitting crumpled in the chair, twisting the sodden tissue between stubby, unmanicured fingers. Sukey felt a wave of anger at the heartless way the dead woman had used her.

'Leonie,' she said quietly, 'are you quite sure there were no men at all in Myrna's life — aside from Paul, I mean?'

'I've just said — '

'Yes, I know — and that's what Myrna told you. But are you sure she was speaking the truth?'

'What are you suggesting?' There was a hint of resentment in the question. 'How many times do I have to tell you? She'd had enough of men, she didn't want anything to do with them any more.'

It was time to shatter the illusion. The well-worn cliché came into Sukey's mind: *This is going to hurt you more than it hurts me.* She would do her best to break it to the girl gently, and at least there was no third party present to witness her humiliation. 'Does the name Doug Brown mean anything to you?' she asked quietly.

Leonie looked blank. 'No. Who is he?'

'A private investigator. There's reason to believe he knew Myrna rather well.'

'I don't know what you're talking about.'

'I'm afraid there are quite a lot of things you don't know.'

'What do you mean?' The tone was belligerent, but a hint of anxiety crept into the red, swollen eyes.

'Six months isn't a very long time to get to know anyone, is it?'

'Long enough for us to fall in love. She confided in me — '

'And you believed everything she told you? That she was finished with men, only wanted you; that sort of thing?'

'Of course.' Leonie was plainly disturbed at the way the conversation was going, but she stood her ground. 'Why would she say that if it wasn't true?'

'Before you turned up just now, there was a call for Myrna — from a man who obviously doesn't know she's dead. He left a message, rather an intimate one. It's pretty clear he was her lover.'

'No!' Leonie shouted. 'No, I can't . . . I won't believe it. There's some mistake. Anyway, how do you know he's a private detective?'

'I checked the number and called back. He answered by saying 'Glevum Investigations' and giving his name.'

'Did you talk to him?'

'No. I just wanted to check where the call came from.'

'Well, that explains it. This man, whoever he is, thought he was talking to someone else, he must have got the wrong number — '

'He knew who he was talking to all right — he'd have recognised her voice on the recording. It's not the kind of message anyone would leave if they weren't sure they had the right number.'

'I don't believe it,' Leonie repeated stubbornly.

'The message is still on the tape. Perhaps you should listen to it, but I warn you, it's very personal — or rather, very intimate.'

Leonie shook her head. Her eyes were full of despair; her mouth formed the words *I don't believe it*, but no sound emerged. Sukey felt a stab of compunction, then reminded herself that she was doing this in the cause of justice and said, 'I'm afraid you have to accept that Myrna wasn't being entirely straight with you. And there's something else. Quite by chance, yesterday I met an old schoolfriend who turned out to be the wife of one of the Maxford directors. She had some pretty harsh things to say about Myrna. For starters, she claims she was blackmailing her husband and almost certainly his colleagues as well.'

'Stop! I don't want to hear any more!' Leonie clapped her hands over her ears and began rocking from side to side. Thin, wailing sobs racked her body and all but choked her while she repeated, 'She wouldn't . . . she couldn't . . . ' like some despairing mantra. Then the weeping abruptly stopped and her distress turned to fury. 'It's a trick!' she shrieked. 'You're making all this up! You're still in love with Paul and you want to turn me against Myrna, make me say something to help him!'

'I want to find out the truth,' said Sukey quietly. 'I'm not in love with Paul any more. In fact, I think he's behaved contemptibly in many ways, but I lived with him for over ten years and I know he couldn't have killed Myrna, not in the way she was killed. He might have lost his temper, injured her accidentally — there are plenty of cases where that's happened — but he wouldn't have gone for her with a knife. Someone else killed her and I believe it was the same person who attacked poor old Mrs Willow with a chopper. Paul would never have done that.'

'Oh no? So why have the police arrested him?'

'Presumably there's some evidence to link

him with both crimes, but it can only be circumstantial or they'd have charged him.'

'They soon will.'

'Not if they can't find hard evidence, and I don't believe they will. I'm convinced he didn't commit either of those murders and I think that whoever killed Myrna had to kill Mrs Willow because she saw something that might have incriminated him. In fact,' Sukey went on as Leonie merely stared with a scornful smile on her face, 'I believe there's more than one person with a motive for killing Myrna.'

'All right, if you're so bloody sure, why don't you tell the police?' Leonie's manner became aggressive again. 'I'll tell you why,' she went on before Sukey could reply. 'It's because there's no truth in it, is there? You've been feeding me a load of garbage. And I'll bet there's no message on that machine.' She leapt out of her chair and rushed upstairs and into Myrna's office with Sukey at her heels. She went over to the desk and jabbed the playback button. 'I'm calling your bluff!' she said defiantly.

Five minutes later she was sitting slumped at the kitchen table, shocked and dry-eyed, her head bowed. She had listened to the tape in a stupefied silence and had not uttered a sound since, passively allowing herself to be led downstairs, mutely shaking her head when Sukey, remorseful at having left Fergus sitting alone in the car for so long, asked if she had any objection to his joining them. The two of them had kept an anxious eye on the stricken woman as they hunted in cupboards for something stronger than tea, only speaking when necessary and then in low voices, as if they were trying to avoid disturbing an invalid.

'Drink that, it'll make you feel better,' Sukey said gently, and Leonie reached out for the glass of brandy without appearing to see it, groping like a blind person, raising it to her lips and drinking with her blank eyes focused on infinity. Sukey waited until she had finished, then said, 'You had to find out sooner or later, but I'm sorry it had to be this way.'

'Why did she do it?' Leonie's pug-like features crumpled. Her voice was hoarse and the words indistinct, as if she was talking in her sleep. For the first time she looked at them directly with a look of bewilderment in her eyes. 'Why?' she repeated.

'That's something we may never know,' said Sukey, with a warning glance at her son. 'The point is, she deceived you about a lot of things.'

'What else?'

'For one thing, she never handed over control of her affairs to Paul. On the contrary, she used him like she used everyone else. She was shrewd and ruthless and she enjoyed having power over other people.'

'You're only saying this, you never knew her — '

'What makes you so sure you knew her? She made you think she was in love with you when all the time she was carrying on an affair with a man.'

'Perhaps that was before she knew me . . . it was probably all over between them.' Leonie began clutching at straws in a despairing effort to avoid facing the truth. 'You heard him say he'd been away — '

'For a week, not six months.' Sukey knew she was rubbing salt into an open wound, but somehow she had to win the girl over.

'She loved me,' Leonie insisted.

'Did she ever say so?'

'Not in so many words,' Leonie admitted reluctantly. 'I just knew, that's all.'

'All right, think about this then. The other directors you spoke about, they had a lot to gain from the takeover, yet she was able to put a stop to it. How do you think she could do that if they were in control the way she pretended?'

'She still had a few shares that she hadn't

made over to them — enough to keep the company nominally in her name. She said it was what her father would have wanted, she owed it to his memory.'

'Do you still believe that?'

Leonie covered her face with her hands. 'I don't know what to believe,' she whispered. 'You're making her out to be so wicked, but what proof have you got?'

'I don't have proof, only hearsay,' Sukey admitted. 'Like I told you, there's a suggestion that she had some hold on at least three people in the company; that she knew something they didn't want made public. That's why Fergus and I are here. We thought there might be something on the computer to give us a lead, but of course, we couldn't access any of the files because we don't know the password.'

'So that's what you were up to when I got here! Is *that* what you meant by a computer game?' Leonie glared accusingly at them, her grief swept away by a further surge of fury. 'I knew this was a bloody con trick!' she shouted. 'You come here, poking into Myrna's affairs, get someone to leave that message just to turn me against her . . . and I suppose the next thing would have been to get me to give you her password — if I knew it, which I don't, but I'd never have betrayed her, not in a million years — !' Her voice cracked and her face was purple; reason and logic had flown out of the window. 'Get out of here, the pair of you, before I call the police!'

'All right, we'll go,' said Sukey quietly. She stood up and Fergus did the same. 'I can understand how distressing this has been for you, but I promise there's been no trickery on our part. And please,' she went on as Leonie gave a snort of contempt and disbelief, 'don't close your mind to the possibility that someone other than Paul killed Myrna. I'm certain she had other enemies, and if you can think of anything she might have said, or that you've heard anyone else say — '

'Such as what?'

'I don't know, I'm groping around in the dark,' Sukey admitted. 'Just the same, if I give you this — ' While she was speaking, she had torn a page from her notebook and scribbled down her phone number. 'If you think of anything at all, will you call me?' She put the paper on the table, but Leonie made no move to take it. 'Please!' she said softly, but there was no response. She took Fergus by the arm. 'Come on Gus, we're leaving.'

17

At about the time that Leonie Filbury was sitting alone with her memories in Dearley Manor, DCI Lord entered DI Castle's office and dropped a document on his desk.

'We've had to let Reynolds go,' he announced, dragging up a chair and sitting down.

'What?' Castle looked up in astonishment from a form he was completing. 'But I thought — '

'That's the pathologist's report. It states categorically that a six inch knife was used to kill Myrna Maxford. The knife we found with his prints on is only five inches long and couldn't have inflicted several of the wounds.'

Castle scanned the details, frowning. 'What about the blood?' he asked.

'Third paragraph down.' Lord reached across the desk and jabbed the report with a carefully manicured forefinger. 'Same group as Reynolds' — and the victim's. That's not conclusive, of course, and we've sent a sample for DNA testing, but you know how long that can take. In any case, since the knife it was found on can't be the one that killed Maxford — '

' — and you're going to tell me there was no six inch knife found in the kitchen — '

Lord scowled. 'On the contrary, there was — and it was as clean as a whistle after going through the dishwasher, apart from the prints the housekeeper left when she put it away. Not that it makes any difference; that couldn't be the murder weapon either. All the knives the SOCOs found are practically new, but the shape of the wounds indicates that the murder weapon had a much narrower blade and the pathologist reckons it's probably quite old and worn.'

'So the killer must have taken it away with him?'

'Or her.'

Castle, who was still scanning the report while digesting its significance, looked up in surprise. 'Are you saying you think Reynolds is in the clear, sir?'

'Not necessarily, but this has left things wide open. There was no other knife of the right size and shape in the kitchen, or anywhere else in the house, or in the flat where Reynolds says he spent the night. Added to which, our inquiries suggest that the dear departed wasn't universally beloved.'

Castle shrugged. 'It must be difficult to succeed in business without making a few enemies. It's a highly competitive world — presumably she'd trodden on a few corns in her time, but — '

'More than a few, I'd say. Radcliffe and Hill have been interviewing everyone who was at the party on Sunday evening, apart from poor old Mrs Willow, of course.' Lord gave a deep sigh and tugged morosely at his moustache. 'We're not getting anywhere with that case, either. Reynolds is our only suspect to date, and if our theory about him killing his wife and being spotted by 'Pussy' sneaking through the grounds at the crucial time doesn't hold up, his motive for clobbering the old dear goes out of the window as well.'

'You were saying about the interviews — '

'So I was. Radcliffe tells me that the three Maxford directors and their wives who were at the party on Sunday evening were all falling over themselves to give the impression that the company was just one big happy family under Myrna Maxford's inspired leadership. When he referred to the way she'd scuppered the takeover at the eleventh hour, thus depriving them of the goodies they'd all been hoping for, they brushed it aside — admitted a certain disappointment but said they understood her reasons and respected her judgement. 'The long-term future of the company and the well-being of the employees' were quoted several times. Radcliffe said it was almost like a mantra.'

'And Paul Reynolds made a point of telling me that they and several people living on the estate were going to be adversely affected by the decision,' Castle recalled. 'He expected them all to be very upset when they were told and said he didn't want to appear to be associated with it, having given his professional opinion that agreeing to the takeover was in the company's best interests. He claimed that was why he left the party and spent the night in the flat. Of course, that might have been part of his plan to divert suspicion from himself.'

'That was my original impression, but since it appears likely he was telling the truth about the knife, we have to accept that he may have been telling the truth all along. It could be that the others, for reasons best known to themselves, decided to conceal their true feelings towards the deceased.'

'In a way, that's only natural. When a murder's been committed, no one wants to admit to having even the slightest motive.'

'True, but I've a hunch — or rather, Radcliffe has a hunch — that it isn't as simple as that. He and Hill interviewed all these people separately — the men in their offices, the women at home — and their stories seemed to agree just a little too much. He said it was almost as if they'd got together in advance and rehearsed them. And there's something else. When they interviewed Ezra Hampton, the estate manager, who was also at the party, he said they all appeared pretty shocked and upset when the news was broken to them, but what surprised him was the way they took it lying down, as if they were scared to argue with the decision. The only person who made any serious protest was one of the wives, who was so furious that she threw a wobbly and went for Maxford with a bottle. He said the others couldn't get her out of the place quickly enough — yet when she was interviewed later she appeared very embarrassed, put it down to having had too much to drink and went on to tell the same story as the others.'

'Speaking of Hampton, was he going to be adversely affected by the sale of the land?'

'Not directly. The proposed development would have been quite close to his house, but it wouldn't have been a serious disturbance and apart from giving him a few acres less to manage it certainly wasn't going to affect his job. He admits that for environmental reasons he's against any proposal to build on what he calls greenfield sites, but that's not a motive for murder.'

'Hardly,' Castle agreed, 'but going back to the others — the Maxford directors and their wives — it does seem as if the dead woman might have had some sort of hold over them, doesn't it?'

'That's my impression, but at the moment we have no idea what it might be. What it means is that instead of eliminating them, we're having to include every one of them on our list of suspects.'

'Are you suggesting that one of them sneaked back to the house later on that night, broke in and killed Maxford?'

'Somebody did smash the back door,' Lord pointed out.

'But all the indications pointed to that being a put-up job. And how would someone who'd been to the house only once — as this lot all maintain — know where the victim's bedroom was, or how to silence the alarm system?' Remembering Sukey's passionate defence of her ex-husband, it came as a shock to Castle to realise that he was reluctant to admit, even to himself, that she could have been right. 'It seems to me that Reynolds is still the most likely suspect — he knew the layout like the back of his hand, and it's the general impression that his wife treated him like dirt. If you ask me, sir, it's a classic case of the worm turning.'

Lord nodded. 'Oh, I agree with you, he's still in the frame, but we have to remember that there's no evidence that the alarm was set that night,' he pointed out. 'And if you're talking about the three directors and their wives, we only have their word for it that they'd never been to the house before. And now we know that knife isn't the murder weapon, we're back to square one there as well. We've already been through the house with a tooth-comb and searched every inch of the grounds. I've told Radcliffe to get on with an investigation into a few directors' dustbins — both literally and metaphorically.' The Chief Inspector gave an ironic chuckle, picked up the report and pushed back his chair. 'I'm going to the Bear for a jar. Care to join me?'

'With pleasure, sir. Just give me five minutes to wrap up this bit of paperwork.'

'Sure. See you there.'

Castle finished his task, cleared his desk, locked it and sat moodily tossing his keyring in the air and catching it while grappling with his own turbulent thoughts. Throughout the day he had been troubled by the memory of the brief spat with Sukey and her hurt, angry expression as she accused him of caring more about his own career than about her feelings. He had been stung by her words and the bitterness in her voice, and made up his mind that he would take the earliest opportunity of reassuring her. What was worrying him at the moment was not the misunderstanding, which he was confident of putting right, but rather the realisation that he found her insistence on Paul Reynolds' innocence profoundly disturbing. It had not occurred to him until now that she might still care for her ex-husband in a way that would seriously threaten his own relationship with her.

She would, of course, be delighted to know that Paul had been released from custody without charge. Too bloody delighted, that was the trouble. Anyway, she'd hear the news soon enough, either through the media or from colleagues tomorrow morning. Then he remembered that tomorrow was her day off. There was no reason why he shouldn't ring her right away and put her mind at rest. In that way he could at least make a start on mending his fences before going to the pub for the promised drink with DCI Lord. After a few moments' hesitation, he picked up the phone and called her number, but all he got was her answering machine. He decided against leaving a message.

★　★　★

Left alone in the kitchen at Dearley Manor, Leonie leaned her head on her arms and wept uncontrollably. For a while she could think of nothing but her own grief as her mind went back over the short time she had loved Myrna and the moments of sheer bliss spent in her company. She recalled the dead woman's smiles, her breathtaking beauty, the gentleness in her voice as they walked together in the garden, talking idly of this and that, or sat side by side watching the television in the little sitting-room that Myrna called her own and that the hated husband was never allowed to enter. It had been so pure and perfect, with hardly any physical contact yet with the occasional hint — unspoken but, Leonie fervently believed, unmistakable — of a more exciting relationship in the future. Myrna had let it be known that for the time being, after two failed marriages, she found sexual activity of any kind repulsive. Leonie, basking in the sunshine of the new friendship, had fought back her own hungry longings and contented herself with dreaming of the day when Myrna would recover from the trauma of having to submit to the disgusting demands of men and the two of them could fulfill their love.

And now a serpent had slithered into Leonie's imaginary Eden — a male serpent

with a lascivious voice whose filthy sugges-
tions had sullied her dream and poisoned her
memories. Over and over again she told
herself that it wasn't, it couldn't be true that
the revolting message on the tape was
intended for Myrna. Surely her darling would
never have stooped to the treachery and
deceit that it implied. It was just a cruel,
underhanded trick on the part of a woman
desperate to clear her ex-husband's name.
But as she sat alone with her thoughts and
her memories, doubts began to torment her.
Odd recollections from the past few weeks
came creeping out of the shadows at the back
of her mind: snatches of conversation
overheard; the occasional hint by a fellow
employee, diplomatically expressed and no
doubt kindly intended; all pointing to the
possibility that, for all her surface sweetness,
Myrna Maxford was not entirely to be
trusted.

She was calmer now and her mind was
working more clearly. Sukey Reynolds had let
drop that she and Fergus had tried to hack
into Myrna's computer, doubtless in search
of proof of their hateful suspicions. It was
quite possible, despite her denials and all her
hard words against him, that Sukey was still
in love with her ex-husband. As for the boy,
Leonie had never actually seen him say or do

anything out of order, but she knew — hadn't Myrna told her more than once, sometimes on the verge of tears? — that he was devoted to his father and that beneath the polite and respectful manner he nursed a bitter resentment and hatred of his stepmother. Between them, mother and son would love a chance to blacken Myrna's name, to make out that she had enemies — do anything, in fact, to turn suspicion away from Paul. Well, they'd been foiled for want of the password, but even if they'd succeeded it wouldn't have got them anywhere, would it? The notion that Myrna held in her computer dark secrets about her employees' past lives — worse, that she had been using such information to manipulate them in ways that she, Leonie, could hardly begin to imagine — was unthinkable. And there was one way to disprove it.

Leonie had studied computers in her degree course and she had picked up quite a lot about passwords and the dodges used to concoct them. The idea was to hit on something that was easy to remember without being so obvious that an outsider, with a bit of imagination, might think of. She remembered telling Myrna about some of them, not long after she began working for her. If you wanted to use your own name, for example, and it happened to include the letter 'I', you could substitute the figure '1'. That wouldn't have worked for Myrna, of course, or Maxford, or even Reynolds — but there was an 'i' in 'Domestic', wasn't there, and in 'Fittings'? Or you could use your own name but move each letter along one place in the alphabet, so that 'Myrna' would become 'nzsob'. They'd giggled over that one; Myrna said it would be easy for her to remember because she had a cousin in New Zealand and the last three letters were short for son-of-a-bitch and reminded her of her husband. Leonie recalled her sudden change of mood, her sorrowful expression and the bitterness in her voice as she spoke his name — almost as if she hated the sound of it — and the way she impulsively put out a hand as if in an appeal for sympathy, saying in a voice that held a hint of tears, 'I know I can trust you not to let this go any further. I have to keep up appearances, you see'. It was at that moment that her love for Myrna was born and, to her almost incredulous joy, it very soon began to appear that her love was returned.

Her thoughts went back to the computer and she began speculating about the information stored in it. There would, of course, be important data concerning the business — data which the remaining directors would need in order to continue running it as Myrna would have wished. It was by no means certain that any of them would know the password or have the slightest idea how to find it. They would have to call in an outside expert, but that would take time. It would no doubt be of considerable help if it could be found without delay — and by someone *within* the company who could be relied on not to reveal anything which should remain confidential. It would save a great deal of trouble if she could find it and inform Mr Dennison right away. There would be no need to let him know how she had come by it — she would simply tell him that Myrna had confided it to her, for use only in case of emergency. Well, if murder wasn't an emergency, what was? Putting to the back of her mind her earlier distrust of the three men, Leonie hesitated no longer. She hurried up to Myrna's office and booted up the computer.

She began by trying the more obvious variants on the company's name and the names of its products. When that failed, she went through some of the other techniques she and Myrna had discussed together, still without success. An hour passed, the light began to fade and she grew steadily more despondent. Turning away from the keyboard, she closed her eyes and tried to recall everything that had passed between her and Myrna that day. Myrna had admitted that she was only using a variation on a simple password suggested by the man who had installed the computer for her and had asked for Leonie's advice on finding something less accessible. When Paul's name cropped up in the conversation it had obviously triggered some unhappy memories. What were her exact words? *Dear Paul*, she had said, with acid in her voice and a contemptuous curl of her lip, and *Paul of Dearley Manor*, this time with unmistakable regret. And then — the picture flashed into Leonie's head with extraordinary clarity — she had given a slight nod and smiled a fleeting, secret kind of smile, as if something interesting had occurred to her. From then on they talked of other things.

It was worth a try. Leonie turned back to the keyboard and tapped out 'dearpaul'; nothing happened. Then she tried 'pauldear' with the same result. She was on the verge of giving up, but something told her she was on the right track and she tried letter substitution: 'dear' became 'efbs'. 'Effing bloody sod,' she said aloud, and suddenly grinned. That would have pleased Myrna. Holding her breath, she continued with 'qbvm' and pressed 'Enter'. There was a bleep and she found herself staring in incredulous delight at a menu.

She ran her eyes quickly over the contents. Many of the files, as she had expected, had names like 'Sales', 'Targets' and 'Accounts' and obviously referred to the business. She scrolled down the list, stopping on one entitled 'Personnel'. After only a second's hesitation, she called it up. A second menu appeared with a list of names, beginning with those of the Maxford directors. She selected one at random: Bradley Ashton. Up on the screen came a report from one Douglas Brown of Glevum Investigations, giving a detailed account of the numerous occasions when Ashton had cheated on his wife with a woman called Glenda Yates and another called Cindy Nash. 'Dirty swine!' she muttered in disgust, but the thought was swiftly followed by the uneasy realisation that what the boy's mother had suggested might be true, otherwise, why would anyone . . . ? She ran the cursor down the page and found a footnote to the report, obviously added by Myrna herself: *DB did a great job for me — in more ways than one. What a man! I haven't been screwed like that in ages!!*

Disgust turned to fury. So Myrna *had* been lying to her. She had angrily rejected the suggestion; now she knew it was true. Sukey had hinted at blackmail; perhaps that was true as well. She returned to the menu and selected another name, and then another . . . horror piled on horror as she at last came face to face with the indisputable truth: so far from being the pathetic, deeply wronged innocent she had claimed, the late Myrna Maxford had been a ruthless, sadistic, manipulative bitch. The final blow came when, determined now to know the worst, she called up her own file. A few lines contained all that was needed to complete her heartbreak: *Stupid little dyke, has designs on my body haha! It gets up P's nose so I've been stringing her along for the hell of it, but she's becoming a bore so she'll have to go soon. I'm looking forward so much to telling her, it'll be great fun watching her squirm.*

Poor Leonie's disillusion and humiliation were complete. She had laid at her idol's feet all the love and loyalty of which she was capable and if death had not intervened it would all have been flung back on her face. Numb with shock and misery, she shut down the computer and left the room, left the house where she had known so much joy and which now held nothing but pain, and returned to the bleak, empty, darkening world.

18

On the way home, Fergus said, 'You'll tell Jim won't you?'

'What about?'

'The phonecall — the fact that Myrna hired a private detective. She must have been up to something we don't know about.'

'We don't know that she hired him to do a job for her. Perhaps she just met him somewhere socially and — '

'Mum! What's up with you?' he broke in angrily. 'That woman you met in the health club — she *told* you Myrna was blackmailing her husband, that's why we went to the Manor, to find out more. It's obvious, isn't it — Myrna got some dirt on him, and the others too most likely, from this Doug Brown? You *must* tell Jim!'

They had reached the junction with the main road and the need to concentrate on the traffic gave Sukey a few moments' grace to decide how to respond. Fergus was too preoccupied with anxiety about his father to be over-bothered at the present coolness between her and Jim and the last thing she wanted was to let on how hurt she was feeling. When they had safely joined the stream of vehicles she said rather feebly, 'I keep telling you, Jim isn't on the case any more, it's DCI Lord.'

'So tell him.'

'I've had hardly any dealings with him and I've no idea how he might react to my poking my nose in again.'

'You don't have to admit you were poking your nose anywhere,' said Fergus impatiently. 'You took me to the Manor to pick up some stuff of mine and while we were there we just happened to hear that message and you thought it might help the inquiry to know who was calling, so you — '

'And how do I account for our being in Myrna's office when your room's at the other end of the house?' Sukey interrupted in exasperation. 'Do get real, Gus.'

'Tell him what I told Leonie — I was just showing you round.'

'You made out to Leonie I'd never been in the house before, but I was the one who found Myrna's body, remember?'

'She didn't know that.'

'No, but DCI Lord does.'

'So you're just going to keep quiet about the whole thing? Even though it could help Dad?'

Sukey winced at the note of bitter reproach

in her son's voice. 'It could do the opposite by revealing that he had an even stronger motive for killing Myrna than they've come up with so far,' she pointed out gently. 'But you're absolutely right about one thing, Gus, the police must be told about the possibility of blackmail. I'll have a word with DCI Lord, but I'll have to be careful what I say. The only thing is, I shan't be in the office tomorrow, it's my day off.'

'You could phone him.'

'That's no good, he'd be sure to insist on seeing me. It's a dodgy situation; I'd prefer not to let on that we were at the Manor, but I can at least tell him about my conversation with June. That ought to start him ferreting around for more information.'

'You won't mention the phone call then?'

'Not if I can help it — and neither will you if Jim rings while I'm out. Promise?'

'But — '

'No buts, Gus. You must leave it to me.' They were back in Brockworth now, but instead of taking the turning for home she drove on towards the city. 'I don't know about you, my lad, but I'm beginning to feel hungry,' she said in response to his enquiring glance. 'And I don't feel like cooking, so why don't we eat out for a change?'

Fergus brightened immediately. 'Great

274

idea. Can we go to that new pizza place?'

'Whatever you fancy. And on one condition — that we talk about anything except the Myrna Maxford case.'

'Okay.'

While they were tucking into their pizzas, Fergus said, 'Did I tell you Anita's folks are taking her skiing during the Christmas holidays and they've invited me to go with them?'

'How kind! How much is it going to cost me?'

'Not too much. Anita's Mum says they'll pay my air fare and hotel, so it'll just be the hire of skis and things. I can pay most of it myself if you could help out.'

'I'm sure I can.'

'And maybe Dad will — ' He broke off and his face clouded again. 'That is, if — '

'Gus, remember the bargain. No more about that tonight. Have you had enough to eat — do you want a dessert?'

'No, thanks.'

'Let's go home, then.'

When they were back indoors, Fergus went into the kitchen to make coffee while Sukey checked the answering machine. There was just one message, from Sergeant George Barnes: '*Sukey, I know it's your day off tomorrow but I'm afraid we're going to need you. Mandy's gone down with gastric 'flu. Eight to four shift, please'.*

'Damn!' Sukey muttered as she reset the machine. Irritation at having her plans disrupted mingled with disappointment that there was no word from Jim. She took off her jacket, hung it up in the hall and went upstairs to the bathroom. Coming down a few minutes later, she heard an excited shout from the kitchen and went in to find Fergus capering round with a spoon in one hand and a jar of instant coffee in the other, oblivious to the steam spouting from the boiling kettle. He rushed at her, half smothering her in a boisterous hug and whooping with joy.

'Mum, guess what!' he exclaimed. 'I just caught the end of the news — they've let Dad go! 'Released without charge', the announcer said. It's what we said all along, isn't it, Mum? We knew Dad couldn't possibly be a killer.'

'It's splendid news,' she agreed, reaching out to switch off the kettle. 'Did they say anything else?'

'I only heard the closing headline. I wonder where he's gone . . . back to the flat, probably. He might not want to stay at the Manor just yet.' He released her and began spooning coffee granules into mugs. 'I expect he'll be in touch soon — perhaps he'll ring us this evening.'

'I dare say he will.' Sukey turned away, ostensibly to fetch milk from the fridge, but in reality to hide the fact that she could not entirely share his excitement. It was good news, of course, so far as it went, but there was no guarantee that Paul had been eliminated from the inquiry altogether and she could not bring herself to spoil her son's euphoria by reminding him of the rules about the length of time a suspect could be detained without charge. She found herself selfishly hoping that they would not hear from Paul that evening. He would — naturally — expect sympathy and support that she felt too drained and exhausted to give him.

As he handed her a mug of coffee, Fergus gave her a keen look and said, 'You are pleased too, aren't you?'

'Of course I am. What makes you say that?'

'You ... I don't know ... you seem a bit — '

'Sorry, I'm just tired, and I've had a message from George to say I've lost my day off tomorrow because Mandy's ill. I was really looking forward to — '

If she expected sympathy, she was disappointed. 'Great!' he interrupted eagerly. 'That means you can go and see Mr Lord and maybe find out a bit more about why they let Dad go. Unless Dad rings to tell us himself, of course. It's not that late, we might hear from him any minute.'

But there was no call from Paul that night, nor from Jim Castle either.

* * *

DCI Lord's office was a few doors along the passage leading to the SOCOs room, and as Sukey approached the following morning a young constable emerged carrying a file. Behind him she saw Lord himself seated at his desk. *Might as well get it over with*, she thought, and tapped on the door.

He gave her a pleasant smile and said, 'Good-morning, Sukey. Come in.' Before she had a chance to do more than return his greeting, he added, 'I was impressed by your work on the Maxford case. Must have been a nasty shock, finding the body, but you went ahead and did everything by the book. Well done!'

'Thank you, sir. As a matter of fact, I'd like to have a word with you about the Maxford case, if I may.'

With a gesture, he invited her to sit down. 'I'm told you're well acquainted with our prime suspect,' he said, with an air of familiarity that surprised her. 'You may have already heard that we let him go without charge yesterday afternoon.'

'Yes, I heard it last night on the local radio.'

'Yes, well, he hasn't been officially named, of course. And for the record, he's still in the frame, so if the media get on to you for any reason — unlikely, but it could happen — you don't know anything.'

'Sir.'

'Good. Now, what did you want to say to me?'

'I bumped into an old college friend a couple of days ago. I hadn't seen her in years and we had a drink together. It came as something of a shock to learn that her husband is a director of Maxford Domestic Fittings.'

Lord sat forward in his chair, his expression sharp and alert. 'Go on,' he said.

'I soon realised she's an alcoholic. She said she was supposed to be on the wagon but meeting an old friend was an excuse to have just one drink. By the time she was on her third she was telling me the story of her life; how her husband was cheating on her and how his career hadn't turned out the way they'd expected. Then she started bad-mouthing Myrna Maxford, said she'd 'scuppered all their hopes and dreams'. I assumed at the time that she was referring to Myrna's decision to reject the takeover bid.'

'How did you come to hear about that?' Lord's round, almost black eyes, narrowed slightly.

'My ex-husband told me — before his arrest.'

'Ah, yes.' An odd expression flitted across the detective's face. 'Right, let me get this straight. You assumed at the time that it was the rejection of the takeover bid that upset this woman — what's her name, by the way?'

'Her first name's June and her husband's called Bradley — she never mentioned her married name.'

'That'll be Bradley Ashton, the Production Director.' Lord made notes on a desk pad. 'Now, are you saying it might have been something else?'

'She said something earlier that suggested Myrna knew about her husband's affairs, and then she went on to refer to his 'fellow sinners' and how she — Myrna, that is — knew about them too.'

'Any idea who or what this woman was talking about?'

'I think it might have been the other directors, but she changed the subject then, asked about what I'd been doing with my life and so on. I didn't let on about my connection with the case, or that my ex had left me for Myrna Maxford,' she added, anticipating Lord's question. 'Then June said she was hungry and I was too so we went and had a meal and nothing more was said.'

'And you're telling me all this now because — ?'

'I've been thinking, if the other directors did have some sort of guilty secret, it would give Myrna a hold over them and might explain why they didn't raise any serious objections to the takeover bid being dropped.'

'You're suggesting she might have been blackmailing them?'

'Not for money — she was a very wealthy woman — but she might have enjoyed wielding power over them. She wasn't a particularly nice person.' For a moment, remembering all the grief that Myrna had caused her, Sukey forgot who she was speaking to.

'We can't allow personal feelings to cloud our judgement,' Lord said. His expression was stern, but his tone was surprisingly gentle.

'No, sir. I'm sorry if I've wasted your time, but I've thought about all this quite a lot and it seemed worth mentioning.'

'You certainly haven't wasted my time. As it happens, we're already working on the assumption that there are matters the Maxford directors would prefer not to discuss, and this would appear to confirm it. So, if you should stumble on any other nuggets of information, I'd like you to pass them on to me straight away.' His eyes searched hers. 'Is there anything else?'

Sukey hesitated. Before dropping off to sleep the previous night, she had spent some time figuring out a way of putting the police on to Doug Brown of Glevum Investigations without revealing that she knew of the intimate nature of his relationship with Myrna Maxford. What she had decided on involved a certain economy with the truth; the weak link was the fact that Leonie Filbury had heard the taped message, but on balance Sukey felt it was unlikely that she would say anything that might blacken Myrna's memory. It was a risk that had to be taken.

'Well?' Lord prompted with a hint of impatience.

'There is one other thing, sir, although it might not have any bearing at all on the case. My son wanted some books and computer disks he'd left at the Manor, so we went along yesterday afternoon to see if it would be okay for him to pick them up. The guard had been taken off the house and Fergus had a key to the back door that his father gave him some time ago, so there didn't seem any reason why we shouldn't go in.' She waited for a moment, half expecting some word of reproof, but Lord merely waited for her to continue.

'We went up to his room and picked up the things. While we were there, we heard the phone in Mrs Maxford's office. It stopped after a minute or so, but it occurred to me that no one who knew about her death would be ringing her private number and I thought it might be useful to know who the caller was, so I went along and checked.' She took a slip of paper from her pocket and handed it to Lord. 'That's the caller's number.'

'Quite the detective, aren't you?' Lord commented as he took the paper and put it under a glass paperweight on his desk. 'As you say, it might be completely irrelevant to our inquiries, but I'll certainly have someone check it out. Any more titbits?'

'No sir, and I hope you don't think . . . I mean, DI Castle warned me not to go poking my nose in — '

'Ah yes, he mentioned he'd had a word with you about your, shall we say, rather too proactive rôle in the discovery of old Mrs Willow's body.'

Sukey gave a rueful smile. 'He was pretty miffed about that.'

'And things haven't been so good between

you since, have they?'

'Sir?'

Lord picked up the paperweight and began fiddling with it. His official manner had suddenly deserted him and he seemed almost embarrassed. He cleared his throat and said, 'Look, maybe I'm the one who's poking my nose in this time, but Jim Castle and I had a drink yesterday evening and I found he's still very interested in the Maxford case. Not just from a professional point of view but, to put it bluntly — ' Lord coughed again, and rather than look Sukey in the eye he began a close examination of the paperweight as if fascinated by the floral design embedded in the glass. 'I believe he's worried about the concern you've been showing for your ex-husband,' he said after a further moment of hesitation. 'Thinks perhaps the old flame may not have completely died out.'

Sukey stared at him with her mouth open. DCI Lord had in the past seemed to her a remote and, despite his faintly comic appearance, slightly forbidding figure, yet here he was adopting an almost pastoral attitude towards one of his inspectors and a lowly SOCO.

'I'm not trying to pry, just thought you should know how Castle seems to be looking at things,' Lord went on. 'I don't like seeing any of my officers under pressure. No offence intended.'

'None taken, sir. In fact, my son Fergus said something to that effect only a day or so ago. He's been frantic with worry about his father and it's partly because he's been leaning on me so hard that I've taken a particular interest in the case. Jim — DI Castle — and I had a bit of a spat because I insisted that Paul was incapable of committing such a vicious murder, and since then . . . maybe I put the point a little too forcefully, but it seemed to me that he — you — that is — ' Sukey broke off, feeling her cheeks grow hot at the realisation that she was in effect criticising a senior officer's conduct of an inquiry.

If Lord was offended, he gave no sign. In fact, Sukey was almost sure there was a hint of a smile lurking beneath the absurd moustache, although his tone was neutral as he observed, 'You think we've all been chasing a decoy duck while the real killer was sitting pretty somewhere else? Well, I hope I've reassured you on that point. And bear in mind what I've said about — that other matter.'

'Thank you, sir, I will.'

He put down the paperweight and reached for the telephone. Taking the action as a sign of dismissal, Sukey left the room and headed for the SOCOs office with her brain in a state of confusion which was not improved at the sight of DI Jim Castle standing beside George Barnes' desk.

'You're late,' said Barnes as she entered.

'Sorry, Sarge, I was with DCI Lord.'

'The hell you were! What was that about?'

'I learned something on the grapevine that I thought might be relevant to the Maxford murder case.' Out of the corner of her eye she saw Castle stiffen and turn his head in her direction, and she took an impish glee in adding, 'Mr Lord was *very* interested in what I told him and asked me to be sure to pass on anything else I happened to pick up that might be relevant.'

'Well, bully for you. Now perhaps you'd like to do some real work?' George handed Sukey a sheaf of computer print-outs. 'Ted's taken an RTA and a burglary at a riding stable and left you with a break-in on the Industrial Estate and a couple of burglaries in Brockworth.'

'That's handy, I can pop home for lunch.'

'Make sure you keep your mobile switched on so I can reach you. Remember, we're a body short today.' The sergeant picked up a file and made for the door. 'I'll be back in five minutes if anyone wants me.'

'Okay, Sarge.' Sukey sat down at her desk and began studying the details on the print-outs, aware that Castle's eyes were on her. He went over to the door, made sure it was closed, came back and stood in front of her.

'I tried to call you yesterday, but you were out,' he said.

'Really?' In an effort to hide the sudden glow in her cheeks, she dived to extract her notebook from her bag that lay on the floor beside her. 'You didn't leave a message.'

'It didn't seem appropriate. I wanted to talk to you personally.'

'I thought you didn't want any personal contact until the Maxford case is closed,' she said, making scribbled notes and hoping he couldn't read upside down because what she was writing made no sense.

'I admit I was a bit over-officious,' he said. There was a slightly awkward pause before he went on, 'No doubt you've heard that Paul Reynolds has been released without charge.'

'Yes. Is that why you were phoning — to tell me?'

'Among other things, but on second thoughts, I imagined you already knew. I mean, I guess he phoned you himself to tell you.'

'As it happens, he didn't.' *Which isn't*

surprising in view of what was said at our last meeting, she thought. Aloud she added, 'Fergus heard it on the radio.'

'You must be thrilled.'

'Fergus certainly is, and naturally I'm very relieved for his sake. I didn't have the heart to tell him it doesn't mean his father's in the clear.'

'But I take it you still believe he's innocent?'

'Of killing Myrna, yes. There are plenty of other things I could charge him with, but they're hardly indictable offences.'

'Meaning?'

'Meaning, that as far as I'm concerned, Paul Reynolds is a complete tosser and the only good thing that came out of my relationship with him is Fergus.' Sukey shoved her notebook back in the bag and stood up. 'Now, if you'll excuse me, I'd better be on my way. If I'm still here when George Barnes gets back he'll kill me.'

'I'll call you this evening,' he said, with a smile that warmed her heart.

She smiled back at him. 'Please do.'

19

The proprietor of Brockworth Agricultural Supplies was a small, wizened individual wearing half-glasses on the end of a reddened, beaky nose. When Sukey arrived, a uniformed constable was patiently trying to curb his querulous complaints about the length of time it had taken the police to attend the break-in and extract from him a list of missing items. A second officer was examining the door, which had been smashed open and lay in a heap of bent metal and broken glass around the entrance.

'Ram-raid,' said Sukey, surveying the damage.

'Looks like it.' The officer glanced over his shoulder at the racks of steel shelving behind him. 'Only certain items missing, according to Whining Willie over there,' he added, lowering his voice. 'They knew exactly what they were after: lightweight machinery mostly, chainsaws, strimmers, that sort of thing. And some special protective overalls he's particularly exercised about. Imported, exclusive new line, worth a lot of money, so he says.'

'Maybe the villains wanted them for some

future jobs,' Sukey commented with a grin as she set down her bag and began examining the debris on the ground. 'Looks as if the vehicle had an oil leak,' she added, squatting on her haunches to take a closer look. 'It was probably fitted with bull bars — with a bit of luck I might find some traces of paint on the remains of the frame. Not that it'd help much, it was probably nicked anyway.'

'Probably. Okay, I'll leave you to it.'

The officer rejoined his companion, who was putting away his notebook and preparing to leave. 'We'll circulate descriptions of all these items,' he assured the disgruntled proprietor. 'The missing machinery is easily identifiable, it's a pity you can't give us a better description of the protective overalls.'

'I told you, they're a brand new line, I only ordered a few to start with because they're quite pricey, but they went well so I ordered more. They're easy to recognise, they've got a special logo on the front — a sort of spider-shaped thing, blue, I think, or was it green — ?'

'Yes, sir, I've got that noted, but it would help if you had a sample to show us.'

'I'm afraid the thieves didn't have the consideration to leave you one,' the man said waspishly.

'Do you happen to remember who you sold

the other ones to?' said the constable in a flash of inspiration. 'Maybe one of your customers would allow our Scene of Crime Examiner to photograph the logo.'

'I'll have to look up my records.' The man appeared to be partially mollified at the suggestion.

'Right, sir. Let us know if you think of anything else. We'll keep you informed, of course.'

The officers departed and the proprietor came over to where Sukey was transferring fragments of broken glass into plastic envelopes. 'You reckon that'll help you catch them?' he asked cynically.

'You never know.' She stood up and went over to the denuded shelves. 'How many people work here?' she asked as she prepared to dust them for fingerprints.

'Just me and my assistant. He won't be in until later, he's gone to the dentist. You're wasting your time there, I reckon,' he added, moving closer to watch what she was doing. His breath was unpleasant. 'They're sure to have worn gloves.'

'Probably, but we have to try. We'll get you both to let us take your prints for elimination purposes. Now, what about that list the officer asked you to prepare?'

'Ah yes, I'd forgotten.' To her relief, he

withdrew behind a glass partition and sat down at a desk. He came out with a scrap of paper in his hand as she was repacking her bag. 'I've jotted down a few names, but I can't remember them all; some were cash sales, you see,' he explained.

'That'll do to go on with. All we need is one purchaser to agree to let us take a photo of the logo.'

'Going so soon?' His manner had subtly changed; he was breathing more heavily and there was an unmistakable gleam in his beady eyes. He moved closer to give her the paper. 'Can I make you a coffee? I could use one myself.'

'That's very kind of you, but I have to get to my next job,' she said briskly, picking up her bag. She took the paper and stuffed it into her pocket without looking at it.

Without warning, he reached out and grabbed her by the wrist. 'You've not taken my fingerprints yet.' His voice had a nasal whine; his hand was calloused and none too clean.

Sukey yanked herself free. 'If you wouldn't mind calling at the station they'll do it there — and your assistant too, of course,' she added and made her escape.

'Dirty old bugger,' she muttered as she drove to her next assignment. It was not until she had dealt with the burglaries George Barnes had given her and was in her own kitchen preparing a cup of coffee to drink with her lunch-time sandwich that she remembered the list of purchasers of the special protective overalls. Of the half-dozen names and addresses scrawled on the grubby sheet of paper, one was especially familiar: Ezra Hampton of Dearley Manor Estates.

★ ★ ★

At about the time Sukey was warding off unwelcome advances, Detective Sergeant Andy Radcliffe was being shown into the Barton Street office of ex-DS Douglas Brown, formerly of Gloucester CID and now offering his services as a private investigator under the style Glevum Investigations. A flamboyant character with a slightly gypsyish appearance and a much-enjoyed reputation as a ladies' man, Brown had left the Force some five years previously under a vague cloud; the precise circumstances were never made public, but it was generally accepted that a woman was involved and that he had been lucky to be allowed to resign rather than be dismissed. Despite his dubious reputation he had been popular with most of his colleagues and kept in touch with one or two of them who occasionally fed him with scraps of information. This time, the boot was on the other foot.

'So, Andy, how can I help you?' he asked. He offered Radcliffe a cigarette, which the older man declined, lit one himself and leaned back in his chair.

'It's about the Maxford murder,' said Radcliffe.

Brown composed his swarthy features into a momentarily sorrowful expression. 'Yeah, dreadful business that. I was in the States at the time, chasing a runaway husband for one of my rich lady clients — only found out about it when I read last night's *Gazette*. Came as quite a shock, I can tell you.'

'I'm sure it did.' Radcliffe's tone was neutral, but Brown shot him a keen look as if suspecting a hint of sarcasm. 'I believe you called her private telephone number at approximately five-thirty yesterday.'

'That's right. Had no idea then that she'd been topped. Left a rather hot message on her answering machine.' Brown gave a suggestive wink. 'Guess your lads enjoyed listening to that.'

'I'm not aware that anyone listened to it,' said Radcliffe stiffly. 'Our informant happened to be in the house at the time, heard the phone ringing and went later to check on the caller. What I'm here to find out is whether you did any professional work for her, or learned anything during your dealings with her that might help us catch her killer.'

'Can I take it you've eliminated the husband?'

'He's been released pending further enquiries, but we haven't written him out of the frame as yet. Now, if you wouldn't mind answering my question — '

'Not at all. To tell you the truth, I'm not surprised Myrna got her comeuppance. She was a gorgeous woman, great in the sack — but an out and out bitch; loved manipulating people, watching them squirm.'

'She told you this?'

'Not directly. Just the odd remark now and again that gave a clue to her motives, particularly her motive in employing my services.'

'Which was?'

'She wanted dirt on one of her directors. She already had some, but she suspected there was more.'

'What sort of dirt?'

'Run-of-the-mill stuff, really. She knew he'd been carrying on with some floozie for several years and she used that to keep him in his place. Then she got the idea that he had more than one iron in the fire — '

'You mean he was cheating on the mistress as well?'

'That's what Myrna thought.'

'And was he?'

'Oh, yeah — and the new bird turned out to be a right little fire-eater who'd have cut off his balls if she knew about the first one.' Brown gave a wheezy laugh and stubbed out his cigarette. 'She's prepared to accept that he's got a wife and kid, but she'd never go along with being part of a harem. Myrna enjoyed that.'

'Would you be talking about Bradley Ashton, by any chance?'

Brown's heavy black brows lifted in surprise. 'That's right. How'd you know?'

'Our information suggests that the wife knew about the first affair, had suspected all along, but had her own reasons for keeping quiet.'

'Well, bugger me!' Another wheezy laugh ended in a fit of coughing which lasted several seconds. When he recovered, Brown said reflectively, 'Maybe Myrna had tumbled to that, or suspected it. Maybe that's why she needed extra dirt on him . . . to keep him well and truly screwed down.' He fiddled with the cigarette packet for a few seconds, took out another and lit it before saying, 'Mind you, I have a feeling that all this was chicken-feed compared to what she had on the others.'

'What others?'

Brown shrugged. 'I don't know, but she used to drop hints that Ashton wasn't her only victim. You know she inherited the business from her father?' Radcliffe nodded. 'By all accounts, the old man was a bit of a philanthropist. Into prison reform, supported organisations for the rehabilitation of ex-cons, that sort of thing. She didn't have a shred of respect for him, used to make wisecracks about how he'd be turning in his grave if he knew what was happening to his 'poor little lame ducks' as she called them.'

'Any idea what she meant by that?'

'I can't be sure, but my guess is that there are maybe one or two people in the company who've done time and been given a fresh start by old Maxford. If she found out when she took over, she could have used the information to keep them under control. You know, threatened to sack them and leak their records so they'd find it difficult to get other jobs. That sort of power would have been meat and drink to her.'

'Not a nice woman,' Radcliffe commented.

'You can say that again,' Brown agreed. 'One of the best lays I ever had, though,' he added with a hint of regret.

'Any idea where she might have kept the

information? We didn't find anything among her papers to give us a lead.'

'She had a private computer in her office. If you can find someone to hack into that, you might get lucky. Now, if you'll excuse me, I'm expecting a client in a few minutes. Another wealthy lady,' he added with a leer. 'Haven't scored yet, but I'm working on it!'

★ ★ ★

Before setting out for Dearley, Sukey put in a call to the estate office. Without giving her name, simply introducing herself as a Scene of Crime Officer, she asked permission to photograph the logo on a suit of recently purchased protective clothing, explaining that it would help the police with their inquiries into a recent burglary. She was almost certain that the woman who took her call was Leonie Filbury, although there was nothing in the way the girl responded to her request to suggest that she recognised her voice. She briefly left the phone to confer with someone else — presumably Ezra Hampton or his deputy — and returned to say that there was 'no problem'.

The estate office was housed in the complex of buildings that Sukey had noticed when driving Emily Willow home on the day of Myrna Maxford's murder. The memory triggered a *frisson* in the pit of her stomach at the thought of what had happened to the old woman only a few hours later. So far as she knew, no evidence had so far emerged to link the two murders, yet she suddenly experienced an uneasy feeling — almost a premonition — that not only was there a link, but that the horror was not yet over. Then she gave herself a mental shake and told herself not to give way to idiotic fancies.

Turning into the farmyard, she parked her van alongside a green pick-up bearing the words, 'Dearley Manor Estates' in white lettering. There seemed to be no one about; she glanced across at the neighbouring house, which was separated from the farmyard by wooden fencing, half expecting to see Ezra's Land Rover, but it was not there. An air of tranquillity hung about the place; everything lay still and quiet, bathed in the afternoon sunlight. The mellow Cotswold stone barns, the farmhouse with its backdrop of trees and its well-tended garden bright with multi-coloured dahlias, the black and white cat washing itself by the open barn door, all combined to present a classic image of English rural life. It suddenly struck Sukey how misleading appearances could be. In the late Grant Maxford's day, such an ideal picture might have been closer to reality. What little she knew about him suggested that he had managed his lands and his business with a blend of firmness and benevolence that earned him the respect and loyalty of his employees and tenants. The same could hardly be said of his daughter. How, Sukey wondered, could such an otherwise shrewd old man have been so blind to her true character? While the picture presented to the world — of a well-run estate and a prosperous manufacturing enterprise — had not changed since his death, from the very heart of his little empire her malevolent influence had reached out in all directions, spreading its insidious poison and arousing a bitterness and hatred that had exploded at last into an act of indescribable savagery.

Following a sign painted with the single word, 'Office' and a pointing finger, Sukey made her way round the back of the barns to a renovated single storey building that might once have housed livestock. A notice on a green-painted door invited her to ring and enter; she did so and found herself in a minute reception area separated from a long narrow office by a wooden counter. At the far end was a computer terminal beside which a printer was churning out paper. Leonie Filbury was standing with her back to the counter; when the machine stopped, she carefully removed the last sheet of paper and put the print-out on an adjacent desk before turning to see who was waiting. Her jaw dropped as she turned and recognised Sukey.

'What do you want?' she demanded. She looked far from well; her face had an unhealthy pallor and there were dark smudges under her eyes.

'I've come to take photographs of some protective overalls Mr Hampton bought recently from Brockworth Agricultural Supplies. I phoned about half an hour ago.' Sukey held up her ID, but Leonie barely glanced at it.

'You're the police? You never said.'

'I'm not, I'm a civilian. I just work for them.'

'You're Paul Reynolds' ex-wife aren't you?'

'You know I am. Does it matter?'

Leonie shrugged. 'I suppose not. I'll go and fetch one of the overalls for you.' She disappeared through a door at the far end of the office and was gone for several minutes before reappearing with a voluminous garment made of a milky-coloured material with a hood, mask, gloves and lightweight boots attached. 'The farm workers wear them for crop spraying or sheep dipping,' she informed Sukey, becoming unexpectedly communicative. 'They're supposed to give complete protection against harmful chemicals and be virtually indestructible. Mr Hampton bought three, but he took one back because it had a split in it.'

'That wasn't much of an advertisement, was it?' Sukey chuckled, and a faint smile flitted across the woebegone features.

'Looks like a costume for a pantomime ghost, doesn't it?' Leonie remarked as she laid the garment full-length on the counter. 'It's the logo you want to photograph, isn't it?' She folded the sleeves across the middle and smoothed out the dull green emblem embossed on the chest. The semi-transparent fabric, through which every scratch and stain on the wood was clearly visible, gave the thing a bizarre, wraith-like appearance, as if the effigy of some medieval knight, with white plastic gauntlets and boots, a masked hood for a helmet and a curious design like a random ink blot for a coat of arms, had wandered away from its tombstone and chosen this place to take a rest. For some inexplicable reason, as she focused her camera, Sukey felt a momentary tingle of gooseflesh.

'That's fine, thank you very much,' she said after taking a succession of shots. 'Is there a manufacturer's label anywhere?'

'There might be. I'll have a look . . . yes, here we are, inside the neckband.' From being taciturn, almost hostile, Leonie now appeared eager to be helpful. She waited while Sukey took some further shots and jotted down the details in her notebook before saying hesitantly, 'I wonder if I could ask your opinion?'

'What about?'

Although the office was empty, Leonie gave a furtive glance round. 'I — I told a . . . a sort of lie — to the police,' she said. Her voice had thickened with embarrassment.

Sukey stared at her. 'A *sort* of lie? What does that mean?'

'It was the day Myrna — ' For a moment, Leonie's voice failed altogether, then the words began flowing out like water running downhill. 'I was frantic when I heard the news, I hardly knew what I was doing, I was so sure Paul had killed her that I went for him. Maybe you heard?' Sukey nodded. 'They arrested me and I told the police-woman who questioned me that I knew it was him because I'd heard him say to Myrna, 'One of these days, I'll take you by your beautiful neck and throttle the life out of you'.'

'Are you saying you made that up?'

'Oh no, he said it all right. But then the

303

woman asked if he'd said anything else, and I said no, that was all.'

'But there was something else?' Sukey prompted, as Leonie hung her head, apparently having difficulty in going on. 'Something important that you forgot to mention?'

'I didn't forget, I decided not to tell.' The girl was still staring at the floor. 'He ended by saying, 'unless someone else beats me to it',' she mumbled. She raised her head and looked at Sukey with troubled eyes that were full of tears. 'I know I should have said, but I was so sure he'd killed her. I didn't know then that she'd been stabbed, not strangled like he'd threatened . . . and you see, I never questioned what she told me about him. I know now it was all lies, but she made me hate him so much, I didn't believe — I didn't *want* to believe it could be anyone else.' Her voice had sunk to a pathetic whisper, the tears overflowed and slithered down her cheeks. 'It was wicked of me — and I feel the police should be told that there might have been other people besides Paul who wanted to kill her.'

'I'm sure they've taken that possibility into account,' Sukey said drily, 'but there's nothing to stop you calling in at the police station and telling them you want to add to your statement, if it'll make you feel better.' Realising that she had just heard something significant, she added, 'By the way, did you say — ?'

Before she could finish her question, Leonie began speaking again. 'There's something else. It could be much more important.' She wiped away her tears and blew her nose. As if getting the lie off her chest had given her renewed confidence, her voice became stronger. 'After you left me at the Manor yesterday, I went back and — ' She jumped and broke off at the sound of an approaching vehicle. Outside, a car door slammed; moments later Ezra Hampton entered.

He gave Sukey a friendly nod. 'Got your pictures, then?'

'Yes, thank you.' She gestured at the overall, which still lay on the counter. 'About twenty of those were stolen early this morning. If by chance anybody offers you one at a knock-down price, will you let us know immediately? And warn anyone else you think might be approached?'

'Sure, always ready to help the police,' said Ezra. 'I don't suppose there's any more news about the barn fire?' he added with a rueful grin.

'Not so far as I know, I'm afraid.'

He shrugged, lifted the flap of the counter

and went into the office. He took off his waxed jacket, hung it on a peg and picked up the printout that Leonie had left lying on a desk. 'These the milking returns?'

'Yes, Mr Hampton. I haven't checked them yet.'

Ezra grunted, sat down and picked up the phone. As soon as he began speaking Leonie leaned towards Sukey and said in an urgent whisper, 'I need to talk to someone, I need advice. Would you come to my cottage later on?'

'Yes, if you like, but why can't you — ?'

Leonie shook her head and put a finger to her lips. 'I can't tell you any more now.' She scribbled something on a pad lying on the counter, tore off a sheet and gave it to Sukey. 'That's my address. It's a cul-de-sac off the village street, just past the church. Promise you'll come.'

'I promise,' Sukey assured her. Her curiosity had been thoroughly aroused and she was itching to ask more questions, but Ezra had finished his phone call and was approaching with a sheaf of papers in his hand. 'I must be going, thanks for your help,' she said, and left.

Back at the station, she bumped into PC Fox, one of the officers who had attended the incident at Brockworth Agricultural Supplies.

'Any joy with the overalls?' he asked.

'Yes, no problem.'

'What's so special about them? You'd have thought they were Vivienne Westwood originals the way that old misery carried on.'

'They look like a cross between a space suit and a shroud, and one had been returned to the supplier because it was faulty.'

Fox grinned. 'Top quality stuff, eh? You'll let me have the pictures as soon as they're processed?'

'Sure, but — hang on a minute!' The word 'shroud' had triggered a signal in Sukey's brain. Convinced that it was the key to something vital, she put both hands to her temples and closed her eyes in a frantic effort to pin it down.

'What is it?' Fox sounded anxious. 'Are you feeling ill?'

'No, I'm just trying to think — ' Something clicked into place and she opened her eyes. 'Mark, would you have a word with our friend at Brockworth Agricultural? I'd rather not speak to him myself, he made a pass at me after you'd left,' she added, anticipating his question.

Mark grinned. 'Cheeky old so-and-so. What do you want to know?'

Sukey explained and he whistled. He agreed that if her hunch was right, it could shed a whole new light on Myrna Maxford's murder.

He returned a few minutes later to say that he had called the firm's number but got no reply. 'They must pack up early on a Friday,' he said. 'I could try again on Monday, if you like.'

Sukey frowned. 'D'you think maybe DCI Lord should know about this?'

'It wouldn't do any harm, but I believe he's out at the moment. Have a word with DS Radcliffe.'

'Good idea, I will.'

20

Bradley Ashton arrived home that evening in a vicious temper, which was not improved by the sight that greeted him as he burst into the kitchen through the personal door from the garage. It was as if a whirlwind had passed, wrenching open cupboards and drawers, flinging their contents into the air and dropping them in haphazard, untidy heaps. Apparently oblivious to the surrounding chaos, his wife was at the stove stirring something in a saucepan, a set expression on her face, a wooden spoon in one hand and a half-finished drink in the other.

'What the hell's been going on?' Spotting the vodka bottle on the table, Bradley gave a snarl of anger, snatched the glass away from her and poured what was left of the contents down the sink. 'You're supposed to be cutting that out!'

'I'm allowed just one little snort before dinner,' she protested, her voice a resentful whine.

'Don't give me that crap about 'one little snort'! That bottle was nearly full last night and now look at it. And look at the state of this kitchen,' he added furiously, glaring round at the disorder. 'It looks as if a bomb's hit it . . . and you're as pissed as a fucking newt!'

'Don't blame me, blame the police,' she snapped, unhappily aware that he was right; the last drink had been one too many. The floor had begun rocking slightly and she grabbed at the bar on the front of the stove to steady herself.

'The police? What have they got to do with it?'

Even in her befuddled state, June detected the note of alarm in her husband's voice. 'You tell me,' she muttered. 'Banged on the door about four o'clock, didn't they? Said they had a warrant . . . turned the place inside out . . . even went through the dustbin. Enough to make anyone need a drink.'

'What were they looking for? Did they take anything away?'

'Knives . . . they took some knives, Mummy's lovely old kitchen knives — ' A wave of sentiment swept over her; tears splashed from her eyes and landed in the sauce. 'I treasured those knives,' she wailed. 'Mummy gave them to me when we were first married — '

'Stop grizzling and look at me!' He grabbed her by the arm and spun her round.

The edge of the spoon caught against the side of the pan and tipped it over. The contents spread hissing and bubbling over the hob.

'You clumsy oaf!' she screamed. 'The dinner'll be ruined and it's all your fault!' She lashed out at him with the spoon, sending gobs of sauce spattering over his sleeve.

Furiously, he wrenched it out of her hand and flung it into the sink. 'Sod the dinner. Look what you've done to my jacket!' He grabbed the dishcloth and began scrubbing the stains. 'Listen, you drunken bitch, remember what I told you the other evening? About all of us telling the same story if ever we were questioned about our relationship with Myrna?'

'What of it?'

'The police know about Eric and Sam. They've been at the office, asking questions. For all I know, they've been searching their houses too. What we want to know is, how did they find out? Someone must have been talking — was it you?'

'No, it wasn't — why pick on me? I don't even *know* about Eric and Sam, except that Myrna had something on them. What is it, anyway? Have they got tarts on the side as well?' June gave a tipsy cackle while making ineffective attempts to retrieve the remains of her sauce.

'Never you mind what it is, it's enough that you knew there was something they didn't want made public. Have you mentioned it to anyone? Irene and Nicola wouldn't say anything, they've got too much sense.'

'Thank . . . you . . . very . . . much!' she retorted with exaggerated sarcasm. She abandoned the sauce and began peering into the other pans, making a great show of checking their contents. Anxiety was having a sobering effect; despite her denial, she had an uneasy feeling that she had said a little too much to Sukey yesterday about her real feelings towards the murder victim. But Sukey wasn't the police, was she? She was an old college friend, someone she'd known from way back when they were both young and happy and pretty . . . at the memory of those far-off, carefree days more tears, this time of self-pity, began running down her cheeks.

'Oh, for Christ's sake don't start snivelling again!' Bradley's voice was harsh and brutal. At the sight of his face she backed away. There was anger in his expression, but there was something else as well — fear. He was afraid, they were all afraid, he and Eric and Sam, because one of them had killed Myrna . . . or maybe they were all in it together . . . and now the police were on to them and if they ended up in prison it would be her fault.

She saw Bradley raise his arm and she turned and rushed blindly out of the room, across the hall and into the downstairs cloakroom. Her one thought as she locked herself in and cowered behind the door while her enraged husband pounded on it, shouting like a madman, was of thankfulness that their daughter was away from home. At least, Alice had not been there to witness the day when their lives fell irretrievably apart.

* * *

Sukey reached home half an hour later than usual. Fergus was sitting in the kitchen with a mug of tea in his hand and a school textbook open on the table in front of him. Pop music blared from the radio and she went over to the set and switched it off.

'Mum!' he protested.

'You can't concentrate on maths with that row going on,' she scolded.

'What's put you in a bad mood?'

'I'm not in a bad mood, just tired. Is that tea fresh?'

'It'll be pretty stewed. I'll make some more.'

'Bless you.' Sukey took off her jacket,

dumped it on the floor on top of her bag and dropped onto a chair. The wave of excitement at having stumbled on a possible new line of inquiry in the Maxford case had receded, leaving her with a sense of frustration at being unable to follow it up in person. She would have loved to be able to present DCI Lord with the vital piece of information which would lead to the arrest of the killer, to be commended for her observation . . . and later to force Jim Castle to admit that this time 'poking her nose in' had paid dividends. As it was, things were out of her hands. DS Radcliffe had listened attentively to what she had to say; he had made notes and thanked her, but it was impossible to tell from his manner whether he considered it of any real significance.

Fergus handed her a mug of tea and she took it gratefully. 'Have there been any calls?' she asked.

'Dad left a message on the answering machine. He's staying with a colleague in Cheltenham for a while, until things settle down. He wants to know if he can see me this evening. You don't mind, do you?'

'Of course I don't mind.' *So long as he hasn't asked to see me*, she added mentally.

'I'll give him a call in a minute. He left a number.'

314

'That's fine. I'm going out myself later on.'

'But you said you were tired.'

'I am, but this could be important.'

'Where are you going?'

'To see Leonie.'

'Leo?' He looked puzzled. 'Whatever for?'

'Something's bugging her and she asked if she could talk to me.'

'Did she say what it's about?'

'Not really. As soon as Ezra Hampton walked in she shut up.'

'I'm not surprised she wouldn't say anything in front of him. Dad told me once that he hasn't much time for effing dykes.'

Sukey raised an eyebrow. 'You've obviously had some pretty uninhibited conversations with your father.'

Fergus gave a self-conscious grin, but ignored the comment. 'Didn't Leo give you any idea at all what she wants to see you about?' he asked.

'She said that after we left her at the Manor she went back — '

'Back where?'

'She didn't say, but before that she said something to suggest that she knew Myrna had been feeding her a load of porkies.'

'Mum!' Fergus exclaimed, his eyes wide with excitement. 'D'you reckon she went back to the office and managed to hack into that computer?'

'If only.' The thought had already crossed Sukey's mind, but she had dismissed it as being too much to hope for. 'Still, I did get the impression that she's learned something she thinks might be important, but can't make up her mind what to do about it. I assume that's why she wants to talk it over with me.'

'Are you going to tell DCI Lord?'

'Perhaps I should have mentioned it, but it's a bit late now. I told him about the phone call — at least, I didn't say we'd listened to it, but I gave him the caller's number. He was quite impressed.'

'What about that woman, the one that got so pissed?'

Sukey was taken slightly aback at his casual use of the expression, but realised there was no point in objecting. Everyone said it these days and thought nothing of it. 'Yes, I told him about that and he didn't seem at all surprised. He more or less admitted that he suspects some of the Maxford directors have something to hide.'

Fergus's eyes shone. 'That's great, they'll soon have to admit Dad's been telling the truth. D'you reckon he can sue them for wrongful arrest?'

'Good heavens, I've really no idea. The

main thing is to catch whoever really did kill Myrna — and poor old Pussy Willow. I'm pretty sure it was the same person, even though the MO was different. All I hope is they get him before he goes after someone else.'

Fergus stared at her in alarm. 'What makes you think he's likely to?'

Despite the mildness of the evening and the mug of hot tea clasped in her hands, Sukey felt a sudden chill. 'No reason, but I had a queer feeling earlier on that it wasn't over,' she said. 'Just my fancy, I expect.' She finished the tea and stood up. 'You call Dad and make your arrangements for this evening. I'll pop upstairs for a wash and then I'll start getting our supper.'

'Okay.'

When Sukey came downstairs again she found Fergus in the kitchen looking glum. 'What's up?' she asked.

'I'm not seeing Dad this evening after all.'

'Why not?'

'He's in a funny mood. We arranged a time to meet and were having a general chat when he suddenly changed his mind and said could we make it tomorrow instead. Something about being behind with his work and having to prepare some figures for a client.'

Sukey felt a stab of anger against her

ex-husband. His habit of casually altering arrangements to suit his own convenience, without considering the effect on others, had often been a source of friction in the past. She had long since ceased to be affected by it on her own account, but she hated to see Fergus disappointed.

'Never mind, you still have it to look forward to,' she consoled him.

'Sure.'

'I'm sorry I have to go out — '

'It doesn't matter. I'll go round to Anita's, we've both got maths revision.'

'Good idea.'

After supper, as Sukey was getting ready to set out for Dearley, Jim Castle phoned. The sound of his voice gave her a thrill of happiness.

'Is it all right if I pop round?' he asked.

In her excitement over the events of the afternoon she had completely forgotten his promise. 'Oh, Jim, I'm dying to see you, but could you make it later on?' she said. 'Say about half-past nine? I have to go out for a while.'

'Do you have to? Can't you put it off?' He sounded faintly aggrieved.

'Not really. I've promised to call on Leonie Filbury. I don't want to let her down, she's very upset — '

'Leonie Filbury? What have her problems got to do with you?'

'Nothing so far as I know, except that she's got something on her mind and wants to talk it over with me.'

'Is it relevant to the inquiry? Shouldn't DCI Lord know?' Jim's voice became sharp, almost peremptory.

'I've no idea what it's about, but she made it clear she wants to speak to me in confidence. She's in a very volatile, distressed state — '

'She's had all week to come to terms with the Maxford woman's death.'

'It isn't only her death. I've a hunch she's beginning to realise that her beloved Myrna wasn't the lily-white angel she believed her to be.'

'What? How d'you suppose that came about?'

Sukey realised that she had strayed on to delicate ground. To reveal that she knew about Myrna's relationship with a private investigator, but had kept the information to herself rather than reveal exactly what she had been doing in Myrna's office, would only give rise to a further spat. It was time to prevaricate. 'Look, Jim, I haven't time to tell you the full story now,' she said hurriedly. 'You can rest assured that whatever Leonie wants to talk to me about, I'll do my best to persuade her to tell the police if it's relevant.'

'It's not up to you to decide whether it's relevant or not — ' he began.

'Please Jim, give me credit. She hasn't sworn me to secrecy, only asked me for advice. Whether she agrees to contact the police or not, I'll write out a full report after I've heard what she's got to say — does that satisfy you?'

'All right,' he said grudgingly. 'Where does this woman live, by the way?'

'In Church Piece, just off the main village street. Woodbine Cottage.' She could tell from the way he repeated the address that he was writing it down. 'Jim, you won't come barging in while I'm talking to her, will you?'

He ignored the question. 'What time did you say you'd be there?'

'We didn't fix a definite time. I said I'd be with her some time after eight o'clock.'

'Does anyone else know about this?'

'Not unless Leonie's spoken about it since. Ezra Hampton was in the office, but he couldn't have overheard because she was speaking very quietly and he was on the phone most of the time.'

There was a short pause before Jim said, 'Right, I'll see you later,' and rang off.

It wasn't until much later that it occurred

to Sukey that Fergus might have mentioned the arrangement to Paul.

* * *

DCI Lord was in the act of clearing his desk when DI Castle entered his office.

'Come in, Jim,' he said. 'You're just the chap I wanted to see.'

'Sir?'

'There's been an interesting development in the Maxford case. I thought you might be interested.' Lord handed him a sheet of paper. 'This fax came in earlier from the Governor of Leighton Open Prison.'

Castle gave a soft whistle as he scanned the message. 'Well, there's a turn-up for the book. Two of the directors with form, eh? I wonder if Myrna knew about it.'

'I'll bet my pension she did — and used it to make them dance to her tune. The trouble is, they all insist she didn't know, or if she did, she never referred to it. They're still sticking to their story that she was a fair but firm employer who had only the good of the company and the welfare of her staff at heart. Just the same, Radcliffe said it was plain they were thoroughly rattled when he tackled them about it. We got warrants to search their houses and found some likely looking knives in Ashton's kitchen.'

'Ashton? He's not mentioned here — he hasn't got form as well, has he?'

'Not that we know of, but he's got at least two mistresses on the go. His wife's a lush, by the way. She'd been hitting the vodka bottle pretty hard when Radcliffe's boys got there and she made a hell of a fuss when the knives were taken away, said they were a family heirloom or some such crap. Methinks we may be getting warmer.' Lord put the fax in a drawer, sat back and made a steeple with his fingers. The expression on his chunky features bordered on the complacent.

'You reckon those three are in it together, sir?'

'It's a bit early to speculate, but it begins to look a distinct possibility. We're going to carry on digging; I want to know whether any other Maxford employees have skeletons in their cupboards, and if so, did the lovely Myrna know about them? Now, did you want to see me about something?'

'I've just been talking to Sukey Reynolds,' Castle began.

Lord gave an approving nod. 'Everything all right between you two now?'

'I think so, thank you, sir. I'm going to see her later on — I was hoping to go straight from here, but she was getting ready to go and see Leonie Filbury.'

Lord was immediately alert again. 'What about?'

Jim explained, and Lord shook his head in disapproval. 'I'm not sure I like the sound of this,' he said, half to himself. He fingered his moustache for a few moments, frowning. Castle could almost hear the neurons buzzing in his brain. 'Does anyone else know about this meeting?' he asked after a moment.

'I don't think so. From what Sukey told me it seems unlikely that Leonie would have mentioned it to anyone else. Just the same, I thought you should know about it.'

'Absolutely right. As a matter of fact, we're checking on something Sukey reported to Radcliffe this afternoon. He didn't attach a lot of importance to it at the time, and I was inclined to agree with him, but — ' Lord pushed the phone across the desk. 'Try and get hold of her, tell her I'd like a word.'

'Right, sir.' Castle was dying to know what was passing through Lord's mind, but he knew better than to ask further questions.

There was no reply from Sukey's home. 'I'll try her mobile,' muttered Castle, tapping out the number as he spoke. 'She must have switched it off,' he exclaimed in exasperation a moment later, slamming down the handset. Lord's evident disquiet was beginning to worry him.

The DCI picked up the phone as soon as Castle put it down. 'I don't want to sound alarmist, but I think we'd better keep an eye on this. I'll get control to send the local man round to Woodbine Cottage to check that everything's okay. We don't want any more . . . incidents.'

The momentary hesitation increased Castle's feeling of unease. He was almost certain Lord had been on the point of saying 'killings' rather than 'incidents', but it was clear that his senior officer had no intention at that moment of sharing his thoughts.

★　★　★

The air had been still and oppressive for most of the afternoon. Thunderstorms were forecast; like an army massing for an attack, a bank of cloud was slowly rising, layer upon layer, above the western horizon. Soon after six, as if in response to a command, it began to fan out, smothering the setting sun and spreading remorselessly eastwards. Darkness was to fall early that evening.

The inhabitants of Dearley counted themselves fortunate on having no street lamps in their village, so that on clear nights they experienced the full glory of the heavens undimmed by illumination from the ground. If they went out on foot after dark they relied on torches to light their way to church, pub, village hall or neighbour's house, none of which was far away. It was a close-knit community in the literal as well as the figurative sense; the few detached modern dwellings that the local planning committee had allowed to be built in this jealously protected conservation area had slightly larger than average plots, but in the centre of the village the original cottages, many of which had been occupied by the same families for generations, were built in terraces with narrow alleys running between their back gardens.

Since the murders of Myrna Maxford and Emily 'Pussy' Willow, a number of the more recent arrivals had expressed disquiet, suggesting that the darkness and the network of unlit paths were an open invitation to criminals. It was, they pointed out, no longer true that crime, apart from the odd theft of a sheep or opportunist break-in through a window carelessly left open, was virtually unknown in the village. There was talk of starting a Neighbourhood Watch scheme; the police had been asked to step up patrols in the area. Yet there were still those who raised their voices against such an invasion of their rural peace or who shrank from any suggestion of 'spying on their neighbours'.

But after tonight, the objectors would be silenced. Tonight, under cover of the gathering storm, a shadow would steal silently along one of those convenient little passageways. The shadow of a killer, intent on claiming another victim.

21

By the time Sukey reached the top of Crickley Hill and joined the Birdlip bypass it was practically dark. Vehicles were travelling in a steady stream towards Gloucester, but for the moment the eastbound traffic was sparse, a mere scattering of rear lights along the road ahead, sparkling in the gloom like a thinly threaded string of scarlet beads. Quite deliberately, she kept her speed down to give herself time to think how best to play the interview with Leonie. There was no doubt that the girl was seriously troubled about something, but this evening's invitation and the request for confidential advice had clearly been the result of a spontaneous impulse which she might already have begun to regret. She might need coaxing to make her reveal what she claimed to have discovered, or even have changed her mind altogether and refuse to say anything at all. This could turn out to be a wasted journey.

It was unfortunate that Jim had telephoned when he did. Sukey half wished she had not told him where she was going; there had been no particular reason to do so, but equally there had been no reason to lie or be evasive. The person she was going to see was not a suspect or a key witness. Just the same, knowing Jim, he was almost certain to mention her visit to DCI Lord — might in fact have already done so. If one of Lord's officers came banging on the door five minutes after she arrived it would probably scupper any hope of winning Leonie's confidence. But if Leonie had, perhaps without realising it, stumbled across some information that could lead to the murderer before he had time to strike again, it was vital to get that information to the police without delay.

The possibility of yet another killing brought a return of the sense of foreboding that had troubled Sukey earlier. She found herself accelerating, as if the need to talk to Leonie had suddenly acquired a new urgency, then slowed down again as her headlights picked out a sign indicating that her turning was only half a mile ahead. As she began to signal, she glanced in her rear-view mirror. A car was overhauling her at high speed. It pulled out, tore past and then braked sharply, swung round the corner in front of her and went racing towards Dearley with its headlights on full beam. Within seconds it had vanished.

'Hooligan!' she muttered as she followed at a more cautious pace along the narrow lane leading to the village. She had travelled only a few yards when a flashing blue light and a blast on a siren sent her diving into a field gateway to make way for a police car. It too was heading for Dearley.

* * *

Ever since she reached home that afternoon, Leonie had been prowling round the cottage, unable to settle. She knew she should be getting something to eat; she had hardly touched a thing since breakfast and it had been an effort then to force down a few spoonfuls of cereal and a slice of toast. But the thought of food made her feel sick, even though her stomach was empty and hunger was making her light-headed. She had no idea when to expect Sukey, except that it would be after eight. She was beginning to doubt whether Sukey would turn up at all, despite her promise. She wasn't sure whether she had done the right thing in asking her.

She had spent a sleepless night, unable to drive from her thoughts the horror she had uncovered the previous day. It was a diary of cruelty, a record of every barb that Myrna had fired at her victims and a detailed, sadistic description of the pain it had inflicted. '*He was like a butterfly writhing on a pin, it was delicious*', was one comment; '*I really enjoyed it, it was like pulling the wings off a fly*', was another. Revolted, unable to stomach any more, she had switched off the computer and fled from the house, overwhelmed by a terrible sense of isolation. The knowledge she had uncovered seemed to set her apart from the normal, everyday world, a world from which her one thought now was to hide. Mechanically, she had got into her car and driven back to the village, her eyes fixed on the road, indifferent to the nods and smiles of greeting from neighbours she passed along the way as she headed for the cottage where she had lived since starting her job in the office of Dearley Manor Estates. In those early days it had seemed like heaven on earth to have her own little domain, free of the contamination of years spent under the roof of a father whose abuse during her childhood had turned her against men forever. Now, it was more than just a home; it had become a haven, a place where she could be alone with her torment.

Comfort of a sort had come from an unexpected quarter. A telephone call, a kindly word of concern, 'I saw you drive past and I thought you looked ill, are you all right?' was all that was needed. Within minutes she was pouring the whole wretched story into a sympathetic ear and begging for advice. And as she spoke, something strange happened: little by little her grief began to turn to anger. Myrna had betrayed her. Had it not been for her death she, Leonie, who had served her so loyally and loved her so dearly, would have been rewarded with mockery, rejection and humiliation. The world at large had known and admired a beautiful and talented woman; only her victims knew that she had been the living embodiment of sadistic cruelty. It was a monstrous injustice to those who had suffered under her tyranny — an injustice that Leonie had the power to put right.

And yet . . . to reveal the truth would only blight the victims' lives still further. 'I don't know what to do', she had said despairingly. 'I feel people should know what a wicked person she was and yet, to go telling would mess up so many lives. What do you think?'

The response was simple and uncompromising: *Say nothing.* What was the point in stripping Myrna's victims naked for the gutter press to gloat over? They had sinned, yes — one of them in a particularly unpleasant manner — but they had, as the saying went, paid their debt to society and deserved the second chance that Grant

Maxford had intended for them, the chance that his daughter had frustrated in every possible way while exploiting them to the full to satisy her psychotic lust for power. Wasn't it better to let sleeping dogs lie?

Thankfully, Leonie had accepted the advice and they had gone on to talk of other things, especially of her own plans for the future. Myrna's death had left her staring into a black hole; she missed her former home and her old friends more than she realised. Perhaps it would be a good idea to go back to familiar surroundings. Why not? It would be a clean break for her, and those who had suffered under Myrna's yoke could get on with their lives while she rebuilt hers. Gradually, the future began to seem less bleak.

But was it really that simple? Later, as she lay sleepless in her tiny, low-ceilinged bedroom and stared into the darkness while the church clock counted the hours away, the doubts returned and brought new terrors. What if Bradley Ashton, Sam Perry or Eric Dennison — or maybe all three of them acting together — had decided that enough was enough, that it was time to remove once and for all the constant threat of exposure that had soured their lives for so long? Had the decision not to accept the takeover bid, with the loss of the promised perks and future prospects, been the proverbial last straw? Leonie had been so certain that Paul was the murderer, so blinded by her love for Myrna, that she had not even considered the possibility that others might have reasons for wanting her out of the way. But she knew now that these men — and their wives — had more to lose than Paul, who could have walked out at any time without sacrificing his career. Now that she understood the true nature of the woman she had once idolised and — in fancy — endowed with every virtue, it was all too evident that theirs was a far stronger motive. If they had killed her, justice demanded that they pay for the crime.

Yet who could blame them if they had? Their past record was enough — in the case of two of them at any rate — to ensure that should it be made public they would face ruin. Although it had all happened long ago and — so far as she could tell — they had lived within the law ever since, they would never have dared to step out of line while Myrna was alive. She had used her knowledge ruthlessly, she had been an evil woman and the world was a cleaner place now that she was dead. Where was the point of causing further suffering by dragging that knowledge out into the open?

And so Leonie's battle with her conscience raged on until at last she fell into an uneasy sleep, waking with a throbbing head and the problem still unresolved. It was the unexpected encounter with Paul's ex-wife, who had struck her as a woman of integrity and compassion, that had prompted the spontaneous request for advice. It had seemed the right thing at the time.

Now, with darkness falling and the air thick with the menace of the approaching storm, she was having second thoughts. From time to time she peered out through a gap in the sitting-room curtains, halfhoping, halffearing to see a car pulling up outside. Once the local bobby went cruising past. There was nothing unusual about that; he was only doing his regular patrol through the village, yet the sight of him made her uneasy. Supposing Sukey had felt it her duty to inform her police colleagues of this evening's visit and what had prompted it? The prospect of another interrogation filled her with dread; she wished she had kept to her original resolve and said nothing to anyone.

She went into the kitchen. There was no drink in the house, but at least she could offer a cup of tea or coffee. She had just filled the kettle when she heard what sounded like someone moving around outside. With hands that shook, she attached the safety chain to the back door, cracked it open and peered through the gap.

'Who's there?' she called anxiously, then relaxed as she recognised the muffled figure looming out of the shadows. 'Oh, it's you!' she exclaimed in relief.

'May I come in for a moment?'

'Yes, of course, but I'm expecting — '

'This will only take a moment.'

Leonie released the chain and stood back while her visitor entered in a gust of wind and driven rain. 'Gosh!' she exclaimed as she closed the door. 'It's going to be a wild night. Shall I take that?' Turning, she held out a hand for the heavy, damp overcoat, then recoiled in horror and disbelief at the sight of what it concealed. One short scream of terror was all she had time to utter before the knife plunged into her.

* * *

The sight of the speeding police car increased Sukey's feeling of unease, even while she told herself that it was probably responding to a burglar alarm. She wound down her window for a moment and listened, but could hear nothing except the sound of the rising wind. Then the first drops of rain began to fall; by

335

the time she reached the outskirts of the village it had become a downpour that reduced visibility to a few yards. Temporarily disoriented, she switched her headlights to full beam and slowed down, searching for a recognisable landmark. The wipers thumped across the flooded windscreen, through which she caught a glimpse of an illuminated window on the other side of the road. That would be the shop, which she recalled was near the church. Leonie had said the turning to her cottage was just beyond the church; yes, there was a sign reading, 'Church Piece'. She turned out of the main street and crawled along, trying to read the names of the dwellings huddled behind stone walls on either side of the narrow lane. In true country fashion, half of them were illegible, others non-existent.

The lane doubled back on itself; the headlights swung in an arc and picked out the two police cars standing on the verge a few yards ahead. Vague unease turned to dread as she pulled in behind them, switched off her engine and scrambled out of the car, dragging the hood of her jacket over her head against the downpour. Light from an open doorway picked out the words painted on the open gate: 'Woodbine Cottage'. The wind drove a sheet of rain into her face as she ran down the flagged path, all but losing her footing on the slippery wet surface. In the tiny hallway she nearly collided with DS Radcliffe. Over his shoulder, she glimpsed an open door leading to a kitchen. Two men, one in uniform, the other in plain clothes, were bending over a figure lying on the floor.

Radcliffe took her by the shoulders and restrained her as she tried to pass him. 'Don't go in there,' he said grimly.

'For God's sake, what's happened?'

'Leonie Filbury's been stabbed. An ambulance is on the way.'

'Is she badly hurt? Is she dead?'

'Not dead, but she's lost a lot of blood.'

'Has she said anything?'

'She was mumbling something when PC Riley found her, but he couldn't make much sense of it. It's thanks to him she's still alive — he thinks he disturbed the attacker before he could finish what he'd started.'

'Please, let me see her. She wanted to tell me something, that's why I'm here. Maybe — '

'She won't be telling you anything for the moment, she's unconscious.'

The man in plain clothes straightened up and joined them; it was DCI Lord. 'There's still a pulse — just. Let's hope the ambulance doesn't hang about. Riley says it hasn't far to come.'

'Here it is now.' A white van had drawn up at the gate, its blue light flashing through the glittering rods of rain. Paramedics carrying equipment came charging through the open door and were directed to the kitchen. What seemed a lifetime passed before they reappeared carrying Leonie on a stretcher. She was lying motionless under the blankets, her eyes closed and her face the colour of marble, but the drip attached to her arm showed that she was still alive.

'You go with her, Radcliffe,' said Lord. 'Sukey, you stay here, I want a word with you.'

'Sir.'

The ambulance drove off with its siren wailing. Outside, the officers from the rapid response car were busy with yards of blue and white tape while attempting to shoo away a group of curious neighbours who had heard the disturbance and braved the rain to investigate. Lord closed the front door and summoned PC Riley from the kitchen. 'You'll no doubt be writing your report when you get back to the station, but I'd like you to tell me now exactly what happened,' he said.

'Yes, sir, it was like this.' The constable was plainly shaken, but he stood respectfully to attention as he spoke to the Chief Inspector, slowly and deliberately, as if he was reciting something learned by heart. 'At seven-forty-five exactly I had a message from control to come along and check on Miss Filbury. No reason given, just check everything was all right. I'd already done my patrol through the village, like I do every evening, but I returned as per instructions and was just approaching the front door of Woodbine Cottage when I heard a scream from inside. I banged on the door and shouted, but I got no response, so I ran round the back, quick as I could. The kitchen door was unlocked, I opened it and found her lying on the kitchen floor, covered in blood.'

'Did you see any sign of the assailant?'

'No sir, not a whisker. It was pitch dark and coming on to rain.'

'Or a weapon?'

'Nor that either, sir. Must've taken it with him.'

'I take it there's a side entrance to this cottage?'

'No sir, it's part of a terrace. There's an alley runs along the end of the gardens, it comes out into the lane fifty yards or so back there.' Riley made a vague gesture.

'So, it would take you half a minute to get there?' Lord considered the constable's portly frame for a moment before adding, 'Or maybe a bit longer.'

'Long enough for the villain to get clear away,' Riley admitted ruefully. 'I shone my torch as I ran, but I never saw a thing. I was more concerned with getting to Miss Filbury, y'see sir, having heard that screaming,' he explained, and Lord nodded approval. 'Soon as I found her I summoned an ambulance, notified control and did what I could to stop the bleeding until help arrived.'

'You did quite right. Tell me, was the victim conscious when you got to her?'

'Just about, sir. She was moaning and clutching her stomach, but her eyes were tight closed.'

'Did she say anything?'

'Just a few words . . . couldn't hardly hear . . . didn't seem to make much sense anyway — '

'Never mind the sense, what exactly did she say?' Lord interrupted. Sukey, who had been silently listening, guessed that he was becoming slightly irritated by Riley's slow and ponderous manner. 'Did she say who'd attacked her?'

'Like I said, sir, I couldn't hardly hear. It being no more than a whisper and the words coming out slowly, one at a time like and all jumbled up . . . I might've got it wrong, y'see — '

'Just tell me what you think you heard.' This time there was no mistaking Lord's impatience.

'Well, sir, if you're asking what I think, it sounded like she was trying to say, 'Dear little Paul'.'

The Chief Inspector inhaled sharply through pursed lips, but all he said was, 'Thank you, Riley, that'll be all for now. Better go back to the station and write up your report.'

'Sir.'

It was all too clear what line of thought the mention of Paul's name had triggered in the detective's brain. It had occurred to Sukey in the same moment and it filled her with dread. Supposing that during the conversation with his father, Fergus had mentioned this evening's arrangement? It could have happened so innocently: *Mum'll be out as well, she's going to see Leo. Don't know what it's about but it sounded urgent.* Was that the reason for the sudden change of plan, the hastily contrived excuse to postpone their meeting? Was it, after all, Paul Reynolds who had killed first his wife and then Pussy Willow, and had now tried to kill Leonie to prevent her revealing something that could brand him a murderer?

But in that case, Sukey reasoned, why

should someone who until yesterday had nursed a corrosive hatred for Paul suddenly refer to him in such affectionate terms? It made no sense, unless . . . Fergus had suggested that Leonie might have hit on the password giving access to Myrna's private computer. 'Dear little Paul' sounded an unlikely combination, but it was possible that Myrna had at some time referred to him in those terms, in contempt rather than affection. To use the expression for such a purpose might have appealed to her warped sense of humour. And if Leonie had happened to hear it, and put two and two together . . .

'Just a moment!' At the sound of Lord's voice, Sukey jumped. For a moment, she thought he was speaking to her, then realised that he was calling to Riley, who was on the point of closing the front door behind him.

'Yes, sir?'

'One other question. You were telling me about the alley running between the backs of the cottages. I assume it's unlit?'

'That's right, sir. Black as a coal cellar it is on a dark night like this.'

'So how were you able to locate Miss Filbury's cottage?'

'Easy, sir. The name's on the back gate and I had a torch — '

'That's probably how the assailant got in,' said Lord thoughtfully. 'He wouldn't have wanted to risk going to the front door and possibly be spotted by someone putting out their milk bottles or whatever.'

'I reckon that's how it was, sir. He could sneak along the alley, do his dirty work and sneak back without a soul seeing him.'

'And he could enter and leave at either end?'

'Yes, sir.'

Once again, the constable turned to go. This time, it was Sukey who called him back. Another possible interpretation of Leonie's cryptic utterance had sent the adrenalin pumping madly round her system. Without stopping to think and with a total disregard for protocol, she blurted out, 'Constable, are there more gardens on the other side of the alley?'

'Yes of course, miss.' Riley's manner became slightly patronising at such an obvious question. 'They belong to the cottages in the High Street — this bit of Church Piece runs parallel, y'see.'

When Riley had finally departed, Lord said, 'Would you care to explain the significance of your question?' If he was annoyed at her intervention, he gave no sign.

'Just something that occurred to me, sir.

Two things, in fact — they might sound a bit far-fetched — '

'I'll be the judge of that. You can tell me while I'm waiting for the SOCOs to get here.'

She suggested that Leonie might have managed to get into Myrna's computer using a combination of the words: 'Dear little Paul'. He looked dubious, but made a note of the suggestion and said he'd bear it in mind. When she told him her second theory, he was openly sceptical.

'It's ingenious, and I suppose it's just about feasible, but . . . can you suggest a motive?' She had to admit that she couldn't. Having promised to see that she was kept informed of Leonie's condition, he ordered her gently but firmly to go home.

22

Church Piece was a cul-de-sac with a turning space at the end. Reversing the car was a tricky manoeuvre, but Sukey managed it without mishap and made her way back to the junction with the main road. The dim lamp burning behind the counter of the shop and the occasional glow from a curtained window were the only points of light along the way; once she was clear of the village, the darkness was complete. Disoriented by the driving rain that reduced visibility to a few yards, she crawled along in second gear with her headlights on full beam, peering through the flooded windscreen and mentally cursing the lack of road markings that made a potential hazard of every twist and turn in the narrow lane.

A car approaching from the opposite direction forced her to pull over on to the verge. It swept past without slowing down, throwing up a shower of mud and spray and leaving her muttering insults under her breath as she watched its rear lights disappearing. She found herself shaking; there had been no real danger, but the violent outcome of the evening's visit had affected her more than she realised. 'Come on girl, pull yourself together,' she said aloud as she gritted her teeth, engaged first gear and let in the clutch, and then exclaimed, 'Oh no!' as madly spinning wheels told her that she was hopelessly stuck on the slippery, muddy grass. She was stranded, several miles from home in pitch darkness and a howling rainstorm.

After several fruitless attempts to get the car back on the road, she gave up, cut the engine and reached for her mobile phone. At least she could rely on Jim to come to her rescue. She was half-way through tapping out his number when she realised that her call was not registering; the battery was flat. Now she really had a problem. There was no public telephone in the village — but the police would still be at Leonie's cottage. They would certainly help her; the prospect of trekking all that way was daunting, but it seemed to be the only solution to her predicament. Then she had an inspiration. The offices of Dearley Manor Estates were only a short distance ahead. Ezra Hampton lived next door and would surely allow her to use his telephone to summon help. He might not be at home, of course, but it was worth a try. She took her torch from the glove compartment and struggled out of the car.

The rain had slackened a little but she had to fight to close the door in the teeth of the wind that roared with the noise of an express train through the trees lining the road and seemed to buffet her from all directions as she set off. The farm buildings were further ahead than she expected, but at last she spotted the external security lights flickering through the flailing branches as if they were tossing up and down on a stormy sea. It was with a huge sense of relief that she saw Ezra's Land Rover standing outside his house and lights in the downstairs windows. She crossed the road and made for the front gate; an extra strong gust of wind threw her off balance and she slipped on the wet path, grabbing the gatepost to avoid falling. At that moment, above the noise of the storm, she heard a wild, almost unearthly howl that made her shiver. Somewhere an animal, a deer perhaps, must have been attacked by a predator or caught in a trap. The cry was repeated; this time it was clearly human — and it came from inside the house.

A man's voice was raised in anger; plainly, he and a woman were engaged in a furious quarrel. She was screeching hysterically and he was shouting back at her, but the words were unintelligible. A dog's frantic barking added to the din. Sukey stood transfixed by the gate, lashed by wind and rain, reluctant to abandon her quest for help yet uncertain whether to approach at such an inopportune moment. While she was debating what to do the front door flew open to reveal two struggling figures. As she had already assumed, the man was Ezra, but for the moment all she could see of the woman was her back. Now she could make out what they were saying. The woman was screaming, 'You bastard, you treacherous bastard!' while he held her by the shoulders and shook her, shouting at her to be quiet. Then, with a sudden effort, she wrenched herself free, staggered and lost her balance.

Ezra uttered a hoarse, anguished cry of 'Annie!' as he made a desperate, futile attempt to prevent her from falling. Sukey dashed forward, but she had no chance of getting there in time. With another wild shriek the woman toppled down the short flight of steps, landed on her back on the stone path and lay still. The light from the doorway shone on the upturned face and closed eyes of the housekeeper from Dearley Manor, Mrs Little.

Ezra fell to his knees beside her and grasped both her hands, calling in a grief-stricken, broken voice, 'Annie, my love, forgive me, I didn't mean it — oh my God, what shall I do?' There was no response from the unconscious woman and he slid an arm beneath her shoulders as if about to lift her up.

'Don't try to move her!'

At the sound of Sukey's voice, Ezra started and turned round. He showed no surprise at her presence, nor any sign of recognition, only relief that he was not alone. 'What shall I do?' he repeated helplessly. 'I can't leave her lying here in the rain.'

Seeing that he had for the moment gone to pieces, Sukey took charge. 'We need an ambulance — where's your phone?'

'In the hall.' He nodded vaguely towards the house.

She started up the steps, then stopped abruptly as she came face to face with the black and white border collie. It had ceased barking, but its bared teeth and menacing growl told her it had no intention of letting her pass. 'Will you call your dog off, please?' she shouted back to Ezra, but there was no response. He was still crouched over Annie Little as if trying to protect her from the rain with his own body, sobbing 'Forgive me!' over and over again. Precious seconds ticked past before Sukey managed to get him to call the dog to his side.

When she came out to report that the

ambulance was on its way he merely nodded without looking at her. 'Where can I find something to put over her?' she asked. 'We should keep her as warm and dry as possible until the paramedics get here.'

'There's a rug on the couch in the front room,' he said, still without turning his head.

'Can I get you a coat? You're getting soaked yourself.'

'Never mind me.'

She returned to the house, found the rug and was about to take it outside when something white protruding from beneath the cushions on the couch caught her eye. She moved one of them aside and stared down, petrified with horror at the sight of a folded heap of white plastic smeared with fresh, wet blood. For a moment, her brain ceased to function; then the truth dawned on her with a suddenness that was like a physical blow. Her wild, intuitive guess that DCI Lord had turned aside so lightly had been right: what Leonie had been struggling to tell PC Riley was that *Annie Little*, not *Dear little Paul*, had stabbed her and the reason could only be that the housekeeper was desperate to prevent her revealing whatever it was that she had discovered in Myrna's office. Sukey's hunch about the 'faulty' overall that was supposed to have been returned to the supplier — the hunch that she had completely overlooked in her own urgent need of assistance — had been right as well. Annie Little had been wearing it to protect her clothing from bloodstains as she carried out the savage attack on Myrna Maxford. That would account for the fact that the blood had been confined to the bedroom; the murderess must have stayed by the bedside of her victim while she removed it before fleeing the house. She had been seen by Pussy Willow who mistook her for a ghost — 'a silent figure, bearing a shroud' — as she made her way home. And there was always a chance that, under careful questioning, Pussy might have recalled sufficient detail to enable the 'ghost' to be identified as Annie, so she had to be silenced. Was it Annie who had subsequently beaten the widow to death with a chopper — or was it Ezra Hampton? He was Annie's lover and he had to be in it too, because she had come straight to him after attacking Leonie . . . and Sukey was at that moment alone in Ezra's house with the man himself only a few feet away . . .

'Couldn't you find it?' She swung round to find herself confronting him. Her mind flashed back to her first impression of him as he stood beside the smouldering remains of the barn fire: sturdy, straight-backed and ruddy-complexioned, a man in authority, now almost unrecognisable in the stricken individual with sagging shoulders and ravaged features standing before her. His eyes slewed from her face to the tell-tale overall and back again; he took a step towards her and she edged away, bracing herself for a murderous attack.

The attack never came. Instead, he snatched the rug from her grasp and rushed from the room like a man possessed by a demon. It took her a second or two to register the fact that his sole concern at the moment was for the injured woman. Then she dashed after him, slammed and bolted the front door behind him and grabbed the telephone.

When she had made her calls, she went back to the front room and peered through the curtains. Annie Little was still lying unconscious on the ground, covered with the rug. Ezra Hampton, with his dog shivering and whining at his side, was kneeling on the ground in the rain, chafing her hands and weeping as he waited for the ambulance to arrive.

23

The ambulance arrived within ten minutes, but to Sukey, peering fearfully through the window of Ezra's front room, the wait seemed never-ending. When at last it came and Annie Little had been lifted onto a stretcher and placed inside, a short altercation followed. Ezra had scrambled in after her, followed by the dog; an attempt on the part of one of the attendants to eject the animal resulted in a show of teeth and threatening snarls which eventually led to the pair of them being ordered out. As the ambulance sped away leaving them standing in the rain, Sukey had a moment of panic at the thought that Ezra might try to re-enter his house with the intention of silencing her and destroying the damning evidence of the bloodstained overall. Her heart was racing as she checked the bolts on the front door before dashing from room to room until she found the kitchen and made sure the back door was secure as well. At the sound of an engine starting up she flew to the front window in time to see the Land Rover heading for the gate. Her relief as it turned into the lane and disappeared almost reduced her to tears and when, a few minutes later, DCI Lord's car appeared on to the drive, she was shaking so violently that it was all she could do to open the door.

'Where are they?' he demanded.

'The ambulance . . . took Mrs Little,' she gasped. 'Ezra . . . Mr Hampton . . . tried to go with her . . . they wouldn't let him . . . because of the dog . . . so he went off in his Land Rover — '

'Which way did he go?'

'Towards Cirencester.' She took a deep breath in an effort to steady her voice. 'He must be following her to the hospital. He was half frantic — all he cared about was being with her, even after he saw what I'd found.'

'Yes, you said you'd found evidence. Where is it?'

'In there.' She pointed to the open door and a wave of nausea hit her. 'Excuse me!' she muttered and rushed back to the kitchen. As she leaned over the sink, heaving and retching, she was vaguely aware of another car arriving, an engine being cut, a door slamming. She rinsed out her mouth, washed her face and hands and dried them on some sheets torn from a roll of kitchen paper. Returning to the hall, she found herself face to face with Jim Castle. At the sight of him, her self-control shattered and she clung to him, trembling.

'Oh, Jim, thank God you're here! I've been so frightened.' Her voice cracked and he held her close, stroking her head until she could speak again. 'I thought he was going to kill me — '

She felt his body stiffen and he held her away from him, bending his head to look at her face. 'Kill you — who? What's been going on, for God's sake?'

'Ezra Hampton.'

'I don't understand — you said your car was stuck and would I come and get you out. I thought you sounded strange but you rang off — '

'I didn't have time to explain everything . . . I had to reach DCI Lord and tell him — '

'Tell him what?'

'That it looks as if Annie Little and Ezra Hampton between them are responsible for the murders of Myrna Maxford and Emily Willow and the attempted murder of Leonie Filbury,' said Lord, emerging from the room where Sukey had discovered the tell-tale overall. 'Mind you, it didn't come across quite so coherently as that when she called me. Okay now, Sukey? Yes, I'm sure you are,' he added, with a sly glance at Jim, who still had a protective arm round her shoulders.

'Annie Little? The housekeeper?' Jim

looked from one to the other in bafflement. 'But why — where's the motive, and where does Hampton come in?'

'That's what we don't know yet,' said Lord.

'And why the attack on Leonie?'

'We don't know that either, but it's likely she knows something they don't want her to talk about.'

'Is she going to be all right?'

'We haven't heard. Radcliffe went with her to the hospital — '

Sukey put a hand to her mouth. 'Annie's been taken there too . . . and if Ezra was following the ambulance — '

'Yes?'

'Ezra and Annie . . . if Leonie's still alive — '

'Quick thinking!' Lord gave a nod of approval. 'I'll get on to Radcliffe and put him in the picture.' He went back into the sitting-room and they heard him talking on his radio. When he returned he said, 'Right, as soon as reinforcements arrive here I'll get over to the hospital and make an arrest or two. Jim, you take Sukey home — she looks all in.'

'Thank you, sir, but there's the matter of her car. It's stuck in the mud somewhere along the lane. That's why I'm here — I've brought a tow-rope to pull her out.'

'Some of the lads will see to that. She's in no fit state to drive. Just get her home and give her some strong coffee — or whatever other restorative you think will help.' His lips twitched beneath the bushy moustache.

* ★ ★ ★

'I told you Mr Hampton fancied Mrs Little, didn't I?' said Fergus smugly as he carried a tray of coffee into the sitting-room where his mother sat on the couch with Jim beside her, his arm round her shoulders. Anita, Fergus's seventeen-year-old girlfriend, followed with a tin of biscuits which she shyly offered while he handed round mugs of coffee. 'I suppose Myrna found out they were planning to get married or something and decided to put a stop to it — '

'How could she stop them?' Anita interrupted. 'I mean, if people are in love — ?' The look she gave Fergus made it clear that she believed it was not only faith that could move mountains. He gave her a fond smile, settled in an armchair and drew her on to his lap. She was a rosy-cheeked girl with cornflower-blue eyes and smooth straight hair that glistened like honey under the lamplight. For a moment, emotion took Sukey by the throat at the sight of young love in all its freshness and optimism. She felt Jim's encircling arm tighten for a second and knew that he understood.

'I reckon one of them had a guilty secret that Myrna knew about,' said Sukey. 'And Leonie somehow found out, and that's what she was going to tell me and — ' she broke off, her brow furrowed as she spotted the flaw in her line of reasoning. 'How could Annie and Ezra have known? She was hardly likely to tell them.'

'Mum, maybe Ezra did overhear Leonie inviting you to her house and got the wind up?' suggested Fergus.

'Not while I was there, he didn't,' Sukey declared. 'Of course, she might have mentioned it after I'd left, but . . . no, it doesn't make sense.'

'You said something on the way back from Ezra's place about how she might have got into Myrna's private computer,' said Jim. 'But when I asked you what gave you that idea, you changed the subject.' He put down his empty mug and with his free hand turned her face towards him. 'I think there's something you haven't told me — what exactly *have* you been up to?'

'Nothing really . . . I mean, when we went over to Dearley to fetch the stuff Gus left behind — '

'Oh, come on, Mum, you might as well come clean!' Fergus broke in.

'So, you're in the conspiracy as well!' Jim's voice was stern but Sukey, giving him a sidelong glance, caught him suppressing a smile.

Fergus, completely unfazed, told of his abortive effort to hack into Myrna's computer, of the compromising call from Doug Brown of Glevum Investigations and Leonie's arrival and subsequent disillusionment. 'She said she didn't know how to get into Myrna's computer, but I'll bet she did, or managed to hit on the password. That's it!' His face grew pink with excitement as he developed his theory. 'After we left, she must have gone and hacked into it and found some dirt about Ezra. I'll bet he's got a guilty secret and Myrna was blackmailing him, threatening to expose him if he married her housekeeper and took her away!'

He looked round for approval and was rewarded by an adoring smile from Anita, but was brought back to earth by Jim, who said quietly, 'If she found something compromising about Ezra, the office is the last place she'd have chosen to arrange to talk to your mother about it.' The lad's face fell, then brightened again as Jim went on, 'But I think you may well be on the right track about the computer — '

'*Dear little Paul*' Sukey exclaimed. 'I was right!'

'What?' Jim gave her a sharp look and made to withdraw his arm, but she grabbed his hand and held it.

'That's what PC Riley said Leonie was mumbling when he found her and I could see that DCI Lord thought she was trying to tell him it was Paul who had attacked her. But 'Dear little Paul' didn't make sense to me — she hated him because she believed he'd killed Myrna. Then it occurred to me that 'little' might refer to Mrs Little, who lives in one of the cottages in the main village street. PC Riley confirmed that their gardens back on to the footpath between them and the ones in Church Piece — '

' — so it would be easy for Mrs L to nip across in the dark, kill Leonie and dodge back again,' Fergus interrupted triumphantly. 'Mum, that was brilliant!'

'DCI Lord didn't seem to think so . . . not at the time, anyway.'

'I'll bet he does now!' The lad's face glowed in admiration of his mother's powers of deduction.

'Never mind that for the moment,' said Jim. 'How does the rest of it fit in?'

'The computer password, of course,' said

Fergus. 'I'll bet it was some variant of the letters making up 'Dear Paul'.'

'I didn't think she and your father were on such affectionate terms — ?'

'They weren't, she was probably being sarky. She was like that.'

'It sounds unlikely to me, but you never know.' Jim's tone was dubious, but he took out his mobile phone and stood up. 'For what it's worth, I'll pass the idea on to DCI Lord.'

'While you're speaking to him, ask how Leonie is,' Sukey called after him as he went out of the room. She felt a stab of guilt at having forgotten, even for a few minutes, that the last time she saw the girl her life was hanging by a thread.

* * *

It was some time before the police were able to piece the whole story together and when they did it was plain that when the case came to court it would provide news hungry journalists with some sensational material.

Annie Little was found to be suffering nothing more serious than severe concussion. On leaving hospital she was arrested, cautioned and charged, together with Ezra, with two murders and one attempted murder, all of which she denied, claiming they had been committed by her lover. On learning how she had betrayed him, Ezra broke down and told the complete story of how together they had decided to kill Myrna, how Annie had prevailed on him to kill Pussy Willow to prevent her repeating what she had seen of their flight through the woods, and finally how the attempt on Leonie's life had ended in disaster. Meanwhile, after major surgery and many hours hovering between life and death, Leonie recovered consciousness and gave the police the key to Myrna Maxford's computer files, where they uncovered some startling information.

'Annie was the driving force from the word go,' Jim told Sukey and Fergus on his first night off after days of intensive inquiries. 'She hated Myrna because she made her life a misery by taunting her about her age and her looks, especially after she found out about the relationship with Ezra. He was completely besotted with Annie, he'd have cut off his right arm for her — and she repaid him by trying to put the entire blame for the killings on him.'

'That's the sort of thing Myrna would have done,' Sukey remarked thoughtfully. 'Maybe beneath the surface they were two of a kind.'

'Maybe.'

'So tell us everything from the beginning.'

'We already knew about Dennison and Perry — and of course, Bradley Ashton. At his previous firm, Dennison was caught with his hand in the till to the tune of several thousand pounds and he was sent down for five years. Old Grant Maxford gave him an office job as part of a rehabilitation scheme and after a while he promoted him, eventually making him secretary of the company.'

'That was taking a bit of a risk, wasn't it?'

'There were extentuating circumstances. The first Mrs Dennison ran off with a car salesman leaving her husband with a load of debts that he had no hope of settling, and he was desperate. He'd been hoping to repay the money before anyone knew it was missing, but his luck ran out. While he was in the slammer he divorced the first wife and later on married his secretary and with her help and support got back on his feet.'

'What about Perry?'

'Ah, he's a different animal altogether. His little misdemeanour was to join a syndicate circulating videos of child pornography.'

'The filthy so-and-so. Why ever would old Maxford employ a man like that?'

'Who knows? Perhaps he saw him as a challenge. Mind you, the man is a salesman so he probably had a smooth line of talk. Maybe he convinced old Maxford that he was more sinned against than sinning.'

'Doesn't Myrna's file on him give a clue?'

'Not really. She was more concerned with exercising her power over her victims than with her father's motives for helping them. If they didn't dance to her tune, she'd threaten to sack them and make sure their records were made public so they'd find it difficult, if not impossible, to get anything like the sort of jobs they had with her. It seems she never passed up an opportunity to rub their noses in it and then recorded their reactions in graphic detail.'

'So what about Ezra and Annie? What did she have on them?'

'On Annie, nothing. She was the faithful family retainer who'd promised old Grant Maxford on his deathbed that she'd stay on and look after his little girl. Ezra was the one with form; he was caught stealing timber by a previous employer and spent six months in the nick.'

'And was then given another chance by Grant?'

'Right. He was in the same boat as the others, except that in Ezra's case, losing his job would have meant losing his home as well, so it was impossible for him to marry Annie.'

'Jim,' said Fergus, who up to now had been

listening intently without interruption, 'did they plan to kill Myrna in advance, or did they just take the opportunity when there was no one else in the house? I mean, they couldn't have known that Dad was going to sleep in one of the cottages that night — '

'Oh, it was carefully planned all right, it was just a case of waiting for the right moment. According to Ezra, Annie was determined to do the deed herself — of course, she's denying it now — but he was the one who hit on the idea of wearing the overall to stop blood getting on her clothes. That Sunday evening, when Myrna dropped her bombshell and upset everyone so badly, plus the fact that once they'd all gone home there'd be no one in the house but her, seemed the ideal time to strike.'

'Annie must have really hated Myrna to attack her so viciously,' Sukey remarked.

'Yes, well, according to Ezra, Myrna went into the kitchen after her guests had gone. She was pretty drunk and kept wanting to know where 'lover boy' — meaning Ezra — had gone. Annie told her he'd gone to see to a sick cow, and Myrna had laughed and said something about a sick cow having more sex appeal. I think that was the moment when Annie made up her mind that tonight was the night.'

'So she phoned Ezra after Myrna had gone to bed and he came over to help put the plan into operation?'

'That's right. Incidentally, it was Annie's idea to leave the knife with Paul's blood and fingerprints for us to find. Normally, she'd have popped it straight into the dish washer. No doubt she wanted us to think it was the murder weapon, which did seem likely at first.'

'The evil cow! And I used to think she was such a kind old duck!' Fergus could not contain his anger at this cold-blooded attempt to incriminate his father. 'What about the break-in? Was that part of the plan as well?'

'Of course. That was Ezra's job. While she was carving Myrna up, he was bashing in the back door to fake a burglary. After that the two of them hightailed it to their respective homes.'

'I could tell at once there was something iffy about that break-in,' said Sukey. 'A genuine burglar would have trodden glass through the house while looking for stuff to nick, but the only fragments were at the point of entry.' She thought for a moment, then said, 'I wonder if it ever occurred to Myrna that sooner or later one of her victims would top her?'

'That isn't recorded, but as a complete psychopath she probably thought she was invulnerable. She only laughed when Leonie warned her that Paul might try.'

'And then Leonie found out what they'd all been up to and how Myrna had exploited her knowledge. Is that what she was going to tell me — and why Annie Little tried to kill her?'

'Yes, but the irony is that she never got around to reading the files on Ezra and Annie. She was so upset when she read her own and saw what Myrna had written about her that she gave up. Annie saw her driving home looking like death, went round to see what was wrong — '

' — and Leonie confided in her.' Sukey exclaimed. The last piece of the puzzle fell into place. 'It must have shaken the old gorgon rigid when she realised what it could lead to. But why wait and give Leonie time to go rushing to the police? Why not get out her carving knife there and then?'

'Leonie says Annie persuaded her at first that there was nothing to be gained by stirring up ancient history. It was clear that Paul was the killer — no point in making people pay twice for their sins, that sort of thing. Then Leonie decided to ask for your advice and made the mistake of telling Annie.'

'And Annie did her best to silence her. Poor girl, she seems to have been betrayed by everyone she trusted, starting with her own father.'

'She'll be all right though, won't she, Mum?' asked Fergus. 'You've been to see her in hospital, you said the doctors were pleased with her?'

'Physically, they say she'll make a complete recovery, but psychologically, she's taken a fearful hammering.' Sukey closed her eyes, still haunted by the memory of the girl's white face and air of utter hopelessness as she lay in her hospital bed. After a moment, she turned to Jim and said, 'I suppose Annie put on the overall again, did the deed and then expected Ezra to hide it. Maybe that's what all the shouting was about.'

'That's right. He claims he was so appalled at the way things were turning out that he blew his top and told her he was sick of the whole business, said he wished he'd never got involved with her, never set eyes on her — '

'So that's why he kept saying, 'I'm sorry, forgive me', after she fell down the steps.' Sukey's throat tightened at the tragic end to an unlikely love affair. 'By the way, did Annie attack Leonie with the same knife she used to kill Myrna?'

'Oh, yes, it was one of her own. We found it

under the overall on Ezra's couch. It was his job to get rid of both things for her. After stabbing Leonie she rushed round to his house with them — '

'Bearing a shroud!' Sukey interrupted. 'That's what Pussy Willow said she'd seen. I wondered if there was a connection when Leonie spoke about one overall being faulty. It wasn't, of course. I'm told the proprietor of Brockworth Agricultural Supplies was very miffed at the suggestion that he sells defective goods.'

'Mum, you should be a detective!' said Fergus admiringly.

Sukey shot a sly glance at Jim before saying. 'You're not the only one to think so.'

He gave an indulgent smile. 'Oh, really?'

'Really,' she assured him. 'DCI Lord said to me the other day, 'If ever you think about joining the Force and doing your two years on the beat, I'd be happy to recommend you for the CID'. I'm giving it some serious thought,' she added.

THE GREENWAY
Jane Adams

When Cassie and her twelve-year-old cousin Suzie had taken a short cut through an ancient Norfolk pathway, Suzie had simply vanished . . . Twenty years on, Cassie is still tormented by nightmares. She returns to Norfolk, determined to solve the mystery.

FORTY YEARS ON THE WILD FRONTIER
Carl Breihan & W. Montgomery

Noted Western historian Carl Breihan has culled from the handwritten diaries of John Montgomery, grandfather of co-author Wayne Montgomery, new facts about Wyatt Earp, Doc Holliday, Bat Masterson and other famous and infamous men and women who gained notoriety when the Western Frontier was opened up.

TAKE NOW, PAY LATER
Joanna Dessau

This fiction based on fact is the love-turning-to-hate story of Robert Carr, Earl of Somerset, and his wife, Frances.